929014

FIC
Mil   Millhiser, Marlys

Murder in a hot
flash

DUE DATE

MURDER IN A
HOT FLASH

A Charlie Greene Mystery

MARLYS
MILLHISER

OTTO PENZLER BOOKS
NEW YORK

OTTO
PENZLER
BOOKS

OTTO PENZLER BOOKS
129 West 56th Street
New York, NY 10019
(Editorial Offices only)

Simon & Schuster Inc.
Rockefeller Center
1230 Avenue of the Americas
New York, NY 10020

Designed by Laura Hough

Manufactured in the United States of America
10 9 8 7 6 5 4 3 2 1

Library of Congress Cataloging-in-Publication Data
Millhiser, Marlys.
  Murder in a hot flash: a Charlie Greene mystery/Marlys Millhiser.
    p. cm.
  1. Women detectives—West (U.S.)—Fiction. 2. Literary agents—West (U.S.)—Fiction.
I. Title.
PS3563.I4225M88 1995
813'.54—dc20   94-27050
                                                          CIP

ISBN 1-883402-29-8

ACKNOWLEDGMENTS

I would like to acknowledge the patience, guidance, and suggestions of producer Mae Woods, screenwriter Lisa Seidman, and editor Michele Slung. Of Bette Stanton, Executive Director of the Moab to Monument Valley Film Commission. Ranger Rock Smith, Park Manager of Dead Horse Point State Park. Royce Henningson of Royce's Electronics in Moab. And Jay Millhiser, the handsomest pilot in the sky. These people all did their best and are not responsible for any screw-ups in these pages.

I have not rearranged the landscape nearly as much as Hollywood would have.

929014

FOR JAY AND MANON

May they fly together always.

MURDER IN A HOT FLASH

Charlie Greene ignored the hooting of an owl somewhere behind her and brought all her weight down on the lug wrench, breaking a fingernail when the last nut gave. Heaving the heavy tire with one flat side into the Corsica's trunk, she pulled out the spare.

She'd always lived in horror of this happening on a crazy Los Angeles freeway. Hard to believe it had happened on an empty desert instead.

Well, the desert wasn't quite empty. Twilight shadows—long and surreal—dotted it, some moving with the light wind that blew Charlie's hair across her face.

A chilly wind so free of pollutants it smelled alien.

Hey, this is cool. I can handle this.

There was something seriously abnormal going on with Charlie's mother. Most people wouldn't have noticed—Edwina never having been what her daughter thought of as normal anyway. But it was the kind of abnormal you could hear over the phone hundreds of miles away without the words being any different. Not something a daughter could put her finger on, but something that created a cold place deep in her viscera that Charlie couldn't have pointed to either.

She'd left the car door open in case one of those shadows moved in her direction. She couldn't remember the last time she'd felt quite this alone.

Charlie was a literary agent for Congdon and Morse Representation, a talent agency on Wilshire in Beverly Hills, and had much better things to be doing. Important things.

But when you're an only child and your only parent calls for help you don't have much choice, right?

Edwina, if I lose my job over this little outing, I'll never forgive you.

The wind whispered an odd whirring plaint in the stunted juniper and pinyon pine, arranged like evenly spaced shrubbery— nature's way of assuring each its claim to scant water rights.

"Lug wrench, jack, spare." The man at the car rental had pointed out each article, speaking in the bored tones flight attendants use when explaining survival procedures in case of a crash— knowing as well as you do that if you need them you're dead meat anyway.

Ignoring the rustling in the scrub bushes beside the road, Charlie tightened down the last of the remaining nuts on the spare. She'd lost only one. She tossed the lug wrench into the trunk and stood staring at a low tree corpse. It hunched black and gnarled, aiming its several dead fingers at the darkening heavens as if in warning.

Oh, *will* you get a grip?

A small rat or a very large mouse staggered out from under the tree corpse and headed her way in an erratic course. Like it had stopped in for twofers this Friday afternoon on the way home from work. Halfway across the road it reared on its hind legs and came down on the run to ram headfirst into a front tire and bounce off. It repeated the crazy antic over and over, as if intent upon ramming the car out of its way.

Charlie was not particularly fond of rats but didn't particularly fear them either. Still, this one could be rabid. It was an unusual time of day for it to be out even when sober. She slipped into the safety of the Corsica until the poor creature admitted defeat and staggered away into the desert. Then she jumped out to lower the jack, throw it into the trunk with the flat, and head the rented Chevy down the endless road. As she drove, she tried to stop obsessing about the bumpy cattle guards irritating the tire on one rear wheel with the missing nut.

And if the nut behind the wheel wasn't missing a few screws she wouldn't be here to begin with.

Edwina Greene was a professor of biology at the University of Colorado in Boulder, specializing in rodents of the high-desert plateau. Which meant she was heavy into rats and bats.

How old was I when I flat out refused to tag along on her field trips? Long before Howard died.

Dusk deepened to evening. Charlie imagined giant bulls ramming the little car like the rabid rat and the spare failing her here in a vast nowhere. She preferred strange cities to strange land-scapes. You could get off the plane, pick up your luggage, and hail a taxi. If you had the great good fortune to speak the same language as the driver (increasingly less likely in this country), you could be en-sconced in a cozy hotel in under an hour without glancing at a map.

Instead, Charlie had driven three hours across Utah from the closest jet-age airport in Grand Junction, Colorado. It would have been four and a half hours from Salt Lake.

Cows wandered along the side of the road now, eyeing her with passive dislike. Did cows ever get rabies? The campground couldn't be much further. A sign loomed ahead next to the first turnoff she'd seen. APC PROPERTY. NO TRESPASSING.

Charlie and the Corsica continued down the main road.

And it was night. A few zillion stars snapped overhead like city lights upside down in the sky. What if a rabid rat bit a big bull on the ankle and . . . Charlie wished the little Chevy wasn't red.

She came to a lighted area, darkened buildings off to the side, and a speed limit sign. An arrow ordered her left at a wye and she passed a truck, a pickup camper, and several monstrous motor homes before coming to a stop in front of a fold-down tent trailer. Howard's old Jeep sat in front of it.

The other campsites appeared deserted, their vehicles dark, but a gasoline lantern flickered and flashed back at the night from the fold-down trailer. It had to be cozier than the backpacking tents of Charlie's childhood that sat right on the cold hard earth. This at least had a metal and wood body on wheels, the canvas tent forming its upper half and folding in on itself when it was time to hit the road. The plastic windows were rolled down to permit the night in through the screens and probably the sour smoke from Edwina's cigarettes out.

Charlie couldn't see her mother inside. Edwina was, no doubt, wandering around the desert looking for rats. She worked mostly in research now, but from time to time still shepherded a few promising grad students. One of them had written a book on the effects of human disturbance on the ecology of the Colorado Plateau of southern Utah and northern Arizona. Edwina was listed as coauthor for reasons known only to academe. A small independent film company out of Phoenix had hired her instead of the grad student as consultant for a documentary on the subject. As Charlie's father had always maintained—them that has, gets.

Charlie sat a moment psyching herself up to face her mother. When she did step out into the cold she reached for her jacket before hauling the duffel bag and backpack, borrowed from her daughter, up to the trailer's door.

"About time you got here," somebody who was not Edwina said behind her. Charlie dropped everything on her foot while trying to smother a startled yip.

A man unfolded from beneath a concrete picnic table. A tall man with a lean face, high cheekbones, sly smile, and possibly the most suggestive eyes this side of the Mexican border. His dark hair was caught in a ponytail tied with a leather thong, and he had on a suede jacket with that corny fringe. "Your mamma's been waiting all day for you, girl."

Why me? I'm so tired.

He pulled on a pair of cowboy boots and reached under the

table for an ax. "Frankly, I was worried she'd bust a few important-type blood vessels in her head."

His voice was low and suggestive too. Who was this guy? Was the ax supposed to be a threat or what? Charlie decided her best tactic was to go on the offfensive. "What were you doing under Edwina's table?"

"Keeps the dew off. Don't like tents." Even in the dark he oozed testosterone. "Let's go find your mamma before she kills somebody, okay?"

"Do we need the ax?" It wasn't one of your little kindling-type hatchets but a full-size, chop-down-trees ax.

"Never hurts to have some protection out here at night. Especially with your mamma loose." But he slid the ax back under the table and held out a hand to shake hers. "Name's Scrag Dickens."

Figures. If your agent thought that one up, your career's in the toilet. "Charlie Greene, but you already know that."

"Yeah, ol' Edwina's warned me to stay wa-ay away from you." His laugh was low and growly too and, of course, wicked. He started off around the corner of the camper. "Now I know why."

Charlie badly did not wish to follow this guy off into the dark but a sudden thunderous clapping swallowed up the night sounds. Flashing lights descended from above while a dimmer glow lifted to meet them from behind a rock barrier ahead.

Charlie grabbed a handful of fringe and found herself in a protective embrace. Scrag kept them moving toward the outcropping.

She'd just recognized the rhythmic thunder for what it was— helicopter blades—when it swooped on ahead allowing the grit it had raised to settle back to earth and, incredibly, the rasp of Edwina's voice to cut through the clamor. Charlie peered over the rock formation down into a natural bowl, ablaze and colorless with floodlights and two cameras filming the underside of the hovering chopper from different angles. It had a false bottom with circling lights.

But the real scene was Edwina Greene pounding a bald man around the head and shoulders while another tried to fend her off with a clipboard. The second man wore a headset with a speaker bar attached.

"You gotta help us, Charlie," Scrag Dickens told her with a certain glee. "Can't nobody control your mamma."

Charlie knew Edwina to be a royal pain in the ass but the woman wasn't dangerous. "She's probably furious because she signed on for a documentary, not this."

"*Return of an Ecosystem*'s shooting on the other side of the mesa. This is *Animal Aliens*. And the guy ol' Edwina's terrorizing is none other than Gordon Cabot himself." Again that hint of misplaced merriment.

Gordon Cabot was a renowned director of grade D flicks you tended not to hear of until they turned up in video stores. Charlie'd never met him, but she was in the process of trying to rescue one of his writers from hackdom. Cabot's reputation was so sleazy, even in Hollywood where sleaze had a reputation to uphold, she'd never have believed the man himself would be so ordinary-looking.

Charlie groaned and skidded down into the overlit bowl to rescue the director of *Animal Aliens*. She'd rather be home fighting cute guys off her teenage daughter. Edwina was a highly opinionated person who'd embarrassed Charlie to death most of her life, but this had to be the worst yet.

Edwina and Cabot were nose to nose in a shouting match by the time Charlie managed to grab her mother's arm. The assistant director stood undecided. He had a very full head of hair and the helicopter "breeze" was making it dance.

"What are you? Crazy?" Cabot screamed over the helicopter. "We're going to have to scrap the fucking shoot."

"You're scaring them all." Edwina sloughed off Charlie without even looking to see who was tugging on her arm. "All these lights and helicopters at night. . . . These are night creatures, you asshole."

"Creatures? I don't see any creatures. Do you see any creatures?" Gordon Cabot asked his AD and then Charlie, showing no surprise at finding a total stranger trying to drag off his adversary.

"This land teems with life and you have no right to interfere with it. You're an ecological disaster. You and your repulsive movies."

Edwina stomped out the remnants of her long brown cigarette and her enemy pointed at it. "Who's the ecological disaster? I'll tell you who. You. You and your stinking smokes, that's who."

The helicopter lifted straight up, cameras following its progress, oblivious to the fact that neither the director nor his assistant were exactly on line here. When Cabot realized this he ordered an end to the shoot and the helicopter wandered off.

And Edwina stomped off. "Come on, Charlie, get away from that creep."

"I'll sue," the director yelled after her.

"You just try it, dickhead."

"You the agent? Can you do anything with her? She needs a straitjacket, what she needs." He wasn't much taller than Charlie, his face bloated with a rage that transformed its bland features. Serious baldness made him look older than he probably was. Altogether an unpleasant little man with piggy eyes and an obviously nasty disposition.

But Charlie, still hung up on *dickhead*, tried hard to assure him she'd do what she could. She had sand in her teeth and in every crevice of her skin. Too bad Edwina's upgraded tent couldn't provide a hot shower.

She was over halfway up the side of the bowl when the floods went out, leaving her blind. As if he'd planned it that way, Gordon Cabot called to her, "Hey, you're with Congdon and Morse, right? I hear they're on the rocks."

A familiar pricking pain stabbed Charlie's middle. Jesus, had they heard about it clear out here? Already?

Chapter
2

Charlie sat across the tiny table from her mother. Wind flapped the canvas ends of the tent trailer, purred through the dwarf forest surrounding the campground.

"Sorry I didn't have anything better cooked up for you," Edwina said. "Wasn't sure when you could get here."

"It's one of Libby and my favorites, honest." We've learned to cook like you, God help us. "Pass the ketchup." Charlie had downed a Mylanta cocktail before picking up her fork, but the beanie wienies did taste good after the trials of that endless road and the embarrassment of her mother's confrontation with Gordon Cabot.

"How is Libby?" Edwina asked, her voice softening.

"Who knows? Since I'm not there to monitor things. Because I'm here instead. Edwina, *why* am I here?" Libby was in full revolt. Libby was sweet sixteen and a natural platinum blonde. Libby was pure unadulterated honey and L.A. swarmed with bees. And they both knew that. "Is it Cabot? I thought you were threatening to have a stroke over some problem with the documentary."

"How about canned peaches for dessert?"

The documentary crew had been straggling in off their evening shoot a few at a time and the smell of other dinners wafted through the screens. Edwina had never liked hard-shell camping where she was closed off to the outdoors no matter the weather. As

18

she'd aged she'd gone from a sleeping bag under the stars, to a backpacking tent, and now to this. Charlie wore two sweatshirts and a jacket and still shivered. Her mother wore a CU T-shirt.

The campground was well lighted over by the concrete toilets but close by all Charlie could see were dark shapes. Two of these now stepped out of a pickup in the next campsite, one saying clearly, "Probably Edwina's agent."

"Edwina's got an agent?" the other asked in disbelief. A distinctive, somehow familiar timbre to that second voice.

Edwina dished up peaches and poured coffee. The gasoline lantern hissed. The coffee felt hot and good, washing down the sweet syrupy taste of the fruit.

"What was so important that I had to rush out to this forsaken place?" Charlie insisted. "Why am I not home where I belong?" If something went wrong there, Edwina would be the first to blame Charlie. And Edwina didn't even know about the trouble at the agency.

"When I signed the contract for this job, Charlie, there was a blank to fill in the name of my agent."

"I don't care what that guy out there said, you don't have an agent. And that was just a boilerplate contract. Nobody handles technical advisers."

Edwina let her half-glasses fall to the end of the cord around her neck. She still had amazing distance vision but when she shortened her view, one eye wandered as she lost focus. It gave her a slightly wall-eyed appearance now across the table. Her iron-gray hair was cut in a short no-nonsense bob with thin bangs to take advantage of the way it grew. It had once been brown but Charlie had never seen it curled. She'd never seen her mother wear makeup or anything but sensible shoes. Edwina was too involved in her work to worry about prettification. "Charlie, you're the only agent I ever even heard of."

"So, you put down my name." Charlie screened literary properties and represented screenwriters contracted for motion picture and television projects, as well as some book authors. She also kept an eye out for possible vehicles for actors the agency had under contract. She did *not* handle technical advisers.

"So when I have trouble with this John B. character, he says, 'So talk to your agent' in a real snotty way. So I said, 'Okay, I will.'"

"You didn't use the agency's name? You don't have a contract with us."

"You are family, Charlie. Where was I supposed to go if not to you?"

"You used the agency's name." Chill out, Charlie, you know how she'll immobilize you if you lose your temper. "What is this problem you had that I had to leave home and livelihood to solve?"

"They're not following the book."

"Edwina, this is a documentary forgodsake. And it's not really your book."

"Keep your voice down. Everybody'll hear you."

"They don't even follow the book when they film a novel. They can't. You brought me all this way because they aren't following the book? Do you know how much plane tickets and rental cars cost?"

"Told you not to buy that expensive nothing house of yours." Edwina focused over the half-rim glasses to nail Charlie dead center against the thin back cushion. "Not my fault it's not worth half what you're paying for it every month."

Charlie took a swig of Mylanta right out of the bottle.

"Now . . . you contracted to check for accuracy on the script and to be available for consultation during portions of the filming. All they're using the book" (which you didn't really write a word of anyway) "for was to learn some general background and to find the name of an expert to help on what they don't understand. And you're that expert and until you've seen the edited film you don't know what they're doing anyway."

"I know John B. Drake is simplifying the material so much

that I can no longer verify its accuracy. Why hire an expert if you won't listen to her?"

"You told me yourself this was to be shown on television to the general public," Charlie said. "I mean we're talking network here . . . not even PBS. And not an auditorium full of stuffy scientists. Of course he has to simplify things." John B. Drake was a noted producer/director of documentaries with a hot reputation for bringing in high-quality product at or even under budget.

"It's no sin to be accurate, even on popular television."

"But it *is* a sin to be boring. All those scholarly qualifications attached to every statement, opinion, or hiccup would have viewers changing channels so fast—"

"If you don't know enough about being an agent to help me, Charlemagne Catherine, just say so. You don't have to be insulting." Edwina slid out from behind the table and then had to squeeze between it and the corner of the sink cupboard.

The place was maybe an eighth the size of a bed-sitter sublet. The sink and a three-burner stovetop filled the counter, mercifully hiding most of the orange Formica. Beneath was an enclosed water tank, the oven that also stored the pots and pans, a tiny refrigerator, and tinier space heater. The rest of the storage, which was precious little, was tucked under the shelf seats. With the tent top folded out, two moderately sized platforms offered hard shelves for bedding. A fold-down table completed the decor. Two adults could barely pass each other in the space remaining.

Edwina put their dishes into a plastic pail with the rest of the day's dishes.

"Okay. Okay. I don't think you've got a leg to stand on, but let me see your contract." Actually, I know you don't.

"I left it home."

"You left it home." Charlie rubbed gently around the disposable contact lenses which she'd had to remove in order to rinse off the helicopter grit.

"I didn't think I needed it out here." Charlie's mother

squirted detergent into the pail, added more water, and set the whole thing outside to soak overnight. Charlie wondered how much of the local wildlife she managed to kill off that way. "Can't carry all those papers around in the field," Edwina said. "Might get lost."

Charlie noted the pile of notes and books all but falling off the bunk at the other end of the camper and mentally counted to fifteen. Slowly. "Why . . . why don't we sleep on this and talk about it in the morning? I'm too tired to think."

But once in bed, Charlie Greene lay awake worrying about what Libby was doing. And what would happen to them both if Congdon and Morse went under. When she did fall asleep she dreamed of a small rat ramming its head against the tire of a car.

Charlie awoke with every muscle aching from being coiled too tightly against the cold.

Edwina was up and dressed. "We're invited out to breakfast. We'll hunt up old John B. afterward. All I've got left is oatmeal and I know how you like oatmeal."

The dishes were washed and draining in the sink. At least Charlie hoped they'd been washed. She dived into jeans, sweatshirts, Keds, and jacket.

At the concrete-block toilets the stools flushed with a minimum of water, the sinks offered only a cold dribble to wash with, and signs warned Charlie to be sparing with that because every last drop had to be trucked in. She tried to brush out her hair but without a shampoo it was hopeless and quite literally all over the place.

"Good morning, ladies." Scrag Dickens, standing in a commercial dumpster, tipped a cowboy hat to them as they left the concrete john. *His* hair looked pretty good. "You certainly have a gorgeous daughter, Edwina. Doesn't look anything like you."

"What's he doing in the dumpster?" Charlie asked her mother. "Scrounging breakfast?"

"Should have offered him the oatmeal but I wouldn't give that shit the time of day."

Charlie lived in a Hollywood sea of obscenities but had, with varying success, forsworn swearing when Libby took it up with a vengeance. But she had *never* heard her mother use language like she'd tossed at Gordon Cabot last night. "Is he a character actor or professional groupie or what?"

"Bills himself as a 'desert rat.' If so, he's the first rat I ever met I didn't like. And if he's an actor, he's a bad one. You stay away from him." That had been Edwina's advice to her daughter since Charlie began to show signs of maturation.

Lot of good it did.

They walked along the road that circled the campground. No one else appeared to be up yet.

"They don't shoot again until this evening so everyone's sleeping in," Edwina explained. "This campground was supposed to be ours, but some of the *Aliens* crew have been moving in because Moab's so full of tourists." Edwina looked wan for so early in the day and Charlie noticed more new wrinkles and pouches than she had the night before.

They turned off at a beat-up Bronco, a one-man backpacking tent, and the aromatherapy of morning coffee. All the campsites had picnic tables under roof shelters made of redwood slats, cooking grates on pedestals, and signs warning campers not to build fires anywhere else in this fragile landscape. A man stood fanning the smoke away from his eyes at this grate. He looked a lot like Mitch Hilsten, the movie star.

"Charlie, this is Mitch Hilsten." Edwina introduced them.

"Figures." Charlie regretted the condition of her hair and lack of makeup.

"He's narrating *Return of an Ecosystem*." Edwina studied her daughter suspiciously. "And he likes sleeping out under the stars."

Edwina had written Charlie one long carping letter and made some boring phone calls about this filming she was about to be involved in. Not once had she mentioned the name Mitch Hilsten.

"One egg or two?" Mitch Hilsten was one of those superstars you always thought of in terms of both names. And his was the voice Charlie had thought familiar last night.

"Where'd you get eggs? I'm down to oatmeal," Edwina said as if she were addressing an ordinary mortal.

"John B. and I went shopping last night, brought back a few good things for everyone." He flashed his famous teeth. "Just visit his rig when he wakes up."

He served them eggs over easy, cold smoked salmon, fresh-squeezed orange juice, and French bread. The sun managed to reach under the slatted overhang in time to warm them as they sat down.

Charlie fantasized telling her daughter and her best friend, Maggie Stutzman, that *the* Mitch Hilsten had once cooked her breakfast. Congdon and Morse did not handle his category of talent.

Except for the gleaming smile and powder-blue eyes, he looked all of a color in khaki pants and shirt, tan sheepskin jacket, California tan, and sandy hair. If this was an attempt to camouflage his identity and blend in with the desert backdrop, it was doomed to failure.

"Don't know how I can get any groceries," Edwina complained. "I'm not speaking to John B. Drake."

"Now that your agent's here, maybe she can straighten things out between you."

"Charlie's also my daughter." Edwina mopped up the last of her egg yolk with the crusty bread and washed it down with coffee before she answered his startled glance between them. There *was* an obvious lack of similarity. "We adopted her when she was a baby. Missed out on all the labor pains but none of the bills, heartache, or hassle, let me tell you."

Charlie shrugged at Mitch Hilsten. He jumped up to bring the coffeepot from the grate. Known around Hollywood as private, reclusive, and rude—on the screen he came off as tortured, in need of mothering, sexy beyond belief, and even mildly intelligent. He was of medium height, which was tall for actors in the flesh. Still,

Charlie was disappointed, as she invariably was with the big stars she'd met. They were so much smaller than on the screen, pathetically human—fearing they'd be recognized, terrified they wouldn't.

Edwina peeled another strip of succulent salmon off the bones. "First time you've ever invited me over. Couldn't be because of my lovely agent here, could it?"

He set the coffeepot down and blew on his hands pretending it was the pot rather than the question that was hot. "Tell you the truth, Edwina, I just had to see what that husky voice looked like. I could sort of see her in your trailer last night but she kept ducking behind you."

They turned to Charlie for a response so she blurted out the first inanity that came to mind. "Like, there must be a sizable budget here . . . I mean . . . for a documentary. Uh . . . to have someone like you hosting."

"I'm practically donating my time. I love this country. I'm a dedicated environmentalist and look for any excuse to get out here."

Someone with your income can afford to worry about saving the wilderness for the beasties. Rest of us have to worry about keeping our jobs and feeding our kids. But she said, "I take it this is not a union project here."

If it were, all meals on location would be catered and cast and crew would be put up in motels despite the number of tourists.

Hilsten pulled a slow grin. "Utah's a right-to-work state. Fantastic natural sets and nonunion conditions make it very popular with filmmakers. Even Cabot's working his crew without benefit of union."

Still, it was hard to believe a star of this caliber, even if fading, would be camping on the ground and doing his own cooking. No hangers-on/assistants. Maybe he really *was* the recluse and outdoorsman the hype proclaimed. Or was this all just a way to keep his face before the fickle public eye?

Charlie recalled reading that he hadn't made any pictures the last few years and that the last few had done nothing spectacular at the box office. But, with the string of smashes from his younger days, Mitch Hilsten would be a household name for decades even if he never acted again. Wouldn't he?

For a guy he wasn't all that old but his name was often used in conjunction with "as good-looking as" and handsome was currently out of fashion in leading men.

"So, now that you've met her," Edwina said, "what do you think?"

"Edwina!"

"Think I'll do the dishes. I've seen what you do with them." He removed his sheepskin, rolled up his sleeves, and reached for their plates—then froze in mid-movement.

Charlie watched the grin in his eyes fade, form a dangerous squint like in *Deadly Posse*.

She turned at the sound of an approaching vehicle. It was desert-camouflaged, military. But instead of uniformed soldiers, Gordon Cabot and another man sat in it, Cabot driving. As they drew closer, Charlie recognized the other man as Sidney Levit, the producer. Were things so bad he had to work with Cabot?

"Christ, it's a Humvee. He's not even on the road." Mitch watched them pass as if stunned then started after them on foot, soapsuds clinging to the hairs on his arms. Neither Cabot nor his passenger seemed to notice anyone else, so deep were they in argument—hands flailing, shouting words Charlie couldn't quite distinguish over the roar of the Humvee.

"That man's got to be stopped," Edwina said in a voice that chilled even her daughter. And Charlie had tangled with this woman all her life.

"**I** have a return ticket on a plane leaving tomorrow afternoon. We're going to have to straighten out your affairs the best we can today," Charlie told her mother at the door of the tent trailer. "And I have to call home. This is Saturday." Libby would be out of school and on her own.

"When's the last time you came to see me?" Edwina turned, her hand on the latch. "You just got here."

"If anyone should know what I'm facing back there it's you. Now I'm the one raising a teenager."

"Well, I hope you do a better job than I did." Edwina pushed Charlie aside and stomped off across hillocks of sand and scrub toward the concrete bathrooms. "There's a phone down at the Visitors' Center."

Charlie's eyes teared again. But this time not because of flying sand. How long must she go on apologizing for her life and for Libby's?

She stood undecided behind Howard's Jeep. Should she try to talk to John B. now or walk down to the Visitors' Center and phone Libby? Charlie ended up doing neither because once again there was a shouting match going on behind the pile of rocks she'd climbed last night.

* * *

The bowl appeared smaller in natural light. Three teenage girls in heavy makeup draped themselves over various rocks on its far side to pout for a cameraman setting up shots. Charlie wondered if they were about to be devoured by alien animals. Two vans were parked next to the Humvee, off the marked roads as forbidden to all vehicles by forest service signs at each switch and turn.

But the real drama staged itself just below her where Mitch Hilsten, Sidney Levit, Scrag Dickens, a man Charlie recognized from pictures in the trades as John B. Drake, and Gordon Cabot formed a rough circle around yet another man—the latter up to his elbows in plasterlike material he was scooping out of a wheelbarrow and slapping onto a grouping of rocks at the base of the wall. Scrag stood to one side as if to break with the circle, arms folded, observing more than participating. Sidney, on the other hand, a man known for his patience in nursing along troubled projects, was obviously still strung out.

"Too much helicopter time for location shots we can do by miniature in the studio. And now this. Gordon, you are making no sense here." Levit wore a white dress shirt with the sleeves rolled up above his elbows. The *Animal Aliens* producer was one of a fast-disappearing breed of old-timers in the industry—tall, thin, white-haired, with pale skin that shouldn't be exposed to a sun trying to get serious here. Even the spooky wind whirring through the pine needles was heating up. God, Charlie hated nature. She took off her jacket.

It seemed strange to see doc and feature crews mixing like this—even in animosity, sharing the same mesa top for location sites, not to mention the campground. There was a definite pecking order here and a feature would take precedence over a documentary.

"Location plus helicopter equals overbudget, drastic overbudget, Gordon," Sidney Levit continued. "You are losing your mind and you are losing mine. And we're going to lose our shirts if—"

"Every project goes over budget, Sid. Everybody knows every project goes over budget. Everybody expects it except you."

"Mine don't." John B. wore a red-and-black-plaid flannel shirt, faded Levi's, and hiking boots. Charlie had heard or read something juicy about him once, a scandal of some kind, she just knew it. She just couldn't remember it. "I use what's available and don't spend megabucks messing with—"

"Look, Drake, much as I appreciate your puny efforts, not everybody can make a living off sticks and cutesy-pie bugs, know what I mean? These rocks are not right for the aesthetic tone I have in mind here."

"They are *right*," Mitch Hilsten said with the low menace that had given Charlie erotic dreams as a teen. "*They* are perfect. Nature *made* them that way." Each statement brought the superstar a step closer to the little director. "You come *this* far. For *this* setting. And then you have to *fuck* it up."

The men who had given way to Mitch's threatening approach grabbed for him now as he appeared about to take a swing at Cabot. Everyone but Scrag, who glanced up to grin at Charlie.

She crawled off her perch and walked away. Somehow, guy stuff had seemed more dramatic on the big screen when she was a kid.

Charlie found herself on a path carefully edged with rocks, an occasional low and unobtrusive sign pleading with her not to leave it and stomp on the fragile ecology.

It was springtime, May, and the morning warmed enough now for her to wish she could shed her last sweatshirt. She also wished she could shed the wash of guilt Edwina invariably induced. That's probably what had so discolored the scene she'd just left. Given her a funny uneasiness. Guilt or no, Mitch Hilsten or no, Charlie would be glad to get on that plane tomorrow.

Scrubby plants and bushes sported flowers, as small and understated as their faint fragrance. Charlie was aware of birdsong because it was so scant—not the usual morning cacophony you barely notice because it blends into a background noise like traffic. Each little trill or chirp or peep was distinct and alone and perfect here, spaced from its companions like the plants and shrubs along the trail, where the sand stretched tidy and clean between.

There were deer tracks though and, if you looked closely and had a mother like Edwina who made a point of such things, you could pick out the faint trails of the ubiquitous desert rodents.

Charlie came upon the stone and mortar parapet without warning. It was only knee-high. She backed away and sat in the middle of the path, head swimming with adrenaline, guilt and sexy superstars long forgotten.

Cavorting around on the expanse of mesa top, she hadn't kept in mind why this whole area was referred to as Canyonlands.

The drop on the other side of that parapet was a good thousand feet straight down.

If you threw a live body over that parapet, you'd never hear it splatter. Even in tall buildings in New York or mountain overlooks in Colorado, she'd had to sidle up to windows or cliff edges. Charlie never took a window seat in an airplane.

She wasn't sure if it was natural curiosity or that she always feared she might be missing something, but she sidled up to the parapet by scooting along on her tush. At the bottom of the first thousand feet was a broad benchland with a narrow ribbon of road. The road had another chasm running along beside it with another thousand-foot drop to a mud-cream river that looked about as wide as a string from here.

"Oh boy."

Sitting down made the parapet more like chest-high. You couldn't trip over something chest-high and go sailing out into space and plummet in agonized dread for thousands of feet knowing—for what would seem like hours—the sure and final outcome.

Still, this was not a comfortable place for Charlie Greene. She slid back to the middle of the path before she stood.

"I don't want to startle you," John B. Drake said behind her, and Charlie whirled to face the red-and-black-plaid shirt. "I assume you're the agent. I'm John Drake."

"Yes, I'm from Congdon and Morse." She wiped the sweat off her palm down the seat of her jeans and shook his hand. "Charlie Greene, Edwina's daughter."

He looked as if he'd been born in the faded denims and solid hiking boots. He hadn't shaved yet and his dark hair needed combing. Guiding her companionably along the path, he said, "I assume you were headed to the Point."

"The Point . . . uh, is it . . . are there sheer drop-offs and cliffs and—"

"The view," he said, "is what's known as breathtaking."

"That's what I was afraid of."

"Don't worry, the parapet must be two feet thick. About Edwina, there's no way to please the lady. I can't meet her demands and I don't really need her that much. But I don't want to hurt the old girl's feelings. Can you help me make her see sense?"

They had reached the Point, the curved bow of their mesa, anchored in a sea of chasm and plumbless shadow and yawning abyss on three full sides. Charlie turned carefully away from the breathtaking view. "I'm here to help Edwina, Mr. Drake. If I could see a copy of her contract, perhaps we can negotiate something acceptable to both sides."

"You're not going to keep up this farce about Congdon and Morse representing Edwina Greene?"

"How about Charlie Greene will represent Dr. Greene?"

"I heard you tell her yourself last night you didn't think she had a leg to stand on."

Charlie peered over the parapet, took a glance at the Colorado River so many heart-stopping fathoms away, and turned her back on it. Now if anybody asked her if she'd been out to the Point she could say yes and forestall another trip. A flash of blue caught her eye. Safely back from the edge of anything now, she gestured toward the distant deep azure, evenly shaped lakes in an otherwise dull russet and beige landscape.

"The APC holding ponds," the director explained. "American Potash Corporation. One of the sponsors of our film. They pump water thousands of feet deep into a mine and when it comes up another hole it's full of potash. They hold it in those ponds and when all the potash sinks to the bottom and the water evaporates they scoop it out. There's a display about it at the Visitors' Center."

"Potash . . . I've heard of it but I can't remember why."

"It's a potassium compound, used in all kinds of things, but mostly fertilizers. What I wanted to—"

"Mr. Drake, I may not be all that up on location shooting, but I'm surprised Cabot didn't get the Film Commission to boot you from this site."

"Oh, he tried." John B. gave the sky a hard look and a grimace, but turned back to Charlie with the rubbery smile of an actor. "However, the Film Commission doesn't decide those things on public land."

This was a state park and the chief ranger at the Visitors' Center did. And he was much more into environmental documentaries than he was science fiction features. The docs were easier on the fragile landscape he was protecting. "They even buried the last twenty miles of the electrical cable that comes out here."

Cabot's crew had just started to move equipment in the day before.

"They use the campsites more for R&R between shoots and to stock supplies anyway. But they did have some problems finding space in Moab for everybody, supposedly," he said with an edge to his voice that belied his cheerful expression. "Sid Levit and I have known each other for years."

The *Return of an Ecosystem* crew had been here four days already and had planned only three but nature'd been uncooperative. "We've had problems with thunderstorms and the critters never show up when they're supposed to. Which is another bone I have to pick with your mother. She ought to be able to flush them for us."

The cinematographer drove his truck off a cliff the first day. He managed to jump out before it went over, but the production lost some equipment. "We had to rent Earl another truck and fly in replacements. And then along come *Animal Aliens* and Gordon Cabot. I'm hoping, Charlie Greene, that your arrival signals a change of luck for this beleaguered production and its director."

Gordon Cabot might need a Sidney Levit to smooth things over, but a good director is charismatic, persuasive, decisive, demanding, wily, and infinitely patient. Able to charm the maracas off a rattlesnake. Drake was really no exception. He had Charlie laughing by the time they reached the campground, had her agreeing to forgo the discussion of Edwina's complaints until lunch in his motor home, and her tentative acceptance to join him and the crew that evening when they hoped to shoot a sunset sequence.

A slender tawny blonde pouted in the doorway of that motor home as Charlie passed it. And Edwina pouted in her tent trailer over a cup of coffee.

"Let's go call Libby," Charlie coaxed. "I know she'd like to talk to her grandma too."

"What'd Drake have to say?" her mother asked suspiciously as they walked down the road toward the Visitors' Center. "I saw you two come back from the Point together."

"We agreed to discuss your complaints over lunch in his rig. That's when lots of business gets done in this business. And you're invited. I told him I represent you. But you're going to have to let me do the talking. He's twice as clever as he wants anyone to think he is." But he's right—this is all a charade.

"You're the agent, Charlie," Edwina said and even managed a smile.

The Visitors' Center was one of those buildings just before the wye in the road Charlie had passed the night before. There were several rangers behind the desk in the lobby, all young and pink with health. One had a loose, silly grin that didn't disappear when he spoke. His name badge announced him as Tim Pedigrew.

"Radio phone's tied up for a while," Ranger Tim told her cheerfully. "We got a new digital but there's still twenty phones on four frequencies and we got a backlog of calls to make. Come back later this afternoon, why don't ya? Or if it can't wait, maybe Mr. Cabot would let you use one of his. He's rented three cellulars and a repeater from Royce's Electric in Moab."

"We are asking no favors of Gordon Cabot," Edwina informed her daughter as they left the center.

"I wanted to catch her after she got up but before she decided to go out somewhere," Charlie insisted. "And I have to get that tire fixed. John B. and Mitch must have phones, too, if Cabot does."

"Mitch doesn't, I know. This is his chance to get away from it all. Drake has one, I think. If not, I need a few things in Moab. You can call from there. We'll tell him our business lunch'll be late. Those people don't keep human hours anyway."

If the director or his blonde were at home they didn't answer Charlie's knock. She left a note on his door and they took off in Howard's Jeep, Charlie driving.

Howard Greene had purchased the Jeep two weeks before his fatal heart attack—which was just under two weeks before Libby was born—and had never traveled in it except for a few forays into the mountains west of Boulder. Since then, Edwina'd rattled it all over the deserts, plains, and mountains of the Southwest but it would always be "Howard's Jeep."

Howard had been a good deal older than Edwina and a full professor before his second marriage. Still, Charlie would always wonder if the shock of her pregnancy had in any way helped bring on his coronary.

Because, although Professor Howard Greene had taken little notice of his adopted daughter as she grew up, Charlie certainly captured his attention when at sixteen she announced she was pregnant.

Chapter

4

Moab was deathly quiet and a long way to go for "a few things," a phone call, and a tire repair. An elongated town swept clean by the sun, its shape defined by red canyon walls, its dark green trees improbable against the desert backdrop and snow-capped mountains on the horizon. A dusty Western town filled with church spires instead of saloons.

Charlie reached only the answering machine at home. So she called Maggie Stutzman—her neighbor, friend, and confidante.

"Tell me she made it home last night," Charlie pleaded.

"I assume so. Doug Esterhazie picked her up about an hour ago. Saturday's orthodontist day, right?"

"Oh Jesus, would you believe I forgot?"

"Yes. How's Edwina?"

The orthodontist made it clear Saturday slots were for high-paying adults too important to take off on weekdays. He explained endlessly that children missing school for appointments was logical because there were so many of them among his clientele. If mothers stayed home to raise children they could take them to and from school for appointments and his life would be easier.

But times were tough in Long Beach and insurance companies less willing to pay even portions of cosmetic orthodontia. He needed the work and Charlie took enormous satisfaction in messing up his schedule.

She could remember cutting her tongue on her own braces during the torture of Libby's birth.

"Charlie?"

"What? Oh, uh . . . she's just being Edwina. And mysterious. And the usual pain in the behind. Tell you all about it when I get back tomorrow night. Thanks for keeping an eye on the scenery, Maggie."

"Relax, Greene, 'the scenery' will be just fine here. You take care of your mom."

Charlie never felt at ease leaving Libby, but she was more comfortable knowing Maggie lived across the driveway and had windows facing Charlie's.

She stepped away from the public phone, her thoughts still in Long Beach. A door slammed and a car pulled away from a Laundromat across the street, bringing Charlie back. Here it was, early Saturday afternoon, and the shops were open. A few cars were parked in the street, most with out-of-state license plates.

"Where is everybody?" she asked Rudy Dichtl at Dichtl's Full Service service station. At least Charlie didn't have to replace the tire. There'd been a nail in it. Rudy stuffed the hole with gluey rubber bands and cut them off even with the surface.

"They been bussing extras out to Dead Horse Point for a twilight shoot. Those who ain't in the scene, or the film even, go to pass out sandwiches or take pictures of relatives and friends in costume and just to watch. Hollywood's big business around here. And more fun than watching tourists all day. About all we have left—tourists and Hollywood." He dumped the tire in a tub of water to look for leaks. "My dad now, he was baptized by Charlton Heston."

"Excuse me?"

He checked out Charlie's expression. "You're probably too young to remember *The Greatest Story Ever Told,* but Charlton Heston was John the Baptist. He dunked Dad and a slew of Rotarians before he lost his head." Rudy made a slicing motion across his throat with an oil-stained forefinger. He was a nice-looking man with thick hair graying elegantly and a thin mouth slanting down at the corners while playful eyes made fun of her city naiveté.

Why did she expect the world to turn predictable once she left Southern California?

"My son's a rat."

"I'm sorry."

"Runs in the family, acting . . . art . . . you know." He turned the tire to check the other half for bubbles. "My grandfather, now he got killed by Cochise—Jeff Chandler. My mother was scalped by his son, Rock Hudson. Well, one of Rock's braves but it makes a better story. *Broken Arrow* and *Taza, Son of Cochise.* Don't suppose you ever heard of them."

"Yeah, well . . . you ever heard of *Phantom of the Alpine Tunnel?*" Charlie countered. It was, at the moment, about the only big thing she and Congdon and Morse had going. Sort of.

He thought for several minutes—most people would have given it a second. "Don't believe I have. Who starred in it?"

"It's still in production." With any luck.

Rudy wasn't impressed. He informed her that he'd done some off-camera lackey work for the more recent *Geronimo* and *Thelma and Louise* himself and carried the repaired tire on its heavy wheel to the Jeep for her. Edwina was already there and they had to rearrange sacks of groceries to make room for it.

"I'm leaving tomorrow," Charlie said, glancing back at the food as they headed down the street. Where are you going to put all that stuff?

"Don't want old John B. thinking he can hold me up, just for a bite to eat. Let's grab some burgers on the way. If I want to get mad and walk out on the negotiations he won't have the satisfaction of hearing my stomach growl."

Charlie pulled the Jeep into a true drive-in, not a drive-through. A girl in blue jeans came up to the car for their order. Charlie hadn't seen one of these in years.

On the way out of town she asked carefully, "Edwina, are you still taking your hormones?"

"Now what's that supposed to mean?" Charlie's mother reached for a sack of potato chips from the pile of food in back.

"I've just never heard you talk like this before. Calling people names and being so . . . so confrontational."

"Ever strike you that you just might not be around me enough to know what I'm like?" They traveled in a dangerous, loaded silence for miles before Edwina spoke again, this time with a hint of restrained tears. "I gave up a lot for you and Libby. Keeping her in good day care while you went to college, supporting you both for all that time. It about wiped me out financially and emotionally. And Howard dying before she was even born."

Oh boy, not this again. "You know I'm grateful. I don't know where we'd be now without you."

"You'd be on welfare, that's where you'd be." Edwina was a staunch Republican and had maintained from the moment Charlie refused to give up her baby that no child of hers was going to be a "welfare queen."

"Edwina, are you having financial problems?" One of Charlie's worst fears was that for some unforeseen reason her mother would decide to chuck it all and come live with them. Another was that Charlie would lose her job and she and Libby would have to go live with Edwina.

"No, I'm not having financial problems," Edwina mimicked in that infuriating way that made Charlie want to slug something.

She pressed down on the accelerator instead, the ancient Jeep responding with relish.

"You think I'm going crazy, don't you?" The unshed tears again.

"Of course not. You're just talking funny and I thought maybe something was wrong."

"Funny—crazy."

"No. Just different than normal is all." Because she resented owing her mother so much already, Charlie didn't want to admit how much she counted on Edwina's stability (preferably at a great distance) to give ballast to her own world. "I mean, like . . . asshole, dickhead. That's not my mother talking."

"I can't believe I'm hearing this from you. You who had a mouth like a locker-room parrot by the time you hit fourth grade."

"I like to think I've matured some since fourth grade." Are you never proud of anything I do? Any way I change? Of what I've become? We both worked damned hard at this you know. "You seem to be regressing."

"Regressing . . ." Edwina absently fished what was left of Charlie's hamburger out of the bag and finished it, "as in senile, crazy . . ."

"Will you *stop* with the crazy? You're going to drive *me* crazy." As I remember growing up, I was one of the few people in Boulder who *didn't* think you were crazy. And in Boulder, crazy is not easy to notice.

"Better slow down, Charlie, or you're going to get us both killed."

They hit the roadblock just after the APC turnoff.

"Sorry, no one's allowed into the park for the next few hours. Afraid you'll have to turn back." The sheriff's deputy was one of those super cool, polite, handsome, totally expressionless types you see often in law enforcement. Charlie wondered if they were cloned in some central warehouse and sent out by the FBI.

Her mother leaned across her to explain that they were with the film company on location here and heading back to their camp with supplies from Moab. He couldn't find their names on the clipboard he rested on his belt buckle.

"The documentary, not the *Animal Aliens* thing," Charlie offered, trying to head off her mother's ire.

He, in all innocence, asked, "What documentary?"

"*Return of an Ecosystem*, shithead!" Edwina chimed.

He registered the epithet with a flickering hesitation in his blink is all. But he registered it. Charlie could only hope her mother never got in any trouble with the law in Grand County.

"Wait here, ladies," the blank-faced cop said, as if they had a choice, and walked back to the two cars forming the roadblock. He pulled a handset out of one of them and spoke into it, his sunglasses trained on Howard's Jeep. Then he waited. It seemed forever before the car radio began spitting back unintelligible sounds again. When the communication ended he stared, mannequin-still, at the handset before replacing it. Then he turned away from Charlie and Edwina and appeared to search the heavens. His fellow clone, leaning against the other car, bowed his head almost as if in prayer. But his shoulders shook.

Edwina said, "Those two are acting very peculiar."

"Just promise not to call them any more names," Charlie pleaded.

She began checking her watch when the deputies did. More than twenty minutes passed before the one who'd stopped them started toward them for no reason. No radio call, nothing. Just checking his watch. She and her mother were going to miss that business lunch with John B. now no matter how strange his hours.

"There's another roadblock up ahead," the deputy informed them. "Sheriff Sumpter would like to speak with you." As he walked off, his cohort backed one car next to the other so they could pass.

Sheriff Ralph Sumpter was small and thin with a big-man swagger, indelibly rural, and as different from his mechanical deputies as could be. He wore his hair clipped so short Charlie could see the origin of each tiny strand. He had a high-pitched voice, spoke slowly but without a drawl. "Now, Mrs. Greene—"

"Miss."

"Now, Miz Greene, I understand you drove in last night about twilight?"

"Well, yeah . . . like, it was dark by the time I reached the campground. What's happened here?" Ambulances, fire trucks, cars, and pickups lined the road. There was enough excitement for a full-scale disaster. But no sign of a wreck.

"Parker, get a reading on this lady," the sheriff yelled and a man came to pass a black plastic object, the size of a gigantic calculator, up and down Charlie's clothes and over her hair. It had various buttons and a small digital readout screen. No ticking, but Charlie had seen something similar in a newspaper photo from Chernobyl.

"Is that a Geiger counter?" she asked, incredulous.

"A trace," the man announced and hurried off importantly.

At that the sheriff made a worried sound and turned very serious indeed.

"A trace of what? Talk to me." The hot sun glued Charlie's bra and jeans to her skin. Mechanical voices spit static chatter on the radios of the emergency vehicles. Edwina stood next to Howard's Jeep, answering questions from yet another deputy. A steady stream of people rushed to and from something off in the desert. Some wore face masks, others men's handkerchiefs tied over mouths and noses, banditlike. Some carried stretchers holding covered lumps that could have been bodies badly disjointed. "Sheriff, did you find a mass grave out here or something?"

"See anything unusual on the way into the campground last night?" the little sheriff asked. "Now don't answer right away, think about it. Try to remember everything you saw. This is important."

"Well, I had to stop and change a tire and I saw this rat—"

"Rat? Oh, God, no." His sigh was devastated. He looked at Parker, who'd returned with his funny box. "What'd I tell ya?"

Parker looked horrified.

"Miz Greene," Sheriff Ralph turned back to Charlie, "what did the rat do?"

"I think he may have been rabid." She described the rodent's drunken behavior and Parker groaned.

"This is worse than I thought," Ralph said with a manly grimace. "Did you smell anything strange at the time?"

"I don't think so . . . just . . . fresh air. We don't get much of that in L.A."

"Did you see anything out of the usual in the sky?"

"Stars. City lights and fog and pollution sort of hide—"

"Miz Greene, I'm going to show you something I want you to look at, but mostly I want you to smell it for me. And that's going to be hard." He took her arm, much as John B. had earlier on the path out to the Point, and led her off into the bush forest. And then he said in a controlled, personal voice, as studied as Mitch Hilsten's had been with Edwina at breakfast, "But what I want most is your word that you won't say anything to other possible witnesses at that campground until we've had a chance to question them. Especially not to your mother."

"She won't have to, because I'm going with her," Edwina said right behind them. "I demand to know what's happening here."

There was an angry staring match between Sheriff Sumpter and Edwina Greene, but he finally grated his molars in an audible "scritch" and guided them toward the scene of activity.

It didn't seem like the sort of landscape where anything much could be hidden but it was amazing how soon they were out of sight of the road. Charlie didn't know what to expect other than a lot of blood because of all the ambulances. Both she and Edwina recognized the smell long before they arrived at the site.

It was just that Charlie couldn't identify it at first.

Chapter 5

At first, Charlie thought an airliner had crashed without burning. Because of the twisted metal and the covered shapes on the ground.

A lone shoe here, a woman's purse there, everywhere broken glass flashing back at the sun.

"Reported missing when it didn't show up at a motel in Moab," Sheriff Sumpter told them. "Probably wouldn't have been found yet if it wasn't for a small plane happening over here at first light."

Charlie remembered what Rudy Dichtl had said about the shoot out here. "Then this wasn't the busload of extras from Moab?"

"No, thank God. I got half my family in that scene."

Still cameras clicked and whirred. One man panned the accident site with a thirty-five millimeter. One put samples of sand in plastic bags. Two worked with acetylene torches and another pried at the wreckage with a crowbar. Several measured things with tape measures and wrote on clipboards. No one spoke much above a whisper. A sheet of gray metal lying up against a crushed juniper had SUNSET TOURS painted across it.

"Tour company claims there were forty-two passengers, all elderly, and the driver," the sheriff said softly. "No survivors we think. Have to put more of the body pieces together before we can be sure. Hard to tell who's what in a mess like this."

You saw them everywhere these days. Comfortable buses hauling groups of retirees, mainly widows, between motel and restaurant stops. Past sights they were now too old really to explore once they had the leisure to do so.

The thirsty sand had soaked up most of the blood and spilled fuel. Charlie didn't let her eyes dwell long on the remaining dark patches or the things still being removed from the wreckage.

"Figure the bus body was scraped off the chassis and then crushed," Sheriff Sumpter said. "Might be whatever did this was the same thing made your rat drunk last night. What I can't figure is the smell. And how that bus got so far from the road without leaving tracks."

Charlie tried to breathe through her mouth. "Reminds me of chemistry in high school or rotten eggs or a chemical spill or—could it be nerve gas?"

"Nerve gas is odorless," the sheriff said with patient condescension. "And we'd be too busy dying to stand here talking."

"Forget chemistry," Edwina prompted with even more condescension and less patience. "Try biology."

"Biology's your thing, I can barely remember chemistry . . . oh. Right. Your lab at CU. And our basement."

"What?" Ralph the sheriff demanded. "Tell me."

"Rats. I knew it was familiar. Rat urine and shit . . . feces. Only ten times stronger. Wait a minute . . . a bunch of little rats did all *this*? Give me a break."

"She smells rats!" Sheriff Sumpter bellowed at the universe and pumped Parker's hand.

"Well, *I* smell *a* rat," Edwina said.

And about then, Charlie did too.

He appeared from behind a scrubby bush, leaping. He high-fived the sheriff and Parker and hugged Charlie before she could get out of his way.

"If we can fool them, we got it just right," Gordon Cabot said. "Anybody knows rats, it's Edwina Greene."

Edwina Greene decked him on the first swing.

"Well, I didn't call him any names, did I?"

"Did you ever stop to think he could sue you like he's always threatening?" Charlie helped stow all the groceries in the cupboards and crevices of the small trailer. "You're lucky the sheriff didn't arrest you on the spot for assault." Charlie was beginning to feel like her mother's mother.

I've already got a kid. I don't need two.

Half the pharmacies in Utah had worked to concoct the right smell to convince the extras that the scene to be shot was really that of a tour busload of senior citizens savagely mushed when a UFO accidentally dropped a Porta Potti on top of it. Even though the extras knew better.

And the sheriff had cooperated in staging a hastily arranged run-through of the evening's shoot to check out on the Greenes what Cabot insisted upon calling *verisimilitude*.

Charlie found the very thought of Gordon Cabot and that word appearing in the same sentence staggering.

"You see," he'd explained to her, between legal threats to her mother, "these rats from another planet are looking for a waste-disposal site for their world and what better place than here? High concept for the ecofreaks, right? But all the rats see anywhere are humans. Who they consider unimportant critters."

"This would take one frigging giant of a Porta Potti."

"No problemo, babe. These are giant rats. That's why they don't notice the little native rats at first."

Charlie still smarted from being taken in so easily. If she hadn't been concentrating on her mother's strange behavior she'd have picked up on it sooner. Sure.

"Ammonium hydroxide," Edwina said now, as she straightened up from a floor-level cupboard still holding a roll of toilet paper. "They used a lot of commercial ammonia to make that stink."

By the time they'd reached the campground, John B. was busy preparing for his own filming. Edwina sent Charlie down to the Visitors' Center for a bundle of firewood for the grate and their dinner later. Then the two walked across the mesa to a grassy pasturelike landscape where the cast and crew of *Return of an Ecosystem* were in the midst of a setup for their twilight shoot.

Edwina introduced her to Earl Seabaugh, the director of photography, or DP, and in this nonunion doc also the chief camera operator, as he set up his equipment on a tripod. He had a shaved head, one earring, sea green eyes, a trimmed beard, and the build of a football player. "Hear you almost got peed on by great big rats this afternoon."

"No secrets out in the wilds either, huh?"

Earl nodded toward Scrag, who stood talking to the blonde Charlie had seen in the door of Drake's motor home. "Our own desert rat's been spreading the word."

Charlie joined her mother, who stood scowling off by herself. Edwina's social skills had never been great but it was hard to imagine what these people thought of her now that she had this delightful new personality. "Where did all the grass come from?"

"You'll only find it on this side of the cattle guard. Taken twenty-five years of no grazing to get it this far. Take it another twenty to get back to normal."

There was plenty of space between clumps, but from a distance the grass looked like a rippling, flowing, solid ground cover. It must drive the cattle on the other side of the fence nuts. It came up to Mitch Hilsten's knees as he stood patiently while the blonde fussed with his hair, talced the shine from his forehead, adjusted his collar. Earl ran a light meter over him.

John B. loped between his crew and a generator truck where two men had strung cables to lights on a tall grid for the night portion of the sequence. With a hand over his eyes, he checked the position of the sun.

"They'll record the sound of the wind in the grasses now and

Mitch'll lip sync his speech again later," Edwina whispered to Charlie. "No wonder movies cost so much. Must already have miles of footage on the sunset colors of that canyon rim and its cliffs behind him."

"Think we got liftoff," Earl said and bent to his camera while an assistant standing off to the side swung a handheld up to a pad on his shoulder to shoot at a different angle.

The blond woman held a clapboard ready. She was certainly a Jill of all trades in this production company.

"Her name's Tawny," Edwina said under her breath. "Just Tawny, no last name. So she says."

"Quiet on the set. Roll camera."

"Rolling."

"Speed."

"Thirty-eight takes one—marker." And Tawny clapped the stick.

Mitch looked small and insignificant in the broad field of grass with the mammoth canyon rim looming from across an abyss beyond it. An endless sky with clumps of floating gray cloud acted as backdrop. Wind ruffled his hair and shirt as it did the grass at his feet.

"Mitch!"

"Wind lays thick deposits of silts and sands on the mesa tops and here a grassland can develop," Mitch said. "The different textures of ricegrass, galleta, grama, and muhly weave a blanket of subtle, moving beauty that stabilizes the dunes. The superficial roots of these grasses seize the moisture before it can percolate out of reach. Over a hundred years of cattle grazing has all but destroyed the fragile grasslands of this desert plateau.

"But here in the park an experiment is taking place. No grazing has been allowed for twenty-five years and you can see the result. With the return of the grasses there has been a slow but steady return of certain insects, rodents, and small birds. And, with them, their more spectacular predators—the fox, coyote, eagle, hawk, and owl."

He wore a safarilike outfit, similar to the one he'd worn at breakfast but clearly less rumpled and camp-worn. He looked intense and sincere, his gestures relaxed but his message vital. Yet with just a hint of the sardonic, just enough to remind an audience this message came from Mitch Hilsten. He was alone in this immense landscape with Earl's camera, seemingly unaware of the handheld and the groups of people behind both.

And the moment he began to speak he was no longer insignificant in the vast landscape—he was the center of it. The natural lighting appeared to be performing for him.

As he explained how the grasses offered seeds to the rodents, their burrows helped give proper texture to the soil layers which in turn helped the grass to grow, the shadows behind him lengthened.

The desert varnish washed blue-black to deep lavender in the depressions on the cliff face of that far rim.

Flat rock walls grew textured and three-dimensional, scarred with crevasse and mystery.

Gray clouds turned pink and deepened to rose.

The grass whispered with excitement now, as if on cue.

". . . and, as the sun sets, creatures of the night—which burrow beneath us in daylight to conserve the moisture in their bodies—stir in their burrows. And their predators rise and stretch in anticipation of the night's hunt. Some take to the sky to begin their search for dinner."

Charlie shifted her feet uneasily at the thought of all those hungry night creatures stirring under her, reminding herself that documentary or no there was a goodly portion of show biz happening here. God help her, she loved this business. Nuts as it was.

He really was impressive. Even with the force of his words diffused by the wind, his backdrop upstaging him again with its gorgeous color, he still held Charlie captive. He was a presence, a professional at work. The tingle of excitement he managed to create despite a nearly expressionless expression, the inflection even at this distance so right, it was perfect, just . . .

And then he blew it.

Mitch Hilsten—who had made her forget the trouble at the agency, her worry over her mother and daughter, even her embarrassment at being sucked in by the tour bus crushed by an alien Porta Potti—suddenly became merely another human.

The clouds behind him lost their color, turned gray at his sudden silence.

"Cut!" John B. threw both arms in the air. "Mitch? What?"

Mitch stared at the sky overhead. The assistant camera operator disobeyed and swung his handheld to follow Mitch's gaze.

Chapter

6

Charlie cringed for a nanosecond, half-expecting an alien outhouse to fall out of the sky.

"I don't see anything," Edwina said.

Charlie didn't either.

"Damn it, if this is a sick joke I'm going to commit some serious murder around here." Drake stomped off to confront Mitch.

"We can edit out the last frames," Earl called after him, wiping a sleeve across his forehead and winking at Charlie. He reached for the camera on his colleague's shoulder. "You're wasting film, Mike."

"Sure got dark fast," Tawny said to no one in particular.

And she was right. Twilight was over. It was night. Charlie'd noticed the suddenness of the same when driving in here the night before.

"All right, children, we'll pack up the lights and go home," John B. said, stalking through the grama and muhly grasses. Time for a directorial tirade. Charlie caught the dance of laughter in Earl's eyes as he pulled a baseball cap out of a pocket to conceal his mirth and naked head. She hoped Edwina would keep her mouth shut.

The wind had gone as silent as the crew, but the generator hummed.

"Never mind that we are nearing budget," the director emoted.

"Never mind that cables are strung and all is ready. Never mind that the night is perfect for the last scene for which we have to pay a superstar on location—"

"Christ, I'm working for practically nothing."

"You call playing jokes with my budget nothing? The years you took off my life just now, nothing? Is that right, Mitch? I thought we were friends. And all because you looked up and didn't see anything?"

"What I said was, I saw nothing. That's not the same."

But when Charlie and Edwina left them, John B. had everyone back to work as if there'd been no interruption—Mitch Hilsten, bathed this time in a golden glow of false light from the grid, talking earnestly to Earl's camera.

"Only in Hollywood," Charlie muttered. She took her mother's arm when they both stumbled on the uneven ground in the dark and was surprised to feel the bones through Edwina's skin. "Have you lost weight since I saw you last?"

"Flesh sags with years, Charlie. I'm just getting old. I don't do it to irritate you. Someday you'll know."

Once, Edwina had said, "I hope you have a daughter just like you someday, Charlie Greene. That will be my revenge. Then you'll know."

Charlie wished her mother would stop with this "old" business. She never knew when Edwina was making a play for sympathy or when it was time to seriously panic. Charlie'd never heard of aging causing people to take up heavy swearing and get physical. Gordon Cabot must have been off balance when this frail woman knocked him down.

They made their way through the grasslands to the road and along it to the resumption of the stunted forest. Every other shadow-shape was a tree skeleton, twisted and grotesque, trying to snag them like something out of a Disney animation.

But Charlie's thoughts slipped off to real life—her regret at missing the screening of *For Whom the Bell Tolls II* back in L.A. tonight. There would be people there she needed to see.

Right, and all they'd want to talk about is the mess the agency's in.

Charlie would have to call Bud Harrington and Toby Davenport for progress reports tomorrow night when she got home. Monday's schedule was too full. They were the only two writers she had on active assignment at the moment. Things had never been this bad for her or Congdon and Morse. Name talent was falling away like dandruff.

As Richard, the Morse in Congdon and Morse Representation, always warned, "Get a name as a bad luck hotel in this town and you're shunned. Superstitious bunch in this business."

At least Jory would be pitching *Willing Hostage* at Universal Monday. Charlie was backed up on her reading and Richard was putting the pressure on her to discover some "wonder" project to help get the agency on its feet. Her Toyota was due at the garage for a physical, there was cleaning to be picked up, and the damn cat needed a new flea and tick collar, and . . . what was Libby doing tonight? Saturday night with Charlie out of town—

Edwina startled her back to the problems at hand with, "Wonder if there was really anything there when Mitch stopped speaking like that. Always impressed me as pretty levelheaded—for an actor."

Mitch had insisted he'd seen only a large patch of sky with no stars in it. Or thought he had.

They picked their way carefully along a shadowed stretch of road hoping not to turn an ankle in a pothole. Charlie was glad for the illumination the parking lot–style lights around the toilets provided the whole campground.

Enough for Edwina to see to light the lantern. Charlie held it while her mother split wood into kindling with an ax like Scrag Dickens had pulled out from under the table last night.

"Why don't you use charcoal?" she asked as her mother slathered sugary barbecue sauce from a bottle onto chicken pieces.

"Takes too long. Besides, this is more like it used to taste cooked over the campfire. Remember those days? How good everything was?"

Charlie remembered everything mostly as cold and tasting charred but didn't say so.

They were at the picnic table crunching burned chicken and gritty corn and pinto beans from cans Edwina had opened and set right in the fire, when both film crews began to straggle in. Even Cabot in his Humvee. He paused behind Howard's Jeep long enough to raise a triumphant middle finger in their direction.

"Don't let him bait you, Edwina." Charlie had been ready to stuff a drumstick in her mother's mouth to keep her quiet.

But Edwina remained ominously silent. Maybe because of the sounds of joviality emanating from John B.'s motor home.

"Damn, I wanted us to go over and talk to him about your little problem tonight." First thing in the morning I'm outta here. "But it'd be hard to do with all those people around."

"My *little* problem?" Edwina said, every line in her face sagging. "Is that what I am to you, Charlie? *Your* little problem?"

"Mom, stop it right now. I've had it." Charlie slammed her spoon down on the plate and slid off the bench seat. "You either tell me what's really wrong here or I'm changing that tire tonight and heading for the airport in Grand Junction." She wrung chilled hands over the warm embers of the cooking fire and realized her mother was wearing only a thin shirt. "Are you sure you're still taking your hormones?"

"What did you say, Charlie?"

"Are you sure you're still taking your—"

"No, before that."

"I'm outta here tonight if you don't tell me what's really wrong. It's not just John B., is it?" I know you. There's more. And somehow it's going to add up to a big guilt trip for me.

"No, before that. You called me Mom."

"Well you are."

"It's always been Howard and Edwina. And then just Edwina. Never Mom."

"Jesus, what do you want? You want me to call you Mom? I'll call you Mom. Just tell me what the fuck's wrong. I have a life, you know. And I have to get back to work."

"Edwina will be fine, thank you." Charlie's mother picked up the paper plates and slipped them into the grate to burn. "You run on along home and don't bother with my little problems. I should have known better than to ask such an important person for help." She slammed the trailer door leaving Charlie alone with her guilt and rage.

"There is no way to win with her," Charlie told John B., Tawny, and Mitch Hilsten, who all sat across from her in the built-in booth in the director's motor home.

"My mother was just like her," Tawny commiserated, "before she died." She managed to drape herself over both men at the same time.

"What is it with women and their mothers?" Mitch asked.

"I get along fine with my mom." John B. Drake shaped a smug face and refilled Charlie's glass with Beaujolais.

"Me too," Earl said. Charlie sat wedged between the cameraman and Sidney Levit.

"Anyway, I'm leaving first thing in the morning and she's all yours."

"Hey, if she's really suffering some kind of personality change, this could be serious." Mitch smeared the edges of the wet rings from his beer bottle around with a fingertip. His makeup was beginning to shed on his collar. "You can't just walk out on her."

"Just watch me." Charlie pushed the glass of wine away. It was her third and it was wonderful but such closeness to the superstar was causing a warmth between her legs.

"Well, I'm livid over Gordon's scaring you two this afternoon with that run-through of the crushed bus scene," Sidney said. "I hope that didn't cause trouble between you and your mother. He's caused nothing but trouble lately, damn him." The producer was the only member of the enemy crew in the crowded motor home.

"He didn't do anything to mess up my shoot tonight, did he?" John B. asked.

"Couldn't have. Too busy with his own. Besides, not even Gordon could block out stars."

"Mitch is the only one who thought he saw something like that," their host pointed out.

He was also probably the only one facing that direction, Charlie thought, but kept still.

"No, Mitch wasn't the only one." Scrag was busy scarfing down leftovers of the cold ham and pasta salad the producer/director had fed his crew. "I saw it too."

"Oh yeah?" Earl's sea-colored eyes turned to Charlie, this time sparking mischief. "So, what do you think caused it, Dickens?"

Scrag put a hunk of cheese on a hunk of bread and poured himself some wine. "I think it might have been some sort of natural gaseous material," he said in a voice so deep it had to come from his crotch. "Looked to me kind of submarine-shaped. Soon as you develop the film in Mike's camera we'll all know."

Mitch, obviously fed up with being teased about this, groaned and stood to leave. Charlie had to nudge Earl to let her out to follow him.

The cameraman hooted as he slid from the booth. "You mean like swamp gas? On the desert?"

"Careful." Drake grinned at Charlie and nodded toward the closing door. "That guy's dangerous."

Mitch stood immobile at the rear of the motor home, half shrugged into his sheepskin, still holding a bottle of beer, peering toward the lighted toilets. "Charlie," he whispered, "you going to tell me you can just walk off and leave that?"

Her mother was leaping around the dumpster flaying the air with a butterfly net. She wore dark brown, baggy polyester slacks and thick-soled oxfords.

Each time she landed, Edwina's pant legs flew halfway up her calves, exposing rolled anklets, and her glasses bounced off her chest at the end of their cord. Her leg movements none too coordinated, Edwina resembled a clown in a rodeo ring.

"What's she doing?"

"I don't know, but she's too old to be doing it."

"Wait, don't tell me—she's chasing flying rats, right?" Mitch drained his beer and, as one of Edwina's springs took her out of the way, tossed the bottle unerringly into the dumpster. "You got a problem, lady."

Chapter
7

Edwina's final pounce bagged something. She twisted the netting on the catcher and leaned against the white cinder-block wall of the toilets trying to get her breath. Piercing squeaks came from the net and it flopped around as if there were a miniature Tanzanian devil inside.

"Thought your thing was rats." Mitch bent down to look in the net.

"Order Chiroptera. Suborder Microchiroptera," Edwina said between breaths and started coughing.

"No," Mitch told her, "it's a bat."

"*Antrozous pallidus*," Charlie's mother insisted. "Notice how he was darting around nearly knocking into the pole? He did once, stunned himself or I'd never have caught him. Something I've never seen before."

"There've been bats zooming around these lights catching bugs every night since I came here," Mitch said. "Desert's full of bats."

"That's your *Plecotus townsendii* and your *Lasionycteris noctivagans*. The *Antrozous pallidus*, or pallid bat, is big and slow, generally a ground feeder, and it doesn't come out this early." Edwina reached into the stilled net to withdraw a panting, terrified creature about five inches long. It had creamy-colored fur and large pinkish ears. It had dark bead eyes and a tiny pig snout. It had long pointy teeth to dream about.

Mitch hunched deeper into his sheepskin. "You wanted to catch him because he got up too early in the night?"

"I wanted to catch him to see why he couldn't fly straight, smartass." Edwina thrust the pallid bat at the superstar and he backed away. "The suborder Microchiroptera orient acoustically by echolocation—bat sonar."

"Won't that thing bite you?" he asked nervously and sent a meaningful glance Charlie's way.

Edwina scowled and went on with her lecture. "Bats emit high-frequency pulses of sound and listen to the echoes bouncing off nearby objects to gauge direction, distance, velocity, size, and even the nature of those objects. They produce laryngeal impulses in the ultrasonic range near two hundred thousand cycles per second. You can't hear them. Rats and a few other rodents can. In other words—bats can see, but they don't see well. What they do best is listen."

"Edwina, get to the point." At least her mother was acting somewhat normal now, lecturing and stuff.

"This bat's not hearing worth a damn is the point, Charlie. Neither is that one." And something shot out of nowhere to mash itself against the white concrete wall. Something small and brown. It slid to the ground leaving a smear.

Another dive-bombed Mitch's ear, missing it by a breath, and plowed into Charlie's chest where it clung helplessly to her jacket before it too fell to earth. "I don't know about you two," Charlie said, "but I'm getting out of here. Edwina, you're not taking that bat of pallor to the trailer?"

"Need to examine it and it's my trailer. Thought you were leaving."

Charlie had spent her childhood with the stench of caged animals wafting up from the basement. Mostly rodents, but also some snakes and a few other critters. The university had laboratories full of them for Edwina to play with, but there were always a few she had to bring home. They seemed to live forever under her care and each new arrival added to a burgeoning crowd. And of course thrived, totally against all city codes.

"Probably get rabies," the superstar complained. "Have to have needles stuck in our navels." But he edged into the tent trailer with Charlie as Edwina sat at the table to examine her captive through a magnifying glass. Its wings, which were sort of its arms, and a membrane that connected its back legs were naked of fur and pink. But it was the teeth that drew the eye.

Edwina mumbled under her breath. Finally, she released the bat outside and followed its erratic flight as long as possible with a flashlight. Then, still mumbling, she wandered off into the bushes with the flashlight aimed at the ground. Charlie and Mitch followed.

"Now I'm *really* worried about her," Mitch whispered.

"No, this is normal. It's when she calls you a dickhead and offers to punch your lights out there's the personality change. This stuff's her life."

"That right? What's yours?"

Please don't whisper in my ear like that. "My work."

"Like mother, like daughter then, huh?"

Well now, there's a new wrinkle. "Why are you doing this?"

"Because I like your mother. Her daughter too. Damn shame you two don't get along better. I thought she was just into rodents. Are bats rodents?"

"I don't think so, but all the beasties have a relationship with the environment and therefore each other."

"Yeah, even people beasties. You know Edwina's the first conservative Republican environmentalist I can remember meeting?"

"Not all Republicans are conservative." And Edwina chooses sides on issues with predictable unpredictability.

Charlie chose to ignore as many issues as possible. Her life was too frantic the way it was.

Moonlight cast long, cold, flat shadows. Mitch Hilsten's eyes were so light a blue they glowed in the dark. How come he smelled like aftershave, beer, and makeup and she smelled like she needed a shower?

Keep your distance, Hilsten, I'm warning you. But she said aloud, "What could leave a track like that, a baby rabbit?"

"*Dipodomys ordii*, Ord's kangaroo rat." Edwina came over to study two long critter prints that narrowed at the heel and had two small round prints between them with a long drag mark behind. "Hind feet are the long ones. Round ones are the front feet. Trail at the back is the tail."

She moved ahead and then stopped so short Charlie bumped into her. The flashlight picked out another set of tracks—two small round prints, each with four flared toes, pointing at two larger prints of the same configuration but with an added toe or thumb. "Big ones are the hind feet and the little ones the front. *Neotoma lepida*."

"Desert wood rat," Charlie explained for Mitch's benefit. "Better known as a pack rat."

Edwina turned to her in astonishment. "Thought you never listened to my jargon."

"You used so much of it, some had to rub off."

"These rat tracks are too clear for desert sand. As if their owners spent time sitting around instead of scurrying for food and avoiding predators like rats of sound mind should be doing," Professor Edwina said, seriously back at work now.

Charlie had to run to keep up with her and the flashlight that guided their way. And once again she bounced off her mother's back when Edwina stopped too quickly.

"Oh, oh my, ohmylord," the older woman said as if strangling.

Both her mother and Mitch Hilsten tried to pull Charlie back so she couldn't see what had stopped them all, but too late. And "ohmylord" didn't *begin* to describe it. Charlie remembered thinking later that no critter could die as messily as a human.

Other than the bloody brain splatter on the shirt, the body looked intact. The trouble started at the neck and went ballistic from there up.

Someone had separated Gordon Cabot's right brain from his left.

"**W**hat I want to know," the little sheriff-bully said the next morning, "is if your mother smoked a cigarette at the scene of the crime after you all found the body."

"I honestly don't remember, Sheriff, but the crime-scene puke three bushes to the left is mine. Blackened barbecued chicken, scorched canned corn, and pinto bean ashes." Charlie wiped the grease off her hand onto her jeans, gave the newly replaced tire a weary kick, and once again stowed the jack and the spare in the Corsica's trunk.

She'd driven it down to the paved parking lot of the Visitors' Center to have a smoother surface to kneel on. Now she and the sheriff faced off under the snapping flags of the United States and Utah. Wind whipped the chain on the flagpole in a steady unnerving clang.

They'd neither of them had much sleep and the dark pouches under his eyes mirrored her own, reflected in the Corsica's rear window. The weird thing was, when she had caught snatches of sleep, she'd dreamed of her daughter instead of rabid rats and crazy bats or sexy superstars or even split skulls.

She dreamed Libby, her face garish with makeup under streetlights and stars, walked alone and helpless in her tiny cheerleader skirt and spankies while a dark car pulled up to the curb beside her.

Charlie dreamed it repeatedly. Charlie had been accused of being psychic several times by unsteady personalities, but she didn't believe in the power of dreams and didn't believe people could know bad things had happened to someone far away before the phone rang and somebody on the spot told them so. But she did know she had to get home today.

"Wasn't much face left and he went down on it. How'd you

know right away it was Mr. Cabot? It was dark and all the three of you had was one flashlight amongst you."

"Because of the combat boots." Probably came with the Humvee. "Look, Sheriff, my plane leaves at three from Grand Junction. This is a rental car to be returned and I've answered all your questions the best I can. I'll come back if you need me, but I have a teenage daughter at home and I never know what she'll do and it's very important that I get to work Monday morning. There are various projects that—"

"You know, Miz Greene, there is nothing so obnoxious as a self-important career woman?"

"What a thoroughly sexist thing to say."

"But thoroughly true."

"I'll have you know," Charlie said under the tightest control exhaustion would allow, "I'm a single mother and that career is our sole support."

"You people going to get your divorces," Ralph Sumpter said smugly, "you're going to have to take your consequences."

"Sheriff, do you have children?"

"Five," he answered and held up a hand with all fingers spread like that pack rat's footprint last night, "and out of those five, three are daughters. And out of those three, three are teenagers. And my career supports a family of seven, Miz Greene. And my daughters all behave themselves, because if they don't their mother will whip them and if she don't I will. And nobody who was in this campground last night is leaving it until I find out who parted Gordon Cabot's hair darn near down to his brainstem. Do I make myself clear? Miz Greene?"

Chapter 8

"Told you they wouldn't let you leave," Edwina said when Charlie trudged back in. Sidney Levit sat with her at the little table over coffee.

"Well, they can't keep all these people out here for long, with no food or showers, no place to wash clothes."

"I think Sheriff Sumpter expects somebody's alibi to break real soon." Sidney slid over for Charlie to join him. He had a low raspy voice like Scrag's but more platonic in tone.

"It has to be somebody from your crew, Sid, the rest of us were all with you at John B.'s."

"I wasn't." Charlie's mother sounded almost smug.

"You were out making a fool of yourself catching bats under the light of the toilet. Mitch and I can both vouch for that."

"Could have done it before then."

Edwina, don't talk like that. "Besides, your clothes would have been all bloody."

The sheriff and his deputies had checked every piece of clothing in the campground last night before they even started on the alibis.

"And Sid here says that party broke up while we were checking over the *Antrozous pallidus* in here. Anybody would have had time to do it then," Edwina said. "I don't think they can tell time of death that close."

"Then there's always weapon and motive," Sidney added.

"Hey, everybody's got an ax." And most everybody was royally pissed at the director of *Animal Aliens*. But not everybody had slugged him in front of the county sheriff yesterday. Or called one of the deputies a vile name. "Edwina, didn't anyone see you before Mitch and I?"

"Not that I know of."

"Oh boy." Charlie heated some milk on the tiny gas stove top. She hadn't been able to face food since she'd lost her dinner at the crime scene last night. Her stomach acids shot warning signals at her navel.

"Want me to poach you an egg?" Edwina asked and explained to Sidney, "Charlie had surgery for an ulcer last year about this time and my granddaughter says when her mother feels sick she eats poached eggs on milk toast." The producer turned even paler at the thought.

"I'll just put bread in the hot milk. And it wasn't surgery, it was a cauterization."

"You've got to learn to avoid stress, Charlie," her mother told her.

"Yeah, right. Meantime I've got to call Libby and my boss but the radio phone is down again. I don't have any more clean clothes and if I don't get a shower pretty soon *I'm* going to take an ax to somebody. My mother prances around catching rabid bats in a butterfly net—"

"It's a capture net."

"—and has no alibi for the grizzly murder of a man she made no bones about hating. And that's just for openers, folks." My livelihood may well be going up in smoke even as we speak and agencies in L.A. aren't hiring right now due to the economy or the taxes or the goddamned weather for all I know.

I have a killer mortgage, even though I've refinanced, on a home into which I've sunk everything, but on which the value is dropping like a rock in a bathtub, but not the payments, because nobody's buying California right now. Too many trying to get out. And I have a daughter with an attitude and an orthodontist. She'll soon be ready for college, but hey, she could have been out last night contracting AIDS and won't need college. "So, relax, Charlie. Stop and smell the cactus."

"Your milk's boiling over," her mother pointed out, calmly.

"**W**anna come with me?" John B. whispered in Charlie's ear and glanced over his shoulder in a theatrical squint.

"Where? They're not letting anybody out of the park."

"Somewhere where there might be a shower." He'd found her pacing in front of the Visitors' Center hoping for word that a radio phone frequency had been freed up. Charlie was used to keeping in touch with life by car phone, office phone, modem, fax. The boondocks drove her nuts. How could people relax when they were so out of touch?

"Where?"

"You're not coming, I'm not telling." He walked off behind the building and she followed to a shiny pickup parked in the scrub forest.

Charlie crawled in beside him. Why not? How much worse could things get?

Edwina would have had a full litter of kittens had she witnessed them weaving around bushy trees and rocks to make forbidden tracks through the virgin land, Charlie riding beside a man who made his living touting the fragility of the ecology. But it felt good to be shedding that trapped feeling. She kept turning to look through the rear window for the sheriff's department in hot pursuit but saw only dust.

Drake wore a cowboy hat, a couple days' worth of dark beard, and a bandanna yet. He leered from under his hat brim. "You must want a shower bad, Charlie Greene."

"I'd kill for a shower."

"You don't have to go that far."

"How far do I have to go?"

John B. pulled an exaggeratedly straight face, patted her knee, and shifted down to eat a gully. "You only have to go as far as Moab."

"Moab's that way." Charlie pointed in the direction of the legal road and its roadblocks.

"No, Agent Greene,"—the pickup careened over a hillock like they do in those insane macho TV commercials and bottomed out with a thud that jarred Charlie's self-esteem and strained her seat belt—"as a matter of fact, Moab am . . . *that* way." And he pointed straight down.

They came to two tracks with a lot of rock in the middle and more than enough under the tires. She looked at him with new respect. "There's a back way into Moab?"

"Sure am looking forward to that shower." He scratched at his chin. "But you know, I think the trip's going to be half the fun?"

And he braked at the very edge of a precipice. Charlie reached for the dashboard with both hands. Drake batted eyebrows and lashes. "Want to walk home?"

She turned again to the rear window. Still no law enforcement. Cops in scripts and novels sure were more efficient than real cops.

The pickup headed down. "You can help hold the dashboard in the truck and squeeze your eyes shut, like you're doing now. Or you can keep watch for boulders on your side. Because one of those suckers could throw us off the road on my side. And that is *way* down there, lady."

Most of the boulders were so big he couldn't miss seeing them himself but Charlie dutifully called out each one to irritate him. He was enjoying this too much.

"Your mother doesn't want us to use the term 'desert,'" Drake said, "wants us to say 'plateau' instead."

"John B., we are all suspects in a horrible murder. I think your problems with Edwina don't count for much now."

"No, they're her problems with me." He turned to look at Charlie.

"Will you watch the road? Why don't you just say 'desert plateau'?"

"Have been. 'High-desert plateau,' too, but that doesn't suit. And there are all sorts of little nitpicky things she's raising a smell over that nobody's going to give a shit about." He had a faint Western twang Charlie couldn't be sure was real. It tended to deepen when he thought he was being funny.

"Dr. Greene's renown in her field is well earned, Mr. Drake. And that is what led you to her to begin with."

"Why are you doing this?"

I don't know. I'm an agent. I'm just not *her* agent. As far as Charlie knew, Edwina was a run-of-the-mill biologist approaching retirement. "And it was that very attention to detail that got her where she is today."

This just happened to be one of those perpendicular shelf roads so beloved of Jeepers. Too narrow to pass when meeting another vehicle and narrowed even further in places by rocks sloughed off the vertical face on one side. Nothing but space on the other side, with little inroads made by washouts to catch tires on so you could get flipped off into eternity.

Sky-diving had to be safer than this road.

By the time they reached the bottom of it, Charlie needed a shower twice as much as she had at the top. "Something crazy has gotten into the bats around the campground," she said in a steady voice to prove to the director that it hadn't really bothered her at all. "And Sid Levit tells me both companies can resume filming tonight. As long as they stay in the park. He's going to take over as director because they're so close to wrapping."

"So close to wrapping *and* because Sheriff Sumpter gets to play sheriff in the film *and* half his family collect as extras *and* the Moab Film Commission represents a major portion of the power behind his paycheck."

They soon joined the ribbon of road she'd seen from above.

It was fairly straight and blessedly flat, crossing that broad bench-land a thousand feet below the mesa tops but still a thousand feet above the river. A middle world—stark, arid, hot. He drove with the window down. Charlie's contacts felt like glue. They passed strange lacy tree-shrubs and an occasional puffy weed, both seem-ing too ethereal for this harsh place. Darker blobs of sage peppered the faint green fur of grasslands on flats and ledges inaccessible to grazing.

"Won't the sheriff have somebody watching this road?"

"He's spread pretty thin, for all his bluster. I'm banking on him and his deputies being unable to keep tabs on everyone at the campground, plus they still have a whole county to cover. I have a few people delegated to cover for me back there too. But not for you. You were sort of a last-minute opportunity."

"They'll notice the truck's gone."

"Earl's rental looks something like this. He's going to park it in my spot. They're more likely to notice my parking space empty than Earl's. But we may be turned back yet. If we are—no big deal—no shower."

Charlie had reached the point where no shower would be a big deal. But John B. stretched a satisfied smile, one arm crooked out the window, one hand on the wheel, eyes squinting into the sun.

The solid rock of the mesa cliffs was easier to take looking up at than looking over. Charlie relaxed, wanted to admit he was right about Edwina's complaints, but she couldn't believe this little trip could go unnoticed. A few phone calls and a shower might just be worth the gamble though.

They came to a downgrade and rounded a curve. The APC holding ponds spread in dazzling blue below, much larger than she'd suspected from up there.

"This business," John B. said, "you have to make it while you're hot. Nobody stays hot forever. Not even Mitch Hilsten." He winked at her. "But do we salt some away for the future? No, we sink it into the next project. One failure and we lose it all. End up eating dog food on Social Security."

"Or you sink it into new pickups, superstar narrators, gigantic motor homes, and sleek blondes. Is Mitch really working for practically nothing?"

"No," Drake said, "he's working for absolutely nothing. But where he's coming from you don't admit these things."

"Why? Because you're good friends?"

"Because he has to keep working. He's got bucks, though not what people imagine, but when you've been in this business so long, you're not fit for anything else. And, when you're living on your talent, any exposure is better than no exposure."

"But *are* you good friends?"

"I don't have good friends, Charlie Greene. I have dreams, lovers, and obsessions. I have causes. But I have no alimony or child-support payments. Don't worry about Mitch. He knows the game."

Here she was thousands of miles from L.A., surrounded by murder and wide and still wider open spaces, alone with one man, and he was talking Beverly Hills.

Chapter

9

They passed the ponds where, in a vast metal shed with hangar doors standing open, a man on a road grader pushed around piles of what looked like salt. Then the road smoothed out to pavement that stretched from the potash mine to a highway.

As they approached Moab, billboards advertised exciting whitewater river trips. And several repeated, *See the RIVER by NIGHT! Nationally renowned Sound and Light Show! Inspirational!*

Drake turned off the main street at the first opportunity and found a motel with dusty stucco cabins. But the one he rented had all it needed—a shower nozzle hanging over the end of a stained bathtub and a telephone.

Charlie borrowed his shampoo and shaving gear while he went out to find some lunch. If a shower had ever felt this good, she couldn't remember it. The hot steam even got her contacts sliding smoothly on her eyeballs. She stood under the water jet so long that when she finally emerged and redressed in her dirty clothes, Drake was back with tuna salad submarines and arguing with someone on the phone.

"Listen, Lew, there has to be something. Mike must have shot sixty seconds. Well, bring it along with the shipment and this time bring some dessert. My sweet tooth is yearning . . . In a motel room in Moab with this agent, see . . . Snuck out the back way. You ever seen hair the color of burnished brass, Lew? Not copper, but brass?"

Charlie managed to duck the hand about to stroke her wet hair and grabbed half a sub and a paper carton of milk. "Cabot has cell phones, don't you?"

"Sheriff's hanging on to them for us." He reached for her again, this time to pat her behind. So she sat on it. "Until after he solves the murder, of course."

Charlie wasn't sure how much of the burlesquelike sneer was for the sheriff and how much was for her.

While he was in the shower, she tried to call Richard Morse, Maggie, and Libby and connected with nothing but answering machines again. She did get hold of Larry Mann, her assistant, at home and outlined what he'd have to do to cover her ass Monday. But there were so many things he couldn't do.

"Settle down, Charlie, or you'll end up in the hospital again. A day or two can't make things any worse at Congdon and Morse than they already are."

"Yes, Mother. Any news on Eric Ashton and the *Alpine Tunnel* deal?"

"We're still hanging by our fingernails on that one. Nothing in the trades. Oh, boss, I have some good news."

"I can sure use it."

"Steve Hunter's going to renew the option on *The Corpse That Got Iced*. Called Friday. Five grand this time out for old A. E. He needs it."

"God, does he." Movie options were rarely picked up, but were found money for some of her older writers on the skids. This author had already made ten thousand against the purchase price of a hundred. Problem was, options tended to get their hopes up to unrealistic levels.

"Want me to call him with the good news?"

"No, let's wait till I get back." Charlie'd known authors to quit their day jobs on the strength of an option, so sure were they their book would be filmed and they were headed for riches untold. This author had already quit his job and his wife was checking out at a grocery store trying to help support them.

"Have any idea how long you'll be out there? What do I tell Richard?"

"Tell him Gordon Cabot got himself sliced and diced last night at the campground where I'm staying with my mother and the law isn't letting any of us leave at the moment."

Charlie was fantasizing that she'd solved the murder and was allowed to go home when John B. stepped out of the bathroom, clean and shaven, fully dressed but with that look in his eye.

"I came here for nothing but the shower," she warned him off and tried to get Libby and Maggie again. Still no answer. All she could do was leave the message that she wouldn't be home today after all. "If you think you're going to—"

"I just want one little kiss. That's all. I swear it."

"Yeah, sure." Charlie opened the door and stepped out into the sun.

He gathered his toilet articles and joined her, making a big production of locking the door. He had a protruding Adam's apple and a dry swallow you could hear. And a dimple in his chin. "I want to be able to say that once I kissed a girl before Mitch Hilsten did. Because once he moves in, the rest of us are left in the dust. And make no mistake, he's moving in."

"I've heard enough come-ons to detect an expert at work here."

"There's no way either of us could get carried away standing out in broad daylight like this. And last I heard you can't get AIDS from a kiss. And look, there's even a witness." John B. pointed to a heavyset woman standing in the doorway of the cabin across the drive. She leaned on an ancient Hoover and watched them with suspicion. "And if not for me you wouldn't have had that wonderful shower."

The director dropped to one knee and put both hands over his heart. The cleaning lady grinned.

Charlie knew better, but she didn't know how to get out of it gracefully. And the shower *was* wonderful. His kiss was warm and enveloping and it felt good. That was the trouble with kissing—damn near always felt good.

Charlie and John B. made it to the Texas Petroleum Company's milling site at the edge of town before the sheriff caught up with them.

They'd stopped to buy some gas, the local weekly newspaper, and a chocolate dip cone at the Dairy Queen for the director's sweet tooth.

"Eat your heart out, Mitch Hilsten," Drake said in mock ecstasy and licked ice milk off his lip.

"Oh, knock it off. And if you mention that kiss around my mother—"

"A career woman of the world worries about a chaste kiss? In this day and age?"

No sense trying to explain that Edwina would never believe it had been only a kiss. Charlie'd allowed this guy too much leverage already.

Edwina had enrolled Charlie and Libby in a program for unwed mothers in a little building next to Boulder High School that had since become a parking lot. The mothers learned birth control, child care, and completed their high school educations. In that order. Volunteers cared for the infants while their mothers were in class. Charlie's girlfriends all gushed, "I think it's wonderful you're keeping your baby," before they wandered off to lead lives that would ignore hers.

"You can forget your dreams about the Peace Corps or being an actress or whatever the last one was," Edwina had said. Charlie never told her mother the last one was to be a cheerleader.

Edwina paid for Charlie's degree in English at Smith and for Libby's day care and nursery school. "You can be a

teacher. You won't be rich but you won't be a drag on the economy either."

But Charlie never became a teacher. Two days before graduation she was offered a job as editorial assistant to a small Washington, D.C., book publisher. Editorial assistants were secretaries given a more prestigious title and more responsibility but not more pay. Edwina still provided half their support when Charlie and Libby moved to a junior editorial position in Boston and then on to Wesson Bradly, a literary agency in New York.

John B. crunched on the last of his cone as they came to the closed uranium mill site just after crossing the Colorado River. The mill looked tan, dusty, deserted. There were a few broken windows. The siren pulsated suddenly behind them.

"Think you're real clever, do you?" Sheriff Sumpter said. John B.'s truck was a big Detroit four wheel and the sheriff had to stretch up to see in at them.

"Had to get out and grab a shower and some ice cream, Sheriff. Got this terrible urge," Drake said in his best good-old-boy persona.

The sheriff slapped the door in emphasis. "There is a serious murder investigation going on here, mister, and both of you are suspects."

"Would you say that man was a cliché," John B. asked Charlie as they drove with an official escort back to Dead Horse Point, "or a stereotype?"

"Yes."

Charlie spent most of the next day pacing and fuming at the waste of her precious time.

"You're getting old enough to learn to control your impatience and if you can't, go for a walk," Edwina told her sharply and bent back to some tome filled with line drawings of animal parts.

Wasn't this the mother who had complained that Charlie never came to see her?

The sheriff's department was much in evidence, questioning everyone a second time. It didn't seem that either film crew was accomplishing much else. There were several card games going and Scrag had dragged out his guitar. He, Mitch, and Earl sang ancient songs, some of which Charlie remembered from her Scouting days. Sounded pretty awful back then too.

But by late that afternoon most of the officers had left the Point and Drake asked Mitch and Charlie to go for the dinner. Edwina was assigned to scare up some night critters for the camera and everyone else was needed for various associated duties. Only Charlie and Mitch were superfluous to this night's shoot.

"Why can't we eat what the sheriff brought out?" Charlie asked him. "Be great for your budget."

"I can't feed my crew Campbell's soup and Velveeta cheese two nights in a row," John B. said. "What kind of an outfit do you think this is?"

So Charlie accompanied Mitch on the circuitous route around the back of the Visitors' Center. The gates were closed on the road coming into the campground. The sheriff's deputy and a ranger leaned against them talking low.

"I'm not walking clear to Moab," Charlie said. Campbell's and Velveeta could taste pretty good if you were hungry.

"Bronco's parked out in the bush there . . . somewhere," Mitch whispered, but down the back of her neck instead of in her ear. "You cold already?"

"They're going to be watching everybody like hawks after finding Drake and me in Moab yesterday. And they must know we've discovered the back road by now." They reached the first shelter of bushes and crouched behind them to peek out at the officers standing guard at the gate. They were still talking and not acting very hawklike.

"Too many of us. The place is too big."

"Don't you think they know that?" Charlie said. "This is their home ground."

"Yeah, but they think of us as city dudes who don't know our way around a wilderness. Stereotypes die hard."

They were out of sight of the gate and able to stand straight in minutes. No one hailed them from behind. It was uncanny how quickly you could get lost out here.

"What makes you think they won't miss two people?" Charlie asked.

"Word has it that since you and I aren't needed on the shoot we're doing embarrassing things in John B.'s motor home because all I have is a tent and that we shouldn't be disturbed."

"Great. The sheriff's department already has a wonderful opinion of me. This ought to enhance it no end."

Mitch was clearly as relieved as she was when they finally bumped into the Bronco. He patted its hood and gave a sigh.

"Bunch of little boys playing out fantasies in the big outdoors," Charlie groused. Her eyes were about level with his earlobe and she concentrated on his earlobe. "There's an ax murderer loose around here, you know."

"Could be me. Could be you. Could be John B., but I notice you went off to Moab with him yesterday."

Then it had been broad daylight and all she could think of was that shower he'd promised her. Only to discover upon her return a line of film crew people waiting in front of the rangers' quarters with towels over their arms. Extra water had been hauled in for those stuck at the Point by the murder investigation.

Charlie strapped herself into the Bronco, still feeling like a fool.

"That guy's the greatest con man ever born," Mitch said as if he'd heard her thoughts. "The world is lucky he decided to do this instead of banking or politics."

"And he says you are dangerous."

Mitch gave his sexy laugh, the scoffing one, the one the entire world knew about. "He sees too many movies."

Here Charlie was in the middle of nowhere with the world's most wanted man and they were talking Hollywood. You couldn't even find reality in the middle of Utah.

"Why is it," she asked, "you're driving a dented Bronco and John B. a brand-new whatever-it-is?"

"Camouflage. People say, 'Jeez, that guy looks just like Mitch Hilsten.' And then they say, 'Naaa, Mitch Hilsten wouldn't be driving a beat-up Bronco. He'd be driving a Jag or something.'"

"Do you enjoy being Mitch Hilsten, the famous movie star?"

"Depends on the mood I'm in."

They came out on the road that led to the precipice she'd traveled the day before. "Why don't they have a roadblock here? It's obviously the way you people are getting in and out."

"They don't have to. They have us all corralled in the campground. They're guarding the road. No city slicker's going to take off on foot. I told you, stereotypes die hard."

He didn't insist she keep watch for boulders, so Charlie kept her eyes closed on this second trip down to the arid benchland. When they reached it the sun was lower and what it had washed out in morning light it lent a golden glow this evening. Mitch turned the wrong way on the ribbon road.

"Aren't we going to Moab?"

"We're going to meet a man named Lew."

They traveled through a *Star Trek* war zone of rocks heaped and piled and stacked and upended. Some looked like empty clam shells discarded after a giants' banquet. Spikes and knobs and turrets and spires—some the size of small buildings—made Charlie think of ruined mosques. Tilted ledges, humongous mushrooms, phallic columns with foreskin or circumcision bulbs—

Mitch said suddenly, "A dollar for your thoughts."

"Umm? Oh . . . uh, that I'd like to get back to my daughter and my job."

He heard it seconds before Charlie did. He had almost stopped by the time she realized there was a roaring sound coming up behind them. It shook the Bronco and vibrated in her ears. Her first thought was that it was an earthquake. She had a quick vision of all those tortured rocks falling off their pedestals and crushing the Bronco.

Charlie cringed and watched a bulb, not twenty feet away, teeter and then topple off its stalk. It landed in a mushrooming cloud of dust.

Chapter
10

"**T**hat's military," Mitch said. "Cabot had this all set for shooting, but I can't believe they'd do that low a fly-over in unstable country like this." He and Charlie stood next to the Bronco, watching the triangular silver object roar off in a curve to buzz the mesa where Edwina was supposed to scare up critters for the camera when darkness came.

"Maybe you have to if you're looking for spaceships full of giant rats that dump on innocent senior citizens," Charlie offered. "And it's not the first time the military has performed for film."

"Yeah, and another reason for Sheriff Sumpter to allow shooting to go on as if murder hadn't happened."

"According to John B. most of the Sumpter family is on the *Animal Aliens* payroll and the Moab Film Commission's a powerful force in the county, other sources of employment having dried up. Like, all that's left is show biz and tourists."

Mitch nodded. "The effects of overgrazing hit the ranching industry hard. Uranium mining went on the skids years ago."

The circumcision bulb had exploded into pieces when it hit and dust lingered above the crash site. Hanging puffs of dust from unstable rocking rocks hovered almost everywhere Charlie looked. She could taste it.

They counted three silver triangles, military jets coming from different directions to skim the same mesa top.

Charlie had assumed Mitch's hairstyle was carefully sprayed to look carefully disheveled. But he ran his hand through it now and it fell right back into place. "Come on, we're going to be late."

"What if more rock falls up ahead?" She pointed toward the debris smoking dust into lowering sun rays.

"Just as liable to do it behind us." They circumvented fallen rock, Mitch gearing down to buck over what he couldn't get around. The old Bronco rattled up off the benchland on another hideous road to what he called the white rim and arrived eventually at a crumbling runway with a small plane at one edge.

The AEC, Atomic Energy Commission, had built airstrips in this no man's land during the years of uranium exploration. They were currently more likely to be used by drug runners, according to Mitch. But this one happened to be John B. Drake's umbilical cord to his film lab in Los Angeles and a source of supplies from the outside world. Now that the sheriff had cut him off from the small legal airport about twenty miles out of Moab in a different direction.

"Drake works out of Phoenix to avoid the unions, but he's hooked on this lab in L.A."

Lew leaned against his airplane, arms folded, an overweight man in faded denim pants and a T-shirt with the sleeves cut out to expose purple and red puckered lips tattooed up and down his arms. He looked like he should be riding motorcycles instead of flying airplanes.

His expression when looking at Mitch denoted pride in the male half of the human race. The two guys spent a long boring twenty minutes verbally showing off what they knew about airplanes and aviation that Charlie didn't.

This apparently undistinguished little aircraft was in fact a "Piper Malibu single engine" and its pilot informed Mitch that it had delivered him here in under two and a half hours and could carry a thousand pounds of fuel.

Sufficiently awed, Charlie helped the two men transfer boxes of supplies and the dailies to the Bronco. Lew'd watched the Air

Force jets buzz the mesa and was much impressed. "Tell Drake the news wires and networks are humming with Cabot's murder."

Mitch handed him a list of needs for the next run. Charlie longed to climb in the plane and escape back to L.A. with Lew but instead dutifully sealed herself back in the Bronco. There were worse fates than riding through the rosy haze of sundown with Mitch Hilsten.

She knew he had two daughters who lived in New Hampshire with his ex-wife. They must be in their late teens about now. "Do you ever see your girls?"

"Used to get them at Christmas and in the summers if I wasn't working, but they're at the ages where they want to lead their own lives. I had Marla this last Christmas but Jena spent the holidays on a ski trip in Switzerland with her new boyfriend. He's not good enough for her, of course."

Mitch was forty-five. Must be awful to have your birthday and age announced yearly over entertainment-news programs. Must be heaven to have whole months of respite from the exhaustion of child-rearing.

"So, who do you think offed Cabot?" Mitch steered the conversation away from his private life. Charlie couldn't blame him. There was so little of it he could keep private.

"Well, I know it wasn't you or me."

"Just how do you figure that?"

"We were together in one way or another the whole time. Gordon Cabot went by and gave us the bird while Edwina and I were eating dinner and you and the others came to John B.'s shortly thereafter."

"Did you see us arrive together?"

"You were all there when I got there." And in the meantime, I was very involved in an argument with Edwina. And I saw you and John B. and Sid Levit square off at Cabot that morning. Come to think of it, you and Edwina seemed the angriest and Edwina wouldn't murder anyone. Well, she might irritate them to death.

Now Charlie decided to change the subject. "Is this all legal—I mean keeping us at the campground? Can a sheriff do that without charging us with something?"

"I don't know, but I doubt he can keep it up for long. And what do you think is making the bats and rats and your mother act so strange? Is it just the filming at Dead Horse Point?"

Dust coated the dashboard. Charlie could see her handprints in it. She was suddenly too tired to even try to come up with an answer. Mitch was acting normal, friendly, nice. Of course acting natural was his acting style. His ex probably never knew when to trust him either. She just shook her head.

And he withdrew. Hard to explain how, but he did. Like he had in *After Hours* with Carly Shepherd, before he got out of bed and blew away the spy hiding in the shower stall. Or with Sally London in *Bloody Promises*, before he got out of bed to go off to be slaughtered in the trenches in World War I.

Sun flamed the upper reaches of the mesa cliffs in orange-red and yellow. But it was shadow-dark down here where the Bronco bumped over rocks and washouts. On the next level down, the river looked like ink sludge. Charlie knew she was vulnerable anywhere, but she felt it more in the middle of such spectacular nothing. Harsh and huge and empty, this whole place reminded her of another planet.

And Edwina sapped Charlie's vitality and self-confidence. She was stymied by her mother's presumption of control and by her own guilt. Richard Morse, her boss, laughed at her dread of going home. "Who would have thought it?" he said once. "Classy chick like you? Didn't know anybody felt guilty about that stuff these days. Unwed motherhood's all the rage."

But Larry Mann, her assistant, understood. Larry was gay. He knew about guilt trips from childhood. And that, no matter what an enlightened world professed to believe, things were different when you went home to face the people you'd hurt.

It was dark by the time they reached an informal parking place outside the campground. Charlie expected the men guarding the gates to hear the engine, but no one challenged them as, loaded down with boxes and cartons, they made several trips between the Bronco and the big motor home, sneaking around behind the Visitors' Center.

By the time a tired film crew trailed in, she and Mitch had the charcoal glowing under five grates and they broiled the lavish T-bones Lew had brought. John B. sent everyone back to their own camps with sizzling steaks, coleslaw, and potato salad. Everyone except Mitch, Charlie, Edwina, Tawny, and the two cameramen, who were invited to eat with him.

Drake was jubilant but Edwina was strangely sullen, considering the director's high praise of her.

"We got rats, we got bats, we even got a fox eating a rat. A bat eating a moth." He gestured wildly with his fork. Excitement animated his entire rangy length. "We'd been trying to find critters for days and all we came up with were ground squirrels and lizards. Edwina's worth her weight in gold."

"I'm her agent and I heard that," Charlie reminded him. The steaks were just right—scorched, salty, and crunchy on the outside, red, juicy, and tender on the inside. Of course they had cooked over charcoal briquettes and not wood, but she refrained from pointing that out to Edwina.

John B. uncorked several bottles of good red zinfandel, which didn't detract from the meal either.

Charlie was glad to see her mother eating heartily, even though so obviously angry about something. Edwina tended to eat from cans since she'd been living alone, too busy with her work to take much of an interest in cooking.

"And, for your entertainment pleasure, with our pie and coffee we will view some smuggled dailies," their host announced. "The ones from the film Mike wasted on that something that wasn't there but that ruined so much of our take night before last."

He set up a video on a small TV and they all sat too close to it and too close to each other.

Charlie was wedged thigh to thigh beside John B. on a booth

seat. She'd eaten only half her steak and a few bites of the pecan pie but felt bloated and stuffed. The odd combination of coleslaw and wine lingered on her tongue.

Drake lifted his arms to ease the sardine-fit of his neighbors, but then brought one arm down to rest around Charlie's shoulders, the other around Tawny's. The dual gesture was not lost on the assembled.

The air reeked of coffee and too many bodies in too small a space. Someone turned off the last light and the glow from the little screen reflected harsh and flat on the faces around Charlie, lending them the look of performers in a rock video. Everybody turned back to stare at the screen except Mitch Hilsten. He stared at her.

A silent moving picture, just John B. clearing his throat. About the only thing that moved on the film was Charlie's unruly hair blowing in the wind and the branches of a pinyon in the distance. Then Mike had moved the camera higher to a patch of sky with only the top of the generator truck showing. Daylight had almost vanished, the light was murky. The few stars out that early barely showed up.

Still, it was obvious that a patch of not quite opaque darkness hovered in the sky above the generator truck. Mike had panned back and forth across it several times and then it was gone, so nebulous that its disappearance was all that proved its existence.

"Looks like the outline of a giant football," Tawny murmured when Earl reversed the clip to show the panning frames again in slow motion. She snuggled deeper into Drake's armpit. So he hugged her and Charlie tighter. Charlie fought the urge to burp.

"More like a hot dog or a bratwurst," Edwina said and turned to glare at Charlie. That's who she was mad at. Why?

"The shadow of a submarine without a conning tower," Earl said, snapping his fingers. Charlie thought Earl's description the most apt of all.

And she noticed Mitch wasn't even looking at the screen. He was still staring at her.

Wouldn't it be interesting if Mitch Hilsten was angry because John B. had his arm around Charlie?

But Sheriff Sumpter arrived just then to arrest Charlie's mother for the murder of Gordon Cabot and all else was forgotten.

Chapter
11

Mitch Hilsten drove Charlie into Moab in his Bronco, Scrag Dickens riding along in the backseat. Ahead of them, Edwina rode with the sheriff.

"Where am I going to find a lawyer this time of night?" was all she could think of to say for miles. They were all pretty quiet. And then—"Will they let me see her tonight? I don't think she's feeling well." Charlie was so numb she didn't realize she was crying until Scrag reached over the seat back to stroke her shoulders in silent sympathy. "How could they tell it was her ax? That someone didn't switch axes? Anybody could have left one of her cigarette butts there. I mean, if you wanted to kill Cabot and blame it on someone else, Edwina was the answer to a prayer. She knocked him on his ass right in front of the sheriff of Grand County. It's such an obvious frame-up."

"You do love her," Mitch said barely above a whisper.

"I never said I didn't love her. Just because I can't stand her, doesn't mean I don't love her." Edwina had accepted the handcuffs and been read her rights without a whimper or a four-letter word. In fact with no word, just that scary gray acceptance. "Which doesn't mean she did it."

"**M**om?" Charlie, accompanied by a female cop, stood in her mother's cell in the Grand County Courthouse in the wee hours of the morning. Edwina sat on the edge of her bunk swaying with exhaustion.

"We're worried too," the officer said. "Does she have any history of heart problems or other ill health? Do you want a doctor, Mrs. Greene?"

"I'm not deaf," Edwina snapped back. "And no, I don't want a doctor."

"She's not that old either." Charlie was offended too. "You don't have to treat her like she's elderly."

"Why not, you do," her mother's voice croaked out of the partial darkness. And then, "Never learn, do you? Thought at your age and being a mother yourself you'd have learned something by now."

"Hello? Are we on the same planet here? You have just been arrested for murder. And like, we're talking about *what*?"

But Charlie knew. Sheriff Sumpter had counted noses while she and Mitch were on the supply run and Edwina had overheard John B. explaining where Mitch Hilsten and Charlie Greene were and why they should not be disturbed. That's what her mother'd been so pissed about at dinner.

"And you believed him. Just because I made a mistake years ago and so should never be trusted again?" Not to mention that at thirty-two I have the right to sleep with someone if I want to. But Charlie knew that argument cut no ice with a parent.

"How was I to know what was bred into your genes?" her mother whispered with that hateful hiss. "Or who was into your jeans before I even knew the damn pants were hot?"

Charlie churned with a familiar impotent frustration, knowing she was breeding the same cancer in her relationship with Libby and helpless to stop it.

"And yesterday you went off with John B. to Moab. Charlie, I didn't kill anybody, but they can hang me for this one and I don't care. I'm worn out. So if you were planning on my raising Libby while you go off and have a wonderful life, you're skunked, aren't you?"

"I wouldn't let you raise Libby if you were the last adult on earth. And I'm not letting you take the fall for a stupid murder you didn't commit and my jeans are my own *goddamned business*."

"**B**etween the campers needing a break from filth and gnat bites, canoers, whitewater rafters, your generic tourist, religious people here for an experience, reporters on the trail of a Hollywood ax murder, and two film companies 'lensing' (God, I hate that word), Scrag and I could come up with one motel room. It's not that great but it's yours for tonight. We'll be back tomorrow morning with your car and your toothbrush, take you out for breakfast, and help you find a lawyer. You gonna make it, Charlie?"

"Hey, you guy types just don't realize how strong we females are when it comes to chin-deep feces." But she hugged them both long and hard before they left her for the night in one of the grossest motel rooms she'd ever smelled.

An old-fashioned double bed, not even a queen size. And the odor—decades of chemical cleaners and air fresheners and cigarette smoke decomposed to stale. And probably other things Charlie refused to think about.

She had the presence of mind to wash out her underclothes in the bathroom sink before crawling naked between the sheets. Despite a gut-gnawing fear for the health and sanity of her mother Charlie slept like a tank.

She was so deeply out of it that she had to answer the door, when Mitch and Scrag returned in the morning, wrapped in the limp bedspread that smelled like discount-store perfume. They'd brought the Corsica and, when she'd dressed, walked her down to the main street for breakfast. Charlie sucked in great thankful gulps of chilly fresh air.

Roses climbed trellises, fences, porches. They sat in clumps and on bushes. Glorious shades of red, peach, pink, and yellow. And poor Edwina sat in jail and couldn't see them. Somehow, unreasonably, Charlie felt it was all her fault.

"How old a woman is Edwina?" Scrag asked.

"Let's see . . . she must be . . . about fifty-seven."

Both men stopped to gape at her.

"I know, she looks ten years older." That's all supposed to be my fault too.

"More like twenty," Scrag said indelicately.

The River Palace Café and Grill was doing a good business but they managed to snag a booth just vacated by the window. Everyone in the room stared at Mitch Hilsten, even the waitresses, not one of whom was under sixty, nor anything other than scrawny with dyed hair molded into place. Maybe the younger ones were out at Dead Horse Point getting eaten by giant rats. Mitch pretended not to notice the attention. Their waitress brought an extra menu for him to autograph and somebody behind Charlie snapped photos using a flash.

But it was Sheriff Ralph Sumpter who came up to the table, bill in hand. With the other he shook Mitch's. "Mr. Hilsten."

"Sheriff."

The lawman gave Scrag a curt nod and turned to Charlie, who sat across from her escorts. "And Miz Greene."

Charlie couldn't tell you what a sneer sounded like but she knew one when she heard it.

"I have just learned something of your history, Miz Greene, and I want you to know I am not impressed. Are you impressed, Arthur?" he said to the big vacant-faced deputy behind him.

Arthur was not impressed. He had his sunglasses on indoors and they reflected a van with a kayak roped on top running the stoplight outside the window.

What, you've learned I'm an UM instead of divorced? UM stood for unwed mother, a label Libby inflicted when in need of heavy artillery.

"I have just learned from a newspaper reporter from Los Angeles that you are a famous psychic. I would like to make it clear that my temperament, my religion, and my common sense do not allow for such foolishness. Any special powers bestowed around here are bestowed by Jesus and I don't believe He believes in psychics either. Do I make myself clear?"

"You do, Sheriff, and I want you to know I think you and Jesus have got it dead right."

"You religious, Miz Greene?"

"No, but I don't believe in psychics. That's a silly rumor that got started for the same reason most silly rumors do and I'll be the first to declare it isn't true. But let me point out, Sheriff, that no one has to be psychic to see you are holding the wrong person for the murder of Gordon Cabot and I intend to prove it." Charlie's shins ached from the kicks the men across from her delivered under the table, accompanied by agonized looks of warning.

"I look forward to watching you do that, Miz Greene. Enjoy your eggs, folks." He slapped his Smokey Bear hat on his ancient-astronaut crew cut, nodded to Mitch, handed his deputy the bill, and grabbed a toothpick at the counter on his way out.

"What do you want to do, get your mother hanged?" Mitch said. "Jesus."

"Jesus doesn't believe in Charlie." Scrag sat back so the waitress could deliver his order of steaming oatmeal, a plate heaped with huevos rancheros plus an extra side of beans and another of tortillas. He obviously was not expecting to pick up his own tab. "Wait a minute," he said, the brown sugar suspended over his oatmeal. "I heard about you I think, wasn't it last year? You with that agency on Wilshire where the receptionist was a witch and they found her body in the alley?"

"Something like that."

"What agency you with?" Mitch dug a pious spoon into a granola, yogurt, fresh fruit combination.

"Congdon and Morse."

"Never heard of it."

"Well, thank you very much." Charlie dumped the poached eggs out of the bowl onto her toast order and poured the hot milk over it all. "Pass the salt and pepper."

"And one of the agents was a psychic and solved the murder."

"Not because she was a psychic and the Beverly Hills PD did most of the work."

"That's not what I heard."

"Hey, I'm sorry," Mitch broke in. "I'm sure there're lots of little agencies I never heard of. And I wouldn't put down psychics if I were you. I've known a few who were good."

Oh boy. "So how about you, now that your part in *Ecosystem* is done? Are you leaving?"

"I'd planned to stick around for a short river trip with John B. and Earl. Scout out sites for another documentary he's got in mind that I'm thinking of backing. Long as we're here. Now with the murder and Edwina in jail I don't know what's going to happen."

"Edwina's my problem."

"**I** already have a lawyer," Charlie's problem told her. This time they sat across a table from each other in a small interrogation room with the same lady cop supervising. "You just go on home and tend to more important business."

"Edwina, you know I can't go off and leave you in this mess."

"Sure you can. Now I've got a lawyer I don't need an agent." Her color was better this morning or else it was the indoor lighting. "Oh, but before you go, tell John B. he can't use the critter footage we shot last night."

"Can't use it? Edwina, that's box office. People eat that stuff up." Next to watching Mitch Hilsten bat his eyelashes, they'll remember seeing those critters doing their critter thing. "How often do you get creatures in the wild to sit still for a camera like that?"

"That's just it," Edwina said. "You don't."

"You don't expect me to go out there and try to tell him those weren't real rats and bats and that fox wasn't really a fox like this isn't really a desert?"

"They're real enough, but that's not the way they really act. The bat would have taken off when we shone a light on it while it was eating the moth. The fox, maybe, was acting normally. He was young and he was curious about the lights and all that food was sitting there waiting for him. But rats don't sit still like that for foxes to catch and eat them."

"Look, those jets flying over just before dark probably upset the critters' habits but the point is you can't expect John B. Drake to keep from taking advantage of it. Who's going to know the difference? Besides, what's a dumb rat know anyway?"

"Never underestimate the intelligence of a rodent." Edwina pushed her glasses up on her nose. "In my lab there isn't a one that isn't more intelligent than the grad student feeding him."

"Then how come the rats are in the cages and the students run free?" Here we are having a totally stupid argument and you've just been charged with murdering a man with an ax.

Edwina peered blankly over her glasses. "Why would anybody want to study a grad student?"

Chapter

12

"**Y**ou mean she really doesn't have a lawyer?" Mitch stood in the bathroom door of Charlie's smelly room, clean clothes draped over his arm. They'd agreed, since he'd found the last room in town for her, he could use her shower. Since the murder had been "solved" everyone was free to leave Dead Horse Point but no longer allowed to use the precious water hauled in to bathe.

"She's going to let the court appoint one."

"She can't do that."

"She says she doesn't care what happens to her. All she wants to talk about is persuading Drake not to use the critter footage he was so proud of last night because the animals wouldn't have acted that way normally. I'm going out to the Point to ask some pointed questions of the *Animal Aliens* crew while they're still around. But first I'm going to call home and buy some clean clothes."

"Tell you what," Mitch said. "I'll scout out a lawyer for Edwina and take your dirty clothes with mine to the Sudzy Duds if you'll let me take you out to dinner tonight. Deal?" He closed the door on his gleaming smile and his dirty bod.

"Maggie, guess what? I'm in a motel room in Moab, Utah, with Mitch Hilsten."

"Oh, right, Greene."

"He's in the bathroom, taking a shower. We're at the Pit Stop Motel, Room Eight."

"Charlie, can I take this call to mean you won't be home to-day either?"

"Yeah. What's happening back there?" You tell me your bad news and I'll tell you mine.

"I would like to apologize for all those cracks I made about you learning to trust your daughter."

"I expected something Saturday night. But Monday? She's not hurt or in jail?"

"No, in fact she's the one who called the police. Just that she should have done it sooner. The damage to your place isn't as bad as we thought at first—that's Larry and me . . . your assistant? He's been so much help. And the cat showed up this morning. I was worried he'd been killed or something and . . . Charlie?"

"Maggie . . . just what was it that happened last night?"

"Too many kids over there and things got out of hand. Nothing meaner than a bunch of immature drunks."

"I told her no drinking and she could have no more than three friends in at a time when I'm not there." Hell, I make a lot of rules, like any good mommy.

"That's all she did at first, but apparently word got out you were away and suddenly half the football team drops by. Of course, she couldn't turn them down. You know how she likes to be popular. I got in about eleven-thirty and the cops were just pulling up. Larry has scheduled a carpet cleaner who's coming in tomorrow and most of the furniture is all right. Some blinds will have to be replaced. Hey, in a few days you'll hardly know anything happened. Larry boarded up the window over the kitchen sink and he's finding somebody to put in glass. And you'd be proud of me, I stood right over Libby and made her clean up the puke herself. Charlie . . . you don't really have Mitch Hilsten in a motel room?"

"When you come in from a campground all you can think about is a shower." MYGODWHAT'STHEDAMAGEGO-INGTOCOSTME?

"If I were in a motel room with Mitch Hilsten, a shower'd be the last thing I'd think about. Is he why you're not coming home to-day?"

Charlie explained about Edwina.

"That's totally ridiculous."

You're always telling me I should trust her more too. "Too bad the sheriff doesn't think so."

"That sucks. You take care of your mom and I'll see to the little cheerleader. She'll spend her nights over here till you get back. And, Charlie, Libby really does feel awful about her friends trash-ing your place."

"You mean guilty. She comes by it naturally." And she wasn't little. She was taller than either Charlie or Maggie. But Libby liked Maggie and just maybe enough to obey the order to spend the night there.

While Charlie was out buying another set of clothing, she found Scrag Dickens lounging on a street corner and agreed to give him a ride back to Dead Horse Point. So, while a superstar was wash-ing her panties with his shorts at the Sudzy Duds, she was driving alone with a prime suspect in an ax murder across lonely desolate no woman's land.

And she thought her mother was crazy.

"So, where do you keep your ax, Scrag?"

"Don't have one. Carrying the damn things makes it real dif-ficult to get a ride when you're hitching. That was your mother's ax I had Friday night." Was it just Charlie or did he sound smug?

"So, where's your home?"

"Oh, I got some parents in L.A. and a brother in Oregon and a sister in Florida and an ex-wife in Kansas. I stop in places more than live in 'em. Hang out a lot around location sites. Pick up work. I enjoy the milieu." A surprising vulnerability softened that last sentence, followed by a nervous glance.

"Acting work?"

"Bit parts, dead bodies, doubles, whatever. Sometimes I'm an extra, gofer . . . done some stunt work. John B. and Earl and I go way back and I met Hilsten years ago too. When he was in *Tortured Prince*. How about you? Mitch tells me you're adopted. Ever had the urge to look up your birth mother?"

"God no, one's enough. Ever done anything else besides travel and hang out?"

"Taught English literature at a private boys' school in Virginia for years. Stood it as long as I could and hit the road. So, you don't think your mother did it?"

"I don't think my mother did it. You have any children?"

"Two that I know about. I don't have the urge to look them up either. Understand your agency's in trouble."

"Who told you that?"

"Gordon Cabot."

"Do you go way back with Cabot too?"

"You going to submit to the old Hilsten line?"

"Who do you think killed Gordon Cabot?"

"Why don't you save us both time and use your psychic powers?"

"I think you're really a studio spy." Or an ax murderer. Or both.

This time it was a relief to be stopped at a roadblock and this time it was much closer to the campground. The stoic deputy checked to be sure they were neither tourists nor reporters and let them pass.

Even before she parked behind Howard's Jeep, Charlie could see her mother's tent trailer was occupied.

"Sorry, Tawny got pissed and kicked me out," John B. explained. He and Sidney Levit sat at Edwina's tiny table over coffee, cream cheese, lox and bagels, and chocolate-coated strawberries.

"You didn't get that from these cupboards."

"No, but we used your mother's gas to boil coffee."

"You better be careful, this woman's a psychic and Jesus doesn't like her." Scrag helped himself to a strawberry.

"What are you doing sitting here, Sid?" Charlie asked. "You're supposed to be playing frenzied director about now." His smile was warm and more fatherly than Howard's had ever been. Charlie liked Sid a lot better than she had Gordon Cabot. He had liver spots on the backs of his hands. Had those hands wielded her mother's ax three nights ago? "Don't you have to get permission from the Directors Guild to take Gordon's place?"

"No, because we're nonunion. Only two major location shoots left. Gordon already had the army set up for this one. Stan, my production manager, is putting the finish on the layout. Want to come watch?"

No one even mentioned Edwina's little problem. Charlie could very well be sitting in Edwina's tent trailer with the murderer. Charlie didn't mention Edwina's problem either. "Wouldn't miss it."

As it happened nobody wanted to miss this one. Charlie found herself driving Earl and Tawny out to the location site in Howard's Jeep right behind Scrag and John B., who rode with Sidney in the Humvee. *Return of an Ecosystem* had nothing on the docket again until tomorrow.

Isn't it interesting, Charlie, that Mitch Hilsten didn't seem worried about you coming out here to snoop out a murderer? Didn't even warn you to be careful? In a book or film, he'd have warned you.

In a film, I'd be in Moab washing the underwear and he'd be here doing the snooping.

Unless he's the murderer, or knows who is and that you aren't in danger.

Oh shut up.

Like most people, Charlie'd learned to ignore her inner voice. It was invariably wrong.

"So, how does John B. come in under budget flying dailies out and chocolate strawberries in and taking a whole day off?" she asked her passengers in the real world. And what is the scandal about him I can't remember?

"Guy that runs the lab, his brother-in-law's Lew. Lew owns the plane with a couple of other guys. He's trying to get flight hours," Earl yelled in her ear and Charlie winced. Her hearing was painfully good. "Just charging Drake for fuel and repairs. We're down to a skeleton crew now anyway."

She was thoroughly lost by the time they turned off the paved road back to the highway and then off it onto a dirt road wandering out across another mesa and down another dirt road to the benchland below it. And by this time she'd learned some confusing things about Tawny and the cameraman and clouds had appeared in what had been a perfectly clear sky when they started out.

Tumbling clouds that propelled color and depth and shadow into an already overpowering landscape. And the other two people in the Jeep transmogrified just as suddenly, became unexpectedly striking and individual.

Charlie knew she had no real psychic gifts because she tended to lump people together in stereotypes, Hollywood fashion, and then believe in these subdivisions because it made life simpler. This was not the first time she'd been brought up short by it.

The clouds had black bottoms. The washed-out sky changed to dirty blue in between them. A distant mountain range grew purple and what had been sandstone-colored cliffs took on a greenish-gray hue. Giant cloud shadows raced across the benchland and the wrinkled craggy mesa faces rearing out of it, turning the green-gray to black and back again. Lightning notched down to the surface of a near rim and Charlie half-expected Moses (in the form of Charlton Heston) to descend with his tablets.

"Pure Cecil B. De Mille, huh?" Earl shouted as if reading her thoughts and damn near put them off the road.

This road down to the benchland was nothing like the one off Dead Horse Point but Charlie already dreaded the drive back up. You can't very well keep your eyes closed if you're behind the wheel.

Earl was an ex-Marine who'd enjoyed the freedom of his service haircut to the point he kept his head shaved now to get even more air and sun to his brain. And his baldness had nothing whatsoever to do with Yul Brynner or Telly Savalas or trying to be different. Right.

The government helped put him through some film classes at UCLA and he'd served his time making recruiting and instructional videos.

Earl had known John B. Drake since his service years and even invested in some land scheme with him. Both lost their shirts on that one, went their separate ways but kept in touch. Earl lived in Phoenix because he loved baseball and it was fun to watch the spring training. He'd never had much contact with Cabot but kind of liked some of his films. "It's like Vegas, you know? If you're going after the gaudy and tawdry don't be half-assed about it. Go balls out and make it an art form."

The beautiful Tawny had gone the predictable route of small-time modeling, big-time waitressing, a few minor roles in films or commercials. She hung around the studios, on the fringes, waiting for a big break that never came.

Tawny was sleek, knew makeup, and had the right bones. Worst of all, she had nothing hips and something boobs. Tight tush even. Skin the color of honey.

She'd done a couple of silent bits for Cabot (nonspeaking bit parts), had seen him at a few parties, thought his stuff sleazy even for Hollywood. John B. now was a jerk, but he at least made "decent film."

Charlie, you're questioning the wrong crew here.

This time her inner voice was probably right.

They stopped behind the Humvee on what was fast becoming a battlefield.

Just before stepping out of Howard's Jeep, Tawny said, "I feel bad for your mom. Like, she can be a real witch, but she wouldn't kill anybody. Not on purpose like that. If there's anything I can do to help, you know where to find me."

And "just" Tawny, in her skin-tight, gold-colored jeans and matching cowgirl boots, sashayed off leaving Charlie with her jaw hanging.

"**T**ell you the truth, I'm glad the fucker's dead," Dean
Goodacre told Charlie and Earl around a wad of chewing gum. Dean was the helicopter pilot for *Animal Aliens*. "Sid's
not going to ask me to kill myself flying a cameraman too deep into
some stupid canyon."

He had curly shoulder-length hair and buffalo-size pectorals
on a short solid build. With his no-nonsense eyes, he conformed to
no stereotype Charlie could muster. Just another suspect, probably
trying to throw her off with all this openness.

It was raining up on the rim but sunlight pierced cloud gaps
to transform the muted color scheme and shadow shapes on the
benchland yet again.

Earl pulled his wadded baseball cap out of a hip pocket and
covered his self-imposed baldness. It was a Rockies cap and he put
it on backward to shield his neck instead of his face. He was a squin-
ter and the sun creases were already as deep as Edwina's around his
eyes.

"Who's the writer on this disaster?" Charlie asked. The way
they're treated in Hollywood writers had great motive for murder.

"Mick Sensenbrenner was the latest sucker." Dean nodded
and chewed harder. "Cabot fired him. Two quit before that."

"Charlie here handles writers," Earl told the helicopter pilot.
"Tell us, how can grown-up people be dumb enough to ask for such
punishment?"

Both men watched closely as Charlie struggled for an answer but she was saved by the assistant director repeating what Sidney Levit had spoken from the Western dolly on its huge rubber wheels that could roll relatively smoothly over rough ground—

"Quiet on the set!"

An actress dressed as an injured forest ranger with torn clothes and false blood patches laid her half-eaten sandwich back in its box. She wasn't plump and pink like the real rangers Charlie'd seen. A man stepped out of a portable outhouse and froze, leaving the door open despite the signs both inside and out pleading with him not to. Charlie remembered the harsh squawking noise it made when closing.

Two harried women at the back of the Moab Whitewater Delicatessen and Bakery catering truck stood watching the silent, stilled battlefield over armloads of white box lunches. The mixer nodded and spoke into the mike on his sound cart. All was quiet but for Dean Goodacre's jaws chewing.

The thunder rumbling above was apparently permitted.

"Rolling."

"Speed."

And Sheriff Sumpter rolled in with screaming sirens and tires and colored lights flashing back at the flashing sky. He leaped out of his four-wheeled Grand County patrol vehicle. He did a rewind and leaped back in to back up out again after speaking to an assistant gofer.

Before everything started over, there was time for the guy to squawk the door closed on the movable outhouse and one of the overworked caterers to shove a box lunch at Charlie.

"Quiet on the set!"

"Rolling."

And this time Ralph Sumpter waited for—

"Action!"

—before rolling in with screaming sirens and leaping out of the Grand County four-wheel to gape dramatically at forty or so "rats" lumbering out of the mock-up of a spaceship. It had no back, sides, or insides and they lumbered because the men wearing the rat suits, one of whom had a father who'd fixed Charlie's tire, were about three fourths the size of their costumes. Charlie couldn't smell any ammonium hydroxide. She could smell some good odors from the box lunch though and cautiously lifted the lid.

Sheriff Sumpter was actively acting but no match for monster rats. Not only did he die in an early frame but would probably do the same on the cutting room floor during editing.

In the next shot, and after the sheriff was cleared away, all hell broke loose, at which exciting point Charlie finished the cream cheese, cucumber, tomato, sprouts, black olive, and cashew croissant sandwich.

Soldiers, who looked no older than Libby and who were duded up in full desert combat camouflage, wielded weapons and launchers that appeared capable of taking out Tokyo during coffee break. But the rats, who had mysterious handgun-type weapons of their own, literally walked all over them in a series of shots that followed with surprisingly few retakes and delays.

It would take some heavy editing to hide the seams in this picture. Sidney Levit must be determined to wrap while the director's murder was hot enough to be remembered and provide a possible box office draw. Or before the backers withdrew. Or the Army went home. Come to think of it, Sid had more motive than anyone to wish Cabot dead.

When their battle choreography and lumbering took them off camera, the rats circled behind the dolly and lined up for the next shoot to enter the set again from the original side, forming a seemingly endless army of giant rodentia.

There were several tanks and every kind of macho pyrotechnics. But without the special effects that would be inserted later, the whole thing was highly hilarious. Galumphing rats with long plastic whiskers aimed what could well have been high-tech water pistols from Toys "R" Us at hapless soldiers who crumpled to earth even though nothing visible came out of the guns. Animators would add the "death rays" or whatever.

Four alien animals surrounded a tank and shot it dead center from every direction with their dry water pistols and then had to back away, their arms and paws in front of their faces to shield them from an explosion that wouldn't happen until the second unit crew blew it up when all the extras were at a safe distance. Insurance costs being what they are. Oh well.

Smoke and little fires were kept flaming with some kind of wires in the grass pulled by crew members off camera. Eventually after many takes but with almost maniacal drive, the end grew near—the U.S. Army being mostly dead by now. The rat marauders kicked at the bodies to make sure and wouldn't you know found one still alive but pretending.

The Western dolly edged in and so did the handheld from a different angle as the giant rats hauled the soldier to his feet. This had to be the star because he was too old to really be in the Army and Charlie'd seen him around someplace. Another good suspect for the murder of Gordon Cabot?

These aliens all had long rat claws and one raked bloody streaks down the captive's cheek, the blood color probably transferring from the claws to the cheek. But our hero grimaced manfully, perfect capped teeth barred in perfect defiance.

Charlie wondered how the rats could hold on to, let alone shoot, their weapons—not to mention fiddle the spaceship controls—with those nails.

While two rats dragged our hero off the set, the wounded ranger carefully settled herself among the dead infantry to be discovered by another rat. She, of course, was carried off in his rat arms in order to look sexy and vulnerable.

"Incoming," the sound mixer said suddenly. Sid called for a cut as a small plane Charlie hadn't noticed until now flew low overhead.

"Who the shit?" the helicopter pilot of the Charlie's crew asked no one.

But Earl answered, "It's Lew. What's he doing here? And this early?"

Lew had decided to fly in on his own schedule with a couple of wire-service reporters instead of John B.'s food order and the dailies. John B. was beyond furious, his mobile face so suffused he resembled her boss when somebody crossed him once too often. Charlie decided he must be the murderer, even though she'd also decided Gordon Cabot's killer must come from his own crew.

God, I wish I really was psychic sometimes.

Drake had commandeered Howard's Jeep to meet the plane while Charlie, Earl, and Tawny copped a ride in the helicopter pilot's Land Rover to get back to the campground early. Dean Goodacre, Charlie, and Earl Seabaugh were poking around the scene of the crime when Sheriff Sumpter arrived back from the dead.

"Out doing a little detecting, are we, Detective Greene? Or doing some divining maybe? When a proper daughter would be busy at the jail showing some concern for a mother who is in very serious trouble."

And a proper sheriff would be investigating an ax murder instead of assuming he had the case solved and there was time to cavort for the cameras.

"You know this little lady is a famous psychic, don't you?" Ralph Sumpter had to add dynamite to the beans.

"You should talk to Hilsten about that," Earl said as Sumpter swaggered off between scrub bushes and fire grates, laughing it up. "He consults one regularly, I think . . . uh, Lady Beverly or something like that." He swiped biting gnats from his naked head with his Rockies hat.

There went another childish illusion. Charlie had imagined Mitch Hilsten to be moderately sensible.

A tiny sunning lizard skittered away when she kicked a toe at the cleaned-up crime scene. Even the crime-scene barf was gone.

Nature had probably done most of the work. Blood, brains, barf—
everything was recyclable in this deprived place.

Dean pointed out the campsites of the *Aliens* crew and who
occupied which. He admitted that most everybody also had a room
in town. Monster RVs, all rented, overwhelmed the dwarf forest
and gave the lie to the term camping. The production manager,
Stan Lowenthall, had shared a two-bedroom with Cabot, mostly as
a base office but sometimes to sleep.

"Most of the rest of these it depends on who's spending the
night here and who in town."

"So it might be hard to tie down who was here the night
Gordon Cabot was murdered," Charlie said.

"No, that was the tour-bus scene—practically everybody
connected with *Aliens* was on hand that night. You really psychic?"

"Of course not. It's just a rumor I can't seem to stamp out."
If I were, I'd have Edwina out of jail by now and somebody else in
it. Maybe you. "Gordon was one of the first ones back in, wasn't
he? Which might cut it down a bunch." She'd been so furious at
Edwina she couldn't remember how many vehicles passed behind
Howard's Jeep after the Humvee that night. And she'd been inside
Drake's motor home after that and wouldn't have seen who came
and went. "How could I find out who was here when he was murdered?"

"Ask me." Dean was still chewing on the toothpick that had
held his croissant together. It was a shredded mess. "I didn't work
that shoot. I was sitting right about here when he drove up, having
me a beer. He was all by himself but he was laughing, sort of like
that prick of a sheriff just now." Goodacre crawled up on a picnic
table and leaned back on one elbow.

A slew of gofers and some makeup people had come in next
and Cabot had headed off through the scrub. There were no water
hookups at these campsites and storage in the RVs was limited.
Dean had figured he was on his way to the toilets. "And that's the
last I saw him alive."

"What did you do for dinner?"

"Chinese take-out from town. We were just reheating everything when you folks stumbled over the body."

"Dean, do you know anyone who wanted Cabot dead?"

"Hell, I don't know anybody who didn't."

Chapter
14

"**I** haven't met anybody since I got here who didn't wish the man dead," Charlie groused to Mitch across the candlelit table. "Which isn't a lot of help when you're trying to clear your mom of a murder she didn't commit. Too many suspects."

He'd spent the day calling contacts to line up a power attorney who would come in from Salt Lake tomorrow. Edwina had refused to see Mitch when he went to the courthouse and refused to see Charlie when she'd returned from Dead Horse Point. If Charlie was reading her mother's strange moods right, she'd refuse the power attorney as well. And whatever was screwing up the woman's head, it had been successfully lodged there before Gordon Cabot's was split down the middle.

And to top the day off nicely, Sheriff Sumpter had presented Charlie with a search warrant that would allow an expert somebody to examine Howard's Jeep and the fold-down trailer for samples. Of what Charlie couldn't imagine. It had been three days since the murder, the obvious weapon had been found nearby, and half the campground had been in and out of both vehicles. Charlie, at least, would be glad when the lawyer turned up.

The restaurant nestled along the Colorado River some miles out of town. It had once been a spacious ranch house and against its aging brick the candlelight didn't seem an affectation.

They sat at a secluded table next to a window with two-foot-thick casements and dim moonlight enhancing a walled garden outside. A central staircase glowed with polished wood in the soft light. Charlie felt underdressed in jeans and sweatshirt, but everyone was staring at Mitch anyway.

"You folks decided?" Their young waitress wore a starched organdy dress and apron intended to suggest a Middle European peasant. Mitch asked about a wine list. She'd just recognized him and stood glued to the floor. "Are you him? Wine? Oh."

The girl returned with a red face and a thin padded booklet. She wrote down his selection, glancing at the wine list every third letter. "And two glasses?"

"Well . . . that'd be nice. Yeah."

But instead of bringing it to their table she led them up the shadowy staircase to what had been a small bedroom crowded now with a mahogany bar and mirrored backbar so tall it tilted forward into the room to fit under the ceiling. Which may have been why there were no liquor bottles on its shelves.

"Rhonda," the waitress announced to her replica behind the bar, "this is Mr. and Mrs. Mitch Hilsten and they would like a bottle of . . . Che . . . of Chat . . . of wine." She handed over her order pad so Rhonda could read it herself.

"And two glasses," Mitch added, grinning at Charlie.

Rhonda couldn't seem to find what he'd ordered but allowed him to choose something else out of cardboard boxes at her feet and explained that, although the wine was a bargain, the glasses were three dollars each. And they wouldn't be allowed to take them home. Imbibing in Mormon country . . .

"From what I could see and with the tree-bushes and rock outcroppings and sand hillocks and dips in the terrain, someone as tall as Scrag or Sid or John B. even could have stood there and had a private conversation with Cabot and not been seen from the camping areas of either film crew," Charlie told her companion when they and the wine and the two glasses were safely ensconced at their table. "Or heard for that matter. Which means anybody could have done it." Including you.

Here sat Charlie Greene in an incredibly romantic setting, the diffused light making the rich aged wood and burnished copper and hypnotic ice-blue eyes across the table lustrous. Excellent wine. Roast rack of lamb for two on the way. And what were they talking? Murder.

"Someone who had the time to drop by your mother's camp-site and pick up her ax, don't forget."

"The last time I saw her use it was to split wood to make a cooking fire to burn our dinner, which we were trying to eat when Cabot came back from the shoot." Charlie rubbed her forehead and around her eyes. "So that means somebody swiped the ax after Edwina and I left the table."

"Here's to the freeing of Edwina Greene," he said in that gentle, personal voice he'd used on whichever young-blonde-of-the-year-now-long-forgotten in *Spy of Wall Street*, right after he'd made love to her and just before he shot her. And raised his rental glass to clink with hers.

The funny part about all this was, he didn't know the funny part. That this was all unnecessary—the ambiance thing. He didn't know guilt was Charlie's chief aphrodisiac. Mitch didn't know that simply being within a two-hundred-mile radius of Edwina automatically made Charlie feel guilty.

Here was the sexiest man on earth, and possibly an ax murderer, coming on to her, and he didn't have a clue to the fact his chances of going to bed alone tonight were right up there with the Pope enforcing birth control. It was even, for Charlie, that particular time of the month she called horny (Edwina would have called it estrus or something) that Charlie so rarely had the chance to satisfy. No man would have been especially safe tonight, but this guy was dead meat.

The cream of asparagus soup arrived in its own tureen, fragrant with subtle herbs, naughty with real cream, garnished with crisp raw asparagus tips.

"How well do you know Scrag Dickens?"

"Well enough to know his real name's Norman something. Good man with a guitar." Mitch shrugged. "Sort of a film bum—as in ski bum. Used to teach. When I arrived at John B.'s for dinner the night in question, Scrag was already there."

"And who else?"

"Everybody but you and John B. He was one of the last off the set, came in with the generator truck."

"It has to have been one of Cabot's crew. Dean Goodacre, the helicopter pilot, says they were all out there for the big tour-bus scene." Even though I saw you act like you wanted to kill him that morning. And Sid too. But you were the most menacing.

When he had cut a section of lamb ribs, he lifted them over to her plate before she could pass it and then held his arms and the knife toward her in that threatening position. "You make a good detective, you know? You suspect everyone. Even me." He withdrew finally to serve himself. "You may be complex, Charlie, but you're not inscrutable."

Great, he'd probably read her plans for the rest of his evening on her face too. Not that it would save him.

"Do you know anything about Mick Sensenbrenner?"

"I know he was the latest chump they had working that dog. His agent's Marty Sheldon. He's divorced, hated Cabot's guts. But he got fired before Cabot came out on location. He wouldn't have the guts himself to pick up an ax and kill anybody anyway."

"How do you know he didn't sneak into the campground, grab the ax, and sneak out after he'd killed Cabot? I mean if he hated him that much—"

"I think that would be stretching it a bit, don't you?"

Actually, Charlie did. But it was her mother sitting in a jail cell, not his. "What about the PM, Stan?"

"Stan Lowenthall. Played poker with him once on the set of *Spy of Wall Street*. Mean man at cards. Used to have a problem with alcohol. Seems all right now, but that's probably why he was reduced to working for Cabot. It's Sid that's got me confused. This isn't his kind of pic. Wonder if he's going to try to pull off a farce, a Mel Brooks or *Killer Tomatoes*."

"He's halfway there already." Charlie described the afternoon shoot. "With the right editing it could be campy as hell." She picked up a rib bone to chew off the last delicate morsel and he did too. "What's the old scandal on John B. Drake I can remember hearing about but can't pin down?"

"Only one I know of was some development scheme years ago. He and Earl Seabaugh and an architect buddy were partners. Earl inherited some prime L.A. property from his dad and they were going to build a bunch of houses on it, make a quick buck. John B. was to be the developer. They lost their shirts. The architect committed suicide."

He rubbed the grease off his lips and fingers and sat back to swirl the wine in his glass. "Now it's your turn to answer some questions. What do you really think is making the creatures go wacko out at the Point? And this time I want an answer."

"Probably show biz. You saw what the flyovers did to the rock formations. Why couldn't they and all the other special effects have upset the rats and bats and whatever too?"

"And what do you think that submarine-shaped shadow was over the generator truck? Swamp gas?"

"Maybe there's such a thing as desert gas. It was very nebulous. If I hadn't been looking for something I probably wouldn't have seen it. Could have been something on the clip itself or on the camera lens."

"Do you ever question the company line, Charlie? Question numbers and statistics, supposedly known facts?"

What, the business I'm in? Are you kidding? But she said, "Like, I don't believe in flying saucers if that's what you're getting at."

He hadn't believed in UFOs either until a few years ago when recurring dreams started reminding him of an incident during childhood. Charlie drew in a deep regretful breath redolent of garlic, rosemary, fresh-ground pepper, and mint sauce. She sighed it out and listened politely, nodded at decent intervals, keeping a stick-straight face. With somebody like this you never know when your leg's being pulled.

It seems that when Mitch was about twelve he went missing from the family summer cabin in northern Michigan and his parents feared he'd drowned in the lake. By the time he was discovered the next morning wandering beside it the sheriff, divers, and dogs were on the scene.

"To this day, my dad doesn't believe my story that I was fishing off a dock as it was getting dark and the next I knew I was standing in the woods without my fishing pole and dog and it was morning. Never saw that dog again."

Years later the dreams began about the dog. And about a pillar of green light that cast no shadow and didn't illuminate anything around it. And in subsequent dreams about being handled by someone he couldn't see, being prodded and poked, answering questions he couldn't remember being asked.

"Those dreams nearly fried me, Charlie. I was in the middle of a shooting schedule and a divorce."

Why me, Lord? "So what did you do?"

"Spilled the whole stupid business to a friend on the set—we were in northern Africa—and he started talking nonsense about aliens and even gave me a reading list. I laughed it off but the dreams grew worse and when I got home I took the list to a few bookstores and libraries." From his reading, Mitch Hilsten learned he was not alone in his misery and confusion.

"So you think creatures from billions of light-years away come to earth to steal dogs and fishing poles and terrorize children?"

"No, Charlie, I think they're here and always have been. I think they live here too. And I'm not sure they know or care what they're doing to people like me. That's the frightening thing about all this."

He leaned forward, elbows on the table, expressive hands

trying to convey what a controlled face seemed reluctant to mirror. Several times people approached tentatively with pens and notepads or napkins but turned away when he ignored them.

"What I'm saying, Charlie, is that all these stories of strange sightings and happenings that have been going on since recorded history and probably before that and all over the planet—all of them can't be wrong. All those people can't be deluded kooks."

I don't know why not. Charlie still held out hope there was a punchline coming here.

"And how many more are there like me who once had something traumatic happen to them they don't remember?"

"You think these beings come from another dimension and just happen to cross over into ours now and then?" Charlie signaled their waitress for a refill of coffee. Hey, you oughta see the stuff that crosses my desk. It's a lot better than this.

What he was pitching here was tired science fiction you couldn't give away these days.

"Look, there's a lot of garbage out there I don't believe," Mitch said. "But mixed up in all that, there's some fact too. You have to separate them."

"Okay, separate them. Tell me some of the things you don't believe in."

"I don't believe in little green men. In fact I don't think they're men, maybe not even solid. Maybe merely energy of some kind. That's why they don't have to follow our laws of physics." Sun and smile creases, a mole, a few shaving errors looked just fine on this man. "And giant rats looking for waste-disposal planets . . . women taken on board flying saucers and raped on examining tables . . . you know. That's fantasy stuff." He placed a credit card on the tray without glancing at the check.

"I give up. I can't tell when you're serious or not," Charlie admitted in the parking lot. "You do realize it doesn't really matter?"

The moon was fully up now, its light cold and blue and sullen. Across the road the river rolled massive and bloated, moon sparkles outlining eddies along its sides, young cottonwood leaves clattering and whispering above.

Mitch Hilsten turned up his chin and the collar of his sheepskin, his eyes locked on hers. He sighed long and stoically. "Guess a woman's gotta do . . . what a woman's gotta do."

Chapter

15

Charlie lay in the smelly room in the too-small bed, needing a shower again, and blinked smears off stuck contacts to watch the dirty curtains brighten with daylight.

Edwina was right. After all the years of fighting to reject it, it was agonizing to have to admit it but there must be something wrong with Charlie's genes. Maybe she *should* try to look up her birth mother.

Oh really? What if she's working the streets? Wouldn't that just make your day? Even worse, what if she's psychic?

She'd be too old to work the streets and there are no such things as psychics.

And if she is or was a hooker? How do you tell Libby?

"There's nothing casual about sex," she'd warned Libby again and again. "Not for the woman."

"You oughta know, UM," was Libby's standard reply.

"You always give away something of yourself that you can never get back."

And here Charlie had slipped between the sheets as casually as a bimbo on a daytime soap, given something of herself, something irretrievable.

Oh, get a grip, you knew exactly what was going to happen the minute you saw him frying your eggs at Dead Horse Point.

Edwina probably knew it too.

Careful with that, you're going to get yourself worked up again. The guy needs his rest.

Mitch Hilsten didn't snore, he whistled.

The whistle turned to a snort when the phone rang. He reached across Charlie's chest for it before his eyes were open but she already had it in one hand and the other clamped over his mouth.

"Richard?" Charlie sat up, losing the sheet but still muzzling Mitch. "What are you doing up this early? How'd you know where to find me?"

"Called Larry the Kid, he'd talked to your lawyer-neighbor-lady. Listen, babe, I'm real sorry about your mother, but don't forget you also got a daughter and a mortgage and a normal load of shit. And you need your job. And your agency is having major trouble here." Richard Morse had a way of verbally transferring ownership of the agency to his employees when he deemed the prospect of unemployment could save it from some threat and then taking it back when all was safe. This time, Charlie feared even "downsizing" couldn't save Congdon and Morse Representation, Inc.

"Eric Ashton's dropping *Phantom of the Alpine Tunnel*."

"Like a hot bagel," her boss said. "And we both know what that means."

The rumors had been rife. Ashton was not a Congdon and Morse client, but his costar, Cyndi Seagal, was. Cyndi Seagal was also about the last major talent the agency could boast. If this project sank, Cyndi would abandon ship for another agency. And Congdon and Morse and Charlie's investment in a condo in Long Beach and the career that fed her and her illegitimate ungrateful offspring could be history. Fortunes change quickly anywhere, but in the quicksand of Hollywood, you can't afford to take time to blink.

"But listen to me, doll, we can still pull the lox out of the fire."

Charlie noticed Mitch's startled eyes and mouthed, "My boss." He relaxed under her hand. No problem. But you mess with somebody's wife, lover, sister, mother, automobile, you can find yourself facing the bore of a gun in this country.

"I'm a literary agent. I delivered on the book and the screen-writer. I've done my part."

"We're in the trades again and for all the wrong reasons again. Right? And all because of you again. You got debts building up to astronomical around here, babe, you don't want to forget that. I been up all night working this out."

"Richard, will you get to the point?"

"I'm also reading that Mitch Hilsten is working the documentary your mother was playing expert on. You didn't tell me that."

"I didn't know that. Not till I got here."

"Charlie, you're always telling me he's your matinee idol." Richard used dated expressions because most of their clients worked for things like false-teeth-glue commercials.

"So?"

"So, if you can talk to him . . . or . . . get him off in a cozy corner . . . you know. He'd be great for the train engineer's part. Hilsten in the picture, Seagal stays. And, Charlie, with the two of them Jack Nicholson is going to take another look at the villain role. Think about it. I know you're over thirty. But you don't look it. And there's a lot at stake here."

"Richard, are you suggesting—"

"Hey, times are tough all round, you know? I mean you don't have to . . . but you could . . . well . . . use your imagination . . . Charlie, if you've already got the hots for him—what's it gonna hurt? Congdon and Morse is counting on you. What can I say?"

"You can say good-bye."

Charlie was in the shower trying to cool off when the phone rang again. She yelled at Mitch not to answer it. What if it was Libby and a man answered this early in the day? Or Edwina calling from jail? Or good old Sheriff Sumpter—Jesus.

But it stopped after one ring and she figured the damage was already done. She'd managed to finish rinsing the shampoo out of her hair when he pulled the curtain aside to join her and steal the hot water. "You answered it, didn't you?"

"I'd already said hello when you yelled at me. I was kind of committed. It was just your boss again."

"Richard? You didn't tell him who you were?"

"Well, yeah."

"Tell me everything he said."

"Said to tell you he was sorry and then he said, 'Wait a minute, who the hell is this?'" Mitch's impersonation was damn close to the reality. "And when I told him, he was quiet for a while and then he laughed, called you a good girl, and hung up. What did he say to get you so pissed anyway?"

"Don't ask." She tried to step out of the tub but he barred her way.

"Look, I spilled my guts to you last night and all I get from you is. 'Don't ask.' What kind of a deal is that?"

"I told you about my getting knocked up in a cemetery at sixteen, didn't I?" And, boy, had that heated things up.

"Why wouldn't you answer my question about why you didn't have an abortion or have the baby adopted out?" Mitch returned her to her place under the hot water and washed her back.

"I was a real little shit, okay? I probably kept her to spite Edwina. It was all a big mess. Might have hastened Howard's death, nearly ruined my life. I decided it wasn't going to ruin Libby's. And I thought I had it made, until she turned thirteen. Then I realized the jury was still out on that one."

The last three years had been hell. If Charlie hadn't had a job she loved, she didn't know how she'd have lived through them. How women who stayed home and raised kids kept their sanity, she'd never understand.

This wasn't the first time she'd considered quitting Congdon and Morse because of Richard Morse and this time the old chauvinist had really shown his true colors. But what if she couldn't find another job in her field? Charlie rinsed off her back and washed his.

"No kid's a 'real little shit' for no reason. Were you spiteful because you were adopted?"

"Howard was sort of distant, but kind. I never lacked for anything important. They loved me, but they were involved in their work. Like I am now." Charlie was rebellious like many kids that age. But Charlie got caught, and then refused to admit she could have been wrong. And, because she'd been through this and understood it, she thought she'd be a perfect guide to help Libby through these difficult years. But Libby had decided her mother didn't know anything, just as Charlie had decided the same about her own parents.

Charlie'd put Libby on the pill at the first scary signs. But Libby stopped taking it when she gained weight.

"Besides, it can't protect you from AIDS like a condom. And even besides that, I'm not doing anything."

Would some potent adolescent have the control to reach for the slender packet as smoothly as had the man whose back she'd just washed? No questions. No apologies. Barely a pause in the foreplay.

What if Charlie became a grandma at thirty-two?

Last night Charlie had forgotten about Libby and Edwina and murder and her job and even that this guy was a superstar. (And possibly a murderer, but that now seemed as farfetched as Edwina's being one. Innocent by reason of intercourse.) Just as Edwina had feared she would forget. Just as Charlie feared Libby would, was doing, with someone else. To Edwina, it was just plain wrong. To Charlie, it was just plain dangerous.

They were toweling when the phone rang again. He didn't even make a move for it this time.

It was Libby. "Like, I guess you're all mad at me. I'm sure Maggie and Larry made everything sound much worse than it was. Of course *my* friends can do no right. *Your* friends can do no wrong." Charlie's daughter started in on the attack before her mother could get in a salvo. Maggie had probably insisted she call and apologize and Libby probably really was sorry, but that tended to make her more defensive than contrite.

And there stood Charlie Greene dressed in her skin and goose bumps, staring back at a naked movie star in a tiny run-down motel room and her with only seconds to make decisions that could affect Libby's life forever and hers too.

She could threaten to make Libby pay for all or part of the damages to the condo with the money she earned on her summer job. Charlie could ground Libby for the rest of the school year. But she knew her daughter would simply run away, as Charlie would have once.

"Mom, you still there?"

"Yes, honey, I'm still here."

And there were streets in L.A. where a nymphet could live and hide a long time before being found. Charlie had read of one who'd lived two years that way before she committed suicide. The autopsy showed her body racked with drugs and venereal disease.

"We'll discuss this when I get home," Charlie said finally. "Meanwhile, you get yourself to school and stay with Maggie at night and—"

"Whoa, no way. You know what that bitch made me do? Scrape crud off the carpets where people got sick. You can't make me stay over there again tonight."

"You still want that driver's license?"

An extended pause and then an outraged whisper, "You wouldn't . . . You have no right. It isn't fair . . . you—"

Charlie hung up, fear making the breath in her chest hurt. Libby was a formidable adversary. And the trouble with this kind of decision was that you might not know if it was the right one for years.

"Hey, let me grab a shave and then let's get you out to breakfast before that phone rings again. You can't take much more of this." Mitch crossed the room to comfort her and Charlie started feeling guilty and one thing led to another. Again.

Well, I'm *not* going to say one word to him about *Phantom of the Alpine Tunnel* and I *am* going to look for another job as soon as Edwina's out of this mess, but before I quit the old one, Charlie thought while watching Mitch shave later. She tried not to admit to herself how marvelous she felt, just hated that sappy postcoital look she knew she wore. He was growing increasingly limp with all this stimulation, but at least he hadn't learned his lovemaking from *Playboy*.

He used foam and a safety edge, his chin screwed up toward the ceiling so he could scrape away the foam and whiskers under it while trying to look down past his nose to see into the mirror. Charlie wondered briefly what it would be like to be married and then clamped her mind shut on that idea. Marriage was not for career-women-mothers. Any more complications in her life and Charlie would drop dead of the strain by thirty-five.

Until last night she'd been celibate for almost two years and preferred that blessed state. But the emotional upheaval and the time of the month and the fact that this guy was the second most gorgeous man Charlie'd ever encountered had ganged up on her.

The most gorgeous was Larry Mann, her assistant at Congdon and Morse. But he was unavailable, untouchable. So every now and then Charlie took him out to lunch just to look at him.

Chapter

16

". . . a sense of serenity and quiet beauty on the mighty Colorado River. Don't miss *The River by Night!*" the local cable TV channel implored them, with scenic wonders and a voice-over and ethereal music, as they dressed.

But when the local news began, Mitch nearly caught himself in his zipper.

A man seated on a kitchen chair behind a wooden table said, "You'll be glad to know that Ed Buchanan, night watchman out at the old Texas Petroleum mill, has been found safe and sound. Missing for three days, Ed was discovered wandering along the cliff road up north of town last night by Bud Hawly and son, Gary. According to Bud, Ed has no memory of where he's been."

The speaker wore a red-and-black-plaid shirt like John B.'s and he leaned forward with his elbows on the table, unconsciously rocking his body from side to side as he talked. A floral arrangement took up half the table and hid most of his face when he rocked to the right, as if he were playing hide-and-seek with the viewer.

"Latest on the gruesome murder out at Dead Horse Point of Gordon Cabot, the famous Hollywood director, is that Rita Latham, noted defense lawyer, is due in from Salt Lake today to decide whether she wants to defend Mrs. Edwina Greene, whose ax it allegedly was that killed Mr. Cabot. Mrs. Greene's daughter, Charlemagne Catherine Greene, a self-styled psychic, was one of those who found the director's body out at the campground.

"Meanwhile, the *Animal Aliens* pic should wrap location shooting in a day or two. Sheriff Sumpter himself agreed to take a minor role and died—I understand very nicely—yesterday while trying to stop the giant rats invading the earth and Mrs. Regina Ottinger over on Fifth Street is due to meet a similar fate today." He went on to note other local notables who either had performed as extras or were scheduled to, but Mitch interrupted.

"Charlemagne Catherine Greene?" His incredulity overcame the story of the watchman found wandering the mesa.

"Howard was a history professor." And who told the local news? Only one person seemed likely. Edwina. And damn it, the news wires were in town and probably everybody's stringers. Charlie's belly burned like the flush on her face. "And I'm not a self-styled psychic." No mention of her real job.

"That's the local gab on this morning's edition of 'Cliff Notes,' folks. We'll go off the air now until three this afternoon when Jake 'Jeremiah' Johnson will bring you his 'River Watch' program. And this evening, there should be an interview with Sheriff Sumpter on the latest developments in the murder investigation."

"I can't believe it, Charle—"

"Oh, knock it off."

But it was a knock at the door that saved the superstar. Charlie yanked it open to stand eyeball to eyeball with Ralph Sumpter.

Her day was complete. And she hadn't even had breakfast.

"**I** didn't think Mormons drank coffee," Charlie told the sheriff, sitting across from him and beside Mitch at the River Palace Café and Grill. The sheriff ordered a pot brought to the table and refilled his cup before she'd taken a sip of her milk.

"Bap-*tist*," he pronounced, drilling her to the back of the booth with a hard stare. "South-*errn*."

Charlie felt instantly like a fallen woman. But he gazed at Mitch with cloying respect.

Hey, you found *him* in that room too, don't forget. It's always the woman's fault because she asks for it. A guy asks for it because he's supposed to. Like nature tells him to.

You're just jealous. It's penis envy.

No, it's privilege envy.

The special was huevos rancheros and you could get it with pinto beans instead of yuppie black, and corn tortillas instead of pasty flour. And they'd all ordered it. Wel-l-l, Charlie'd used up a lot of energy last night. And the doctor had warned her not to skip meals.

"Wanted to tell you how much the wife and I enjoyed *Bloody Promises*," the official prick told the superstar. "When you died I didn't think I was ever going to get her to quit bawling." He nodded as if thinking about it awhile and then refocused on the present. "Suppose you heard about the watchman out at the mill? That's all we need on top of a murder. Getting to the bottom of that one's going to gain us nothing but ridicule." He poured himself more coffee. "Why in my county? Why?"

"Plenty of lawmen have lost their jobs over this kind of thing," Mitch said importantly.

"Don't I know. No matter how things appear during a scare, they look pretty silly by the time the next election rolls around. You're damned if you do and damned if you don't."

And of course good old Mitch had to tell good ol' Ralph about the sort-of-shadow thing over the generator truck and they proceeded to argue over whether unidentified flying objects came from outer space or another dimension.

"Oh stop it," Charlie worked up the nerve to say, refusing to be seen and not heard. "If there was really such a thing as UFOs somebody with a camcorder would have captured them on video long ago. And they'd get something more recognizable than nebulous shadows too."

That at least gave them pause and gave her time to do a jump cut. "Sheriff, you never did tell me why you came to my room at the Pit Stop. Was there something you wanted?"

Other than to discover me *en flagrante*.

"Well now, yes, there was, Miz Greene. Two things. Just want you to know the serologist has finished with your mother's camper and Jeep. He took samples out at the campground and the vehicles are still there. You can move them when you're ready. Serologists study body fluids of all kinds. He can pin down identities even from dried semen, sweat, blood . . . and the other thing is your mother wants to see you." He goggled meaningfully between Charlie and the limp hunk beside her. "If you can spare the time, that is."

Charlie sat in the tiny interrogation room again with the woman cop and Edwina. Edwina looked rested, almost happy, as if she thrived on jail cells. And she knew exactly what she wanted.

"I want you out of here, Charlie. As a mother I have the right to request that. I want you home looking after my granddaughter and I want the high-falutin' lawyer to stay in Salt Lake. I'll take care of my own problems, thank you."

"What should I do with Howard's Jeep?"

"What?"

"And the tent camper? And your house in Boulder? I mean, if you're going to fry for a murder you didn't commit they're going to come after me to help make decisions on your possessions. The state takes a third, the lawyer takes a third—have you left a will for what little taxes and legal fees won't eat up? Oh, and then there's CU. Do you want me to call the head of the department or the president of the university? I don't know the protocol here. And do you want to be cremated or buried next to Howard?"

"Charlie, stop it."

"No, I'm not going to. You may not care what happens to you at the moment, but I'm the one left to deal with it if you cop out."

"I always thought I'd be the one to say that. What do you want?"

"Talk to me."

"I can't. You don't understand."

"Then talk to the lawyer. But talk to somebody."

Rita Latham was a slender, graying woman in a Chanel suit of red and black. Her gaze was direct and mischievous, her lips thin and pressed tightly between thoughts as if working hard not to grin. "So, what's the score here with your mom? She's holding back on me."

"Yeah, me too. But I've got a gut feeling," literally, "that it doesn't have anything to do with Gordon Cabot."

"She's going to 'let' me represent her only if I promise to help you and your daughter take care of the aftermath of her state-induced demise for the axing of Cabot, which she claims she didn't do but doesn't care if she 'fries' for. This is a university professor?"

"Please stick with us, Ms. Latham. I can't get anything out of her either but I haven't talked to everyone else involved yet." Charlie described the meager results of her search so far. "I haven't talked to anyone who couldn't have picked up her ax on the way by or anyone who might not wish to use one on Gordon Cabot. And I'm sure the sheriff is sure he has his murderer and isn't looking any further."

"Your mother's in really deep, Charlie, I won't lie to you. You keep asking questions and help me and I'll help her. But we have to find out what's behind this brick-wall attitude she's putting up. She doesn't really come on as suicidal so much as—"

"Resigned."

"That's it. Resigned. Why? Help me."

Charlie and Mitch headed out of town in his Bronco that evening to find the cliff road where Ed Buchanan had been found wandering. Charlie visualized the night watchman as an older man, in his sixties maybe, wearing bib overalls, his eyes red-rimmed and lonely-looking.

She'd spent the afternoon out at Dead Horse Point, with little useful result for Rita Latham but with a dismaying revelation for Charlie Greene.

They were traveling along a highway next to the river and deep in the bottom of a canyon. Fading sunlight still highlighted the canyon wall above them but the river was shadowed for night. Mitch turned off on a rutted road that started up a side canyon and Charlie wished she'd stayed in Moab.

"The police will have gone over it pretty thoroughly," she said.

"Doesn't mean they'd tell us if there was something there. Even Sumpter knows something's up but can't admit it or he'll lose the next election. You heard him this morning."

Get real, the watchman drank too much and some mean-spirited jokesters drove him up there and left him. Of course he couldn't remember how he got there. But Charlie didn't have the heart to dump on Mitch's fantasies and didn't voice the obvious aloud.

This was not a very good road to be traveling on at night.

Charlie wondered what Libby was up to about now. She'd have had cheerleading practice after school. And that exam in chemistry. She probably went to Lori Schantz's after practice.

Lori's parents had never been married to anyone else. Lori's father was a lawyer who could afford to keep his wife home raising Lori and her younger brother. The woman played bridge and even baked cookies. And she didn't approve of her daughter's coming home with a latchkey Libby. Which made sense.

"Mitch, the fact that all those noted scientists say the whole UFO thing is a lot of bull, that there's no proof any of it exists— doesn't that mean anything to you?"

"Only means they haven't proven it exists," he said. "Doesn't mean it doesn't."

"I suppose you believe in ghosts and the whole enchilada."

"I don't even believe in life after death."

"Just because no one has proved that ghosts exist," Charlie countered, "doesn't mean they don't."

"That is not fair."

Charlie concentrated on wondering why handsome was out in actors. Not the classic, perfect, surgically induced kind—but the natural with warts and unaffected charisma kind. Mitch had lots of moles on his back but it was still gorgeous.

They were on a shelf road again, one big rock with a ledge cut in its side, rather than merely a rocky shelf. Their ledge tilted toward the abyss like ledges always do. Charlie closed her eyes and breathed a lot. But she could see the faded orangy-red tint of the rock in her head.

Soooo . . . she concentrated on wondering what Larry might be doing with her job. How the *Hostage* project might have fared at Universal. She didn't want to think about the road or about the afternoon's earlier revelation. She'd talked to only two people out at Dead Horse Point and both from the wrong crew.

Earl Seabaugh and Tawny had sat with her on Edwina's concrete picnic table and argued with each other across her face.

The revelation was that the director of photography believed Edwina murdered Cabot. It hadn't occurred to Charlie that anyone but the stupid sheriff of Grand County could conceive of such idiocy.

"Earl's a guy, he doesn't understand women," Tawny hastened to assure Charlie. "Besides, he and your mother had a blowout, and we're talking major."

"Charlie, everybody within twenty miles of the woman had major trouble with Edwina." Earl had looked serious for once. "I like you and I don't want to hurt you, but you have to consider the possibility that the sheriff is right about this. I'm not sure she's quite sane, are you?"

Charlie'd had about enough time to grab the pain in her middle before John B. came up to claim his employees.

"Did you love Libby's father?" Mitch asked now, breaking into her mental replay. Why was he so fascinated by Libby's father?

"We were totally unsuited. I could see that even at sixteen."

"Then why did you have sex with him?"

"I wasn't thinking of having his baby . . . it was just . . . it just happened." It had been a fun, freaky night in the local graveyard—Columbia Cemetery where the famous outlaw Tom Horn was buried among staunch pioneer families and only one block from the little brick house with the rats in the basement. The night had been unusually quiet and unusually warm—several couples, several six-packs. And a mood of some kind, Charlie supposed now. Libby had been conceived on the outlaw's grave. Charlie'd always wondered if there was something symbolic in that. "Do you usually ask such personal questions?"

"I don't usually let myself get so curious about people," Mitch said. "Must be the scenery."

Charlie opened her eyes and regretted it. The mammoth rock they were on overlooked the river and its canyon and the tiny road below. There was a corresponding rock cliff across the river and a millennium of sky with a helicopter hovering insectlike.

The cramping in her stomach and the tingles under her skin from breasts to thighs subsided when she looked away from "the scenery."

"Did I ever tell you about the problem I have with heights?"

"And all the time I thought you were closing your eyes and breathing that way because you were fantasizing about me," Mitch said and the Bronco rumbled on to the next switchback.

At the top of the mesa the scenery was, predictably, even worse. But the road ended on a broad flat expanse that lured her out to see what Mitch was investigating by flashlight.

The sun was nothing more than a colorful display in the west and even that was paling. The inevitable chilly breeze sneaked inside Charlie's clothes with her to dry the sweat induced by her trip up here, and harden her nipples. She wore a sweatshirt and he his handy sheepskin. Both smelled heavily of Room Eight at the Pit Stop Motel.

There were whorls in the rock dust under their feet mixed with car tracks and shoe prints.

"Probably a dust devil or two or three," Charlie assured him before he could come up with something ridiculous.

"How would Ed Buchanan get here?" he asked. "Walk it the whole way?"

"Mitch, you realize that if you're looking for evidence of something . . . stranger than science will admit to, that's what you'll find, don't you?" How could normal rational people fail to see the obvious?

He studied her face with that mesmerizing scrutiny he was famous for on camera and left her to inspect other whorls in the dust.

She watched night advance on dusk. "Mitch, do you think Edwina has really gone crazy enough to kill someone?"

His answer came measured and thoughtful. "You're the one who's pointed out the personality change, Charlie. This is the only personality of Edwina's I've known. I like her anyway and don't want to think she could do that. But if Rita has to go after an insanity plea to save her, well—Charlie?"

His shape was a shadow above the cone of light at the end of his flashlight. It came up behind him as he came toward her. A dark piece of night that grew ever larger as it rose slowly above the rim. It was only a patch of dense fog. A cloud. Early dew. Ground mist rising up from the valley on the other side. It had distinctive nonwispy edges. Didn't it?

No, it didn't. Charlie was susceptible to suggestion. She realized she was pointing at it, the other hand over her mouth.

"Very funny, Charlie. All you cynics gotta be wise guys." But Mitch turned to look over his shoulder. "I don't see anything. Jesus, Charlie, stop!"

It took a second for Charlie Greene to realize she'd been backing away from the dark thing she couldn't see now either. It was a miracle she hadn't tripped on the uneven rock surface. Just as her brain ordered her feet to stop her backward progress, her rearmost foot hit empty space. Charlie lost her balance and followed it over the side.

Chapter
17

"**C**harlie, stop screaming. Find some cracks to stick your fingers and toes in and hold on to, or you'll pull me over."

Charlie had pulled some ohshits in her life but this had to be the granddaddy of 'em all. "I'm not screaming."

Oh, right, then how come your throat's so sore?

Charlie couldn't see anything but black. "Uh, there's nothing to hang on to."

Then why aren't you plummeting through space? Why are you still here to hear him?

Charlie opened her eyes. Wild panicky visions of her impending free-float out and down to doom ricocheted about her brain. Dizziness and nausea and dread washed over her in surging breath-stopping waves.

"There's not a lot to hang on to up here either." Even with the ringing in her ears, Charlie could hear his swallow come drier than John B. Drake's.

He had hold of some part of her sweatshirt, the sweatshirt trying hard to choke her. She knew she could have heard threads and seams ripping if fear wasn't bludgeoning her ears with the din of a terrified heart.

"Oh, Libby, baby, I'm sorry." Charlie wished Mitch hadn't caught her. He was only drawing out her agony of anticipating the fall, forcing her to live it over and over before the final, real one.

Mitch was face down above her. But she could feel him slipping. Charlie should tell him to let go but couldn't quite form the words. She'd be a murderer if she didn't. A dead one.

"Kick your shoes off, see if you can get a toehold." She could hear in the straining of his voice the enormous exertion he used to hold them even this tenuously. "But don't jerk or anything. Hurry, Charlie, we're running out of time."

One of Charlie's Keds was half off already. Carefully, oh so carefully, she scraped the sole down the rock face and felt the prick of cold air on her toes when it fell. She heard a thump as the rock repelled it somewhere below. But she never did hear it land. It was that far down there.

How would she endure the wait once she was launched herself?

With little hope that it would be of any use, Charlie pried off her other shoe with her bare foot and then used her toes and fingers to search for cracks and crannies. At least it gave her something to do other than contemplate the inevitable.

Charlie'd always considered rock climbers raving lunatics, but could remember pictures of lunatics plastered to smooth cliff faces like spiders and with no discernible handholds. She moved one foot gradually back and forth, and then the other, and met with no opening for her toes. But the fingers on her right hand found an indentation with a warm, mossy feeling to it and grabbed its edge.

For some reason this caused Charlie to raise her left foot a smidgen and it found a slanted crack that cramped and pinched but was deep enough to slip in to the instep and support her weight. This in turn released the choking pressure of the sweatshirt and, unable to believe her luck, Charlie hugged the cliff.

Could this be merely another cruel extension of her dying?

"Charlie, I can't feel your weight. Tell me you didn't fall out of the sweatshirt?" He sounded oddly reconciled.

"I've got one foot and one hand reasonably secure. I can hold on for a while. Is there anything in the Bronco you could use to pull me up?"

"There's a rope, but I can't get to it."

"Whadaya mean, you can't get to it? Mitch, I might have a chance here."

"See if there's room for your free hand to get a hold where your other one did," he told her.

Charlie didn't like the deadly calm of his tone. "Why can't you go get the rope? Are you stuck or something?"

"Christ, do I wish. If I so much as cough, Charlie, I'm coming right on down past you headfirst."

"How can that be? You were holding me up a moment ago. Every last ounce of me." But she moved her left hand over toward her right with sweating care.

"That was a moment ago. When I made that suicidal dive for you I didn't have time to set myself up too well here. Any luck there?"

Charlie's hands met and she held her breath to put more weight on the aching foot pinched in the crack and to move the right hand, finger by finger, over to make room for the left. "I've got it, Mitch, I've got it. If I can just find a place for my other foot."

It was the smell that Charlie registered first. She thought of ammonia and then discarded that notion. The squawk and flutter on the air, the pricking jabs at her fingers and then at her hair signaled bird.

She'd found the ledge of a nesting bird and this was spring and the bird was a tiny dangerous mother type. Why had it remained quiet so long?

This wouldn't have been half the problem if the commotion below hadn't disturbed the tenuous hold of the man above. He suddenly fell in a shower of grit and with an anguished cry. Charlie's sweatshirt dropped back over her head to scare off the bird.

Mitch's body brushed her shoulder, his fingernails raked down her jeans and leg. He clutched her ankle for a split second as if to take her with him, and then let go.

Charlie screamed silently and clung to what was left of her world. A dark world now, even when she opened her eyes. She didn't dare look down and she didn't dare look up.

She didn't hear Mitch Hilsten land either.

Charlie wanted to let go and join him. She couldn't cling to this cliff forever. It would be better to get the terror over with. And she was the cause of a good man's death, an unnecessary death. Who would want to live on with that guilt? Not that anyone would see her hanging here in the dark and come to her rescue.

She hadn't the strength to hang on until morning. Still, she was too much of a coward to release her small hold on life. And then there was Libby. If there was the remotest possibility Charlie could survive, she had to try for Libby.

When Mitch grabbed her ankle, he'd forced her foot deeper into the narrowed end of the crevice. It was going numb. But the leg above it ached and tweaked with shooting pains, gave off involuntary jerks as Charlie now moved her dangling foot up and down in a cautious sawtooth pattern in search of another crack or protrusion or anything.

She found a slight niche that would reluctantly accept her big toe and leaned her weight on it enough to relieve the pressure on the other foot.

Whatever had formed the slight niche gave way almost instantly and Charlie scraped skin down the rock face, finding nothing else to stop the skid. She pulled herself back up by her hold on the bird's ledge and hissed at the pain the renewed weight caused her left foot.

Clinging back in her old position, Charlie found some tears that hadn't dried up with her mouth and throat. "I'm sorry, Mitch. That was such a dumb thing to do, back off a cliff like that . . . I'm so sorry."

"Well, you sure as hell ought to be."

Charlie listened to see if the voice would repeat itself and when it didn't, she whispered, "Mitch? Aren't you dead?"

"Let's put it this way, my hold isn't as good as yours, Charlie, and yours doesn't sound so wonderful from where I'm hanging."

Hope tried to niggle its way back into her life. "Where are you hanging?"

"Somewhere below and to the left of you. I'm even right side up somehow. But I can't hold on here much longer and I can't find anything big enough to stick my boots into."

"Can't you get them off?"

"Not without letting go with my hands to untie them." Then after a long silence he said, "Just tell me one thing? Why did you do it? Panic and back up that way? I looked where you were pointing and I didn't see anything."

"I thought I saw something dark rise up behind you." Another long silence while his boots scuffled against rock and he grunted with the exertion of hanging by his hands and arms. "Mitch, in your reading . . . did 'they' ever save people they scared and got in terminal trouble like this?"

"Do you notice every ant you step on? Now that it's too late, the cynic believes."

"Right now I'd believe in anything if I thought it would save us." That little bit of hope, resurrected when she realized he wasn't dead—yet, kept her mind searching for a possible way out. "Have you ever done anything like this in a film?"

"Yeah, watched stuntmen," he said. "*They* have nets. And this isn't a film."

"I don't suppose anyone could hear us yelling for help."

"You have any idea how far it is down there?"

"What have we got to lose?" Charlie started yelling. Mitch soon joined in.

And when their chorus stopped for breath, there came an answer.

Chapter
18

"**A**nd God said, 'Let there be light!'" a melodious, resonant voice proclaimed from out of the night below. The cliff face to their left lit up like a stage. Charlie squeaked and Mitch Hilsten whispered profanity—but reverently.

The strains of an entire symphony orchestra swelled up out of the canyon. And the light went out.

"'In the beginning God created the heaven and the earth.'" The voice swelled above the orchestra. "'And the earth was without form and void. And darkness was upon the face of the deep. And the spirit of God moved upon the face of the waters.'"

Cymbals clashed. "'And God said, "Let there be light"'!"

And sure enough, the light came back to the cliff face. It began moving toward Charlie and Mitch. Charlie reassessed her religious beliefs.

"'And God saw the light, that it was good. And God divided the light from the darkness'!"

"Charlie, when the light gets to us, try to wave with one hand and not fall."

"Wave to who? What's happening?"

"'And God called the light DAY!'"

"Try, Charlie. All I can do is kick my feet."

"'And the darkness he called NIGHT!'" And the light went out.

"Oh boy."

"Hang on, Charlie."

Charlie hung on. And God went on about the firmament splitting the waters from the waters and calling the firmament heaven and gathering all the water together so dry land could appear. "'And God called the dry land EARTH'!"

And the light returned, catching Charlie full on. She waved one arm and yelled, knowing no one could hear her over the mighty music. There was some scuffling below her and she supposed Mitch was swinging his feet to attract attention.

But the light moved off down the cliff face and God continued creating as though He hadn't seen them. He was creating grass and flowers hundreds of feet down the canyon when the voice cut off in mid-sentence and the music stopped.

Charlie thought she heard tiny voices shouting below. The light started creeping back along the cliff toward them. "Mitch, I think they've seen us. How much longer can you hold on?"

"I don't know." He sounded exhausted. And like he might be giving up.

The light reached them and stopped. Cliff birds stirred and complained from holes and ledges above Charlie's head.

"I think I've figured out what all this weirdness is." If she kept talking to make contact with Mitch, maybe it would give him the strength to hang on longer. "Remember the advertising on that *River by Night* show?"

"They take people in big flatboats on the river and a light truck runs down the road next to them. The speaker and the music are canned. I'd already figured that out. I can't talk anymore."

"Please don't give up now. There, hear it? It's a siren."

He just groaned. It had taken them twenty minutes to traverse that steep, winding road up here. If help was that far away she wasn't sure she could make it and Mitch didn't sound like he had twenty minutes in him.

Then, from the other side of the canyon rim, came the rapid thudding of helicopter blades.

"Oh great." Mitch Hilsten had tears in his voice. "Damned heroes . . . they'll blow us off the fuckin' rock."

Charlie jammed her face against the cliff face and tried to cringe into it. She clamped her eyes shut but could feel the dust in the air. The wind stirred up the odor of bird nests.

Something slapped against the rock next to her, but Charlie couldn't force herself to turn her head to see what it was.

A few minutes later, something slapped her in the back so hard she almost lost her grip. Hands jerked at her waist. "Let go."

"I can't."

"I'm in a sling chair," Mitch yelled. "You can sit on my lap and they'll pull us up. Damn it, Charlie, let go."

God, Charlie hated cliffhangers.

If Dean Goodacre called himself the cavalry one more time, Charlie was going to slug the television. A lavish, large television with a remote yet. She sprawled on one of the two queen-size beds in a room that didn't stink. It adjoined Rita Latham's and Mitch was watching the same thing on the lawyer's TV. Least they left the door open.

Charlie discovered that nearly getting a man killed did nothing for a relationship. They were both aching, bruised, silent, and embarrassed. Charlie with her feet wrapped in bandages and her fingernails surgically trimmed to the quick. Mitch with both hands wrapped in bandages.

Rita Latham must have clout to get two rooms like this. He'd probably sleep in Rita's room tonight, which would be fine with Charlie. Men as a gender were okay at work, but in personal life they were a disaster.

Both sets were tuned into CNN for godsake, not the little local cable, which would have been bad enough. And every gory embarrassing detail of Cabot's murder, Edwina's arrest, and Mitch Hilsten's latest "affair" with the woman with whom he almost died.

Charlie imagined Libby watching this with Lori Schantz and her traditional family, Edwina by herself in a jail cell.

To have come within 99 percent of dying was bad enough, but to watch Dean Goodacre, the helicopter rescue cavalryman, who had seemed like a normal nice guy the day before, burlesque all their lives in front of the whole world . . .

Charlie was not speaking to anyone and she tried to ignore Rita Latham, who appeared suddenly to sit beside her on the bed and proffer a small plate filled with delicacies—peeled shrimp, sliced boiled egg, raw veggies already dipped, and crackers already spread with herbed cheese.

Rita's expression of shrewd amusement was enough to make Charlie wish she still had fingernails. Gray streaked the attorney's hair, cut short but with a stylish flair around a long bony face and eyes that saw more than they should. Small and slender, too old for Hollywood maybe—still, the woman was unquestionably striking.

Rita wrapped her thin lips around her teeth and squinted. "The doctor thought you should eat if you could. The champagne was my idea." And she raised the other hand with a glass of pale bubbling liquid.

"So, what is it we're celebrating? That?" Charlie pointed to the television screen but managed to snag the plate as she withdrew the gesture. There was even a slice of forbidden pickled beet.

"No. Life. Your life, Charlie. Your mother and I need you so much, I, at least, am celebrating your survival."

"Yeah, but himself in there . . ." Charlie took the proffered glass before Rita could spill it all over the bed.

" . . . is feeling embarrassed and guilty," the lawyer finished for her.

"Why should *he* feel guilty? I'm the one who nearly got us killed."

The phone rang and Rita picked it up. "No, this is Rita Latham and we have no statement on anything." She hung up. "Reuters—wire service."

Charlie groaned and Rita went back to her room to return with the champagne bottle and top off Charlie's glass. "He feels guilty because he didn't save the two of you. Because his belief in UFOs is probably what frightened you into seeing one and backing off the cliff. Because he should have realized how serious your acrophobia was, how it would have affected your weakened state after the trauma of seeing Cabot's mutilated body and having your mother arrested for murder." Rita Latham could barely control her skepticism. "Funny, you do not strike me as weak. I think he's reinventing Charlie Greene in a new form he can comprehend."

"You seen the size of the cliffs they got around here? It's a miracle anybody saved us."

"Men solve problems, overcome obstacles. Men conquer, Charlie. Women cope." The phone rang again and Rita said as she reached for it, "We'd better have the desk hold all calls until morning."

But Charlie took this one. It was Maggie.

"You weren't kidding about holing up in a hotel room with Mitch Hilsten. Did you really see a flying saucer?"

"No. And how did you know where I was?"

"Right now I'm watching a head shot of some chick 'reporting from' Moab, Utah, and standing in front of a sign that says, RIVER ROOST MOTEL NO VACANCY. I called information. Were you hurt?"

"Mostly my pride. What's Libby think of all this?"

"Who knows? She's coming over here to sleep but right now she, Lori, and Doug are supposedly studying over pizza and Cokes at your house. TV's probably on, but that crowd doesn't watch the news. Libby is worried about her grandmother. I had to tell her that much. Won't be long before somebody tells her the rest. Larry's worried about you. I'll call and tell him you're okay. And your boss wanted me to congratulate you on your new boyfriend. Is this going to be something serious, Charlie?"

"God, no. And you can tell Richard to go to hell."

* * *

Mitch slept in Charlie's room that night in the other bed. They shared the bathroom the next morning but weren't really speaking. Charlie's self-esteem was flatter than a rug. He just seemed embarrassed.

The swelling in Charlie's feet had gone down enough to get on the ugly black rubber cloglike things provided by the local medical clinic. But she limped as she walked the gamut of reporters, refusing to speak to them too, and slipped into Rita's car.

"Mitch has an added problem with all this," the lawyer confided as she drove to the courthouse.

"His image."

"Right. One of the nation's most respected heroes ignominiously rescued by a helicopter pilot. Doesn't seem to me the press is playing it that way. But he thinks that's the way it must look, poor guy. He didn't even save the girl."

Charlie couldn't help asking, "How come he tells you all this?"

"Mitch and I go back a long way, Charlie. Before I became a defense attorney, I handled divorces. I represented his ex in their divorce."

Edwina was gray and quiet again. She kept looking at Charlie as if she'd actually fallen to her death last night. There was no television in her cell but there are few secrets in a jail.

"I'm going back out to the Point and stay in the tent trailer, ask questions before everybody leaves. Both films are wrapping."

"No, Charlie, he might kill you too."

"Who?"

"Whoever killed Cabot."

"I'll be careful. But I need to know if you saw anybody near enough to your campsite to pick up your ax after I left to go to Drake's motor home."

Edwina had not, her resignation tinged only with worry for Charlie.

Chapter

19

Charlie had hoped to avoid the press by going to the campground but that was not to be. No barricade guarded the road and several pushy guys wearing that telltale jaded/superior expression tried to engage her in conversation. They dogged her steps to the tent trailer where she left the side curtains zipped up and opened the roof vents for air, ignoring the taunts outside intended to provoke an answer.

She found the milk still sweet in the little icebox and made a cheese sandwich to go with it from the white bread and Velveeta Sheriff Sumpter had distributed to the captive crews. Charlie's first food of the day.

She sat in the cramped space and looked around at signs of her mother as if for clues, fragmented emotions demanding priority and threatening to get out of hand.

Charlie had been so stupid she'd almost gotten herself and someone else killed.

The campground was already clearing out and the real murderer could be gone by now. A truck made a roaring sound over by the concrete toilets, either delivering water or cleaning out the sewage. By the faint smell on the air Charlie rather thought the latter.

Mitch Hilsten was embarrassed and ashamed by what little they had shared. Charlie had put in her last pair of disposable contacts this morning.

Leave it to Charlie to sleep with a man for one night and have it broadcast worldwide.

And somewhere under all this was a bubble of joy that she still lived.

Why hadn't Edwina been furious about the coverage of her "affair" with Mitch?

"Charlie, it's me, Earl. Let me in?" Charlie opened to him and Tawny slipped in behind.

"If you want to ask me a lot of dumb questions about UFOs and Mitch Hilsten, forget it."

"Nah, I just wanted to apologize. You got any more of that?" He was looking at her unfinished sandwich.

Tired of John B.'s gourmet deli food, Earl actually hungered for the sheriff's offerings. "Hey, I grew up on Velveeta on Wonder Bread and Campbell's Tomato Soup."

Then again he liked Cabot's movies.

Before the party was over Tawny had found two cans of the tomato soup, used up the rest of the milk with it, and Scrag Dickens had joined them.

"Needs pickles," Scrag decided and was soon back with a jar of dills.

"And beer," John B.'s voice said from outside and they let him in with some. The table seating was more than full already so he perched on the shelf bed across from them.

Charlie totally lost interest in eating and wondered why her companions had rallied around her this way. Maybe they hadn't. Maybe they had their own goose to fry, as Richard Morse might have put it, or fish to goose or some other corruption he'd pretend not to know was one.

People and air were too close with the windows zipped. Charlie reached for a pickle and thought better of it when she remembered Scrag Dickens scavenging in the dumpster for food.

Scrub tree shadows stood still against the plastic windows and canvas walls under the glaring sun.

"Nobody talks about UFOs or Mitch," Tawny told her

lover. They exchanged looks similar to Charlie's and Mitch's in the bathroom a few hours before.

"Isn't anybody working today?" Again? Charlie asked.

Return of an Ecosystem had wrapped for location and would go into postproduction.

"I've dispatched most of my crew. Going to scout another location for a project upriver before I leave the area. Sid's got another major scene in Moab, which will be mostly second-unit stuff so his people are leaving in droves." John B. wasn't eating either and he too was watchful.

"And the sheriff's just letting them go?" Charlie asked accusingly.

"And the sheriff's just letting them go," Earl Seabaugh said and dunked his sandwich in his soup.

"This is your apology?"

"Jeeze, I didn't mean you should jump off a cliff. I just thought you needed to know . . . about things." He said this with a hint of condescension Charlie found puzzling.

"What things? Apology for what? You guys got secrets you're not letting me in on?" John B. pulled a sardonically hurt face that didn't fool anybody. He was really searching theirs and something in his tone set the rest of them glancing quickly at him and then at each other.

Or was it something they weren't letting Charlie in on?

"I didn't jump off a cliff," she told Earl. "I lost my footing and fell off one. People have stupid accidents all the time."

Earl nodded and winked a bright green eye. "That one was a doozy."

"We came here to make her feel better," Tawny reminded him. Her eyes were almond-shaped and almond-colored. Her lashes long and lightly mascaraed. The unfriendly flashes between her and the producer/director were like electrical charges in the crowded space.

Yeah, John B. would wear thin after a while—one of those guys who need constant attention.

Charlie, that's not why you're here. People are leaving. Time is running out.

Earl studied Charlie, a dribble of sweat slipping down in front of one ear from under his stained Rockies cap. "Oh, I think Charlie knows what she's doing. She'll work things out. Just be sure you don't trust anybody, Charlie, till you know who killed Gordon Cabot."

"Not even my mother."

"Not even me or John B. here."

"You can trust me, Charlie." Scrag was sitting beside her and he scooted a little closer—there really wasn't any closer left. He smelled faintly of sweat, mostly of Velveeta. "I wouldn't kill anybody, darlin'."

Okay, boys, let's put our money where our mouths are. "Will you guys help me then?"

Much to her surprise, and probably theirs, Scrag and Earl shepherded her around what was left of the *Aliens* crew campsite, introducing her to everyone they knew, helping her introduce herself to everyone they didn't, and sidetracking reporters as if it was all a game.

Eventually, despite the press and her aching feet, Charlie managed to question a gaffer, two gofers, a half-dozen assistant everythings, three stuntmen, two makeup artists, and a driver in what was now Sid's RV, all with the help of the production manager, Stan Lowenthall.

He went out of his way to be helpful. Gaunt, handsome, in that petrified-scraped look people take on when they begin to fight nature with plastic surgeons. His hair was thick and cut short around the ears leaving a bouffant wave in front set rock solid with setting gel. Even his eyebrows were dyed.

And what did she learn from an entire afternoon of such sleuthing? Everyone was anxious to get back to California or excited about the climactic scene in preparation in Moab. They knew who Charlie was, and at least a fourth of them had seen an unidentified flying object at some point in their lives. Seventy-five percent were psychic too.

Everybody was packing up to leave Dead Horse Point. Nobody mourned Gordon Cabot. Two wanted to know if the problem at Congdon and Morse was so bad that the agency might take on untried clients. Three were writing screenplays and would she just look at them? And four had novels in progress and needed an agent. One of the latter was Stan Lowenthall, the helpful PM.

In other words Charlie had discovered nothing this afternoon. Zippo. She could feel the noose tightening around her mother's neck.

Charlie sat cross-legged, Indian style, on Edwina's concrete picnic table watching the *Aliens* crew depart in a caravan passing behind Howard's Jeep and the rented Corsica, now heavily overdue at the airport in Grand Junction, Colorado. Her new jeans were too tight and she'd lost all circulation from the knees down, but she didn't give a shit. The press had apparently given up and left too.

The murderer was probably long gone.

What if Edwina really is the murderer?

I'm not speaking to you.

What if somebody was trying to get at Edwina by framing her for Cabot's murder? What if Cabot was simply a convenient vehicle because she'd slugged him that very day in front of so many witnesses? But is Edwina the real target here?

Oh now, that is totally stupid. Edwina's not important enough for anyone to get that worked up at.

How do you know? How much time have you actually spent with her in the last ten years?

Edwina is not capable of murder.

Everybody's capable of murder. Even you. You very nearly

killed Mitch Hilsten by not ordering him to let go of your sweatshirt.

Charlie never knew if her internal dialogues were between her right brain and her left, her conscience and her guilt, or her anxieties and her phobias. She did know there were times when she'd gladly crawl inside her own head and strangle one of them though.

And if Edwina was really the target here, Cabot's killer could still be around. The murderer could be a member of the *Return of an Ecosystem* crew. And some of them were still here.

As if summoned, Earl, Tawny, John B., and Scrag suddenly clustered around her table. They'd decided Scrag would drive Howard's Jeep and pull the tent trailer into Moab, after Tawny and Earl helped her pack it up and fold it down. They all wanted to get into town for Sid's big power station scene.

Charlie limped beside Rita Latham through Moab's darkening streets. They passed commercial structures with such names as the Energy Building, the Uranium Building, the Atomic Motel, and the Yellow Cake Bar and Grill, which spoke of Moab's vanished glory days of uranium prospecting and mining.

Frame houses and double-wides mingled on their own full lots. All had square "swamp" coolers on their roofs, the larger ones had two. The coolers sent up a mantralike hum to replace the absent background noise of traffic.

Charlie's feet hurt and she wished she could have driven but city police and sheriff department flyers had been stuck on every windshield, motel room door, and store window in town pleading there be no driving during the evening except for emergency vehicles. Schoolkids had raced around on bikes distributing the flyers that afternoon.

Above the treetops on a rise at the end of the side street ahead of them, where the canyon wall swung around to stop the town, lights flashed and dimmed, arced and snapped already.

Mighty Hollywood flexing its muscles. People walked in quiet groups up to the electrical substation to watch the show that would make the show.

The town's power would be shut down selectively and accidents could happen because streetlights and stoplights would be going out for brief periods. Everyone was invited to view the shoot but asked to walk to the site, to stay behind the barricades, and to keep quiet. A civil defense siren would announce when the shoot was over for those who did not attend.

There was a good crowd when they reached the barricades but Rita took Charlie's wrist and wound their way through one end of it to a spot up front with taller men behind. Charlie could see only one TV reporter working the crowd, flanked by his faithful midget cam, lighting, and makeup lackeys.

Charlie had reported her lack of investigative success to the attorney and now she added, "Could we be looking at this from the wrong angle? Could Edwina have been the intended victim? I know it sounds savage, but could someone have been trying to get even with Edwina by killing Cabot and laying the blame on her?"

Rita Latham stared long and hard into Charlie's face, her own expression serious for once. "Murder is savage, Charlie. An ax murder, violently savage. We are faced with, as I see it now, four choices. Someone hated Gordon Cabot enough to do this thing, using your mother's ax because it was handy. Someone hated him enough to do this thing but used your mother's ax to protect himself and to implicate her. Someone hated Edwina enough to kill Cabot with her ax so that she would be tried and sentenced for murder and Cabot merely used to ensure her humiliation."

The crowd was respectfully quiet. But the hum and buzz of transformers inside the fenced compound drowned out the sound of Moab's swamp coolers. A sudden lightning streak above the transformers haloed Rita's hair. "But if someone hated Edwina Greene that much," the lawyer said, "why wouldn't he have axed her instead of Cabot?"

"That's only three choices." Charlie didn't really want to hear the fourth.

"The state serologist has found chips of dried blood in your mother's car."

"We went into Moab for groceries Saturday. I know there was raw chicken, could have been some ground beef—probably leaked out of the bags."

"My sources say the preliminary lab reports suggest human blood. If they test out to be Gordon Cabot's . . ."

"But the body and the weapon were found at the scene. And believe me, that was the murder scene. I was one of the first to see it. Nothing was moved. There was no car involved."

"That was a messy murder, Charlie. It's unlikely the murderer came away from it clean. No bloodied clothes have been found. They could have been transported out by car."

And of course it was Edwina's car they searched. The killer probably dumped the clothes down a hole in the concrete toilets. Maybe the sheriff had thought of that too. Charlie remembered the truck roaring next to them this afternoon.

"The fourth choice, Charlie, is that your mother axed Gordon Cabot and if I'm to be of any help to either of you, you are going to face that possibility. Either help me prove that wrong or prove her insanity. I'm not God."

Chapter
20

A patch of white lightning jagged along a metal beam of the substation's open superstructure high above the transformers. The red cliff wall behind it glowed and darkened, shadows dancing across it to disappear in deeper shadow.

A used condom glowed too, but dully, on the barbed-wire baffle that topped the chain-link fence under a security light.

John B., Scrag, Earl, and Mitch Hilsten hunched close in a protective covey not far from Charlie and her mother's lawyer. All but Earl turned their backs when any of the roving lights threatened to expose them. He trained a tiny camcorder or mini/micro camera of some kind on the second unit crew working under the substation's lights.

Sidney Levit and Stan Lowenthall conferred with a city policeman beside a patrol car.

Tawny and the heroic Dean Goodacre talked earnestly at the other end of the crowd behind the barricades.

Charlie wondered what the pilot had been doing up in the helicopter last night. God, was it only last night? That feathery sensation in the sudden crater of her interior merely at the memory— Charlie switched thought scenes fast.

Tawny caught her eye, waved, smiled. She'd ridden in from Dead Horse Point with Charlie in the Corsica. One of those beautiful women other women love to hate, but she'd tried hard to lighten

Charlie's mood, to lend a sympathetic ear. Charlie felt guilty now for having been so single-minded.

Of course Edwina hadn't killed Gordon Cabot with an ax, Tawny assured Charlie. "Earl and John B. and Scrag think it's highly likely but they're guys. You know, the almighty law can't be wrong stuff."

She and John B. were breaking up. Remembering the director's randy handiness last Sunday in the motel room with the shower, Charlie wasn't that surprised. But she had the good grace to ask why.

Tawny sighed. "Too much water under the bridge, I guess. We kind of slipped into a relationship we shouldn't have. Been friends for years. This will probably kill even that."

They'd met through Tawny's husband, the architect partner who'd taken his own life when the land deal fell flat. "I was only fifteen when I married Ben. John B. helped me finish school and got me interested in modeling and makeup and here I am. He's forty something and sort of going through a change of life. I can't deal with it. Life's too short."

Sidney Levit crawled onto the platform of a crane with a camera operator and they rose grandly into the air. Another cameraman on the ground moved into position with a steadycam on a body frame. Second-unit crew members made last-minute adjustments and backed out of camera range. A camera on a tripod in the bed of a truck was trained on the town in the opposite direction. Assistants fanned out to hush the crowd, who were, in fact, an inordinately orderly bunch.

Charlie didn't know all that much about the technical side of the business but even she could tell there was a lot of expensive equipment here. The crane would have cost a bundle to ship to location. No wonder Cabot and his producers had squared off. Or perhaps so much science fiction was filmed in this alien countryside one was kept here to rent out.

Sid spoke into his headset and motioned to his first AD on

the ground. It could have been the funny lighting on the crane, but he looked strangely jubilant.

In Hollywood, everybody wants to be a director. Sometimes even producers. It's considered the highest form of artistry in the business. Worth chopping up somebody with an ax?

"Why does this look like a civil trial attorney's dream?" Rita whispered.

"Most of it's smoke and mirrors." But this setup was asking for trouble. It would have been no use to try to keep people away. Better to invite them and try to control them. And Moab was pathetically eager to cooperate.

Why couldn't this be done by miniature in a studio as Sid had wanted Gordon Cabot to do with some of the helicopter scenes? Or even a mockup? Maybe Sid too was going for "verisimilitude" instead of common sense. Was he now feeling a surge of power, of ultimate control?

The sky was clear of clouds and suspicious shadow-shapes, the moon and stars not yet showing. Standing around and waiting took up most of the time on any shoot, especially on location. Charlie was absently watching the condom, trying not to think of Mitch Hilsten, when the globed security light above the flaccid rubber sheath exploded with a pop.

Street- and houselights in the town below blacked out in sections. But the substation grew brighter. Balls of fire bounced from ceramic knobs to wires to the DANGER! KEEP OUT! signs. One by one the rest of the globes on the security lights exploded. Lightning fingers traced every wire of the chain link. Sparks showered into the night.

It was like fireworks, only in black and white.

Charlie's clothes grew stiff and abrasive. Her skin pricked and tingled. Her hair felt like it wanted to stand on end. The smell of sulfur saturated the air.

Two figures writhed and staggered between transformer bases, aflame with Hollywood magic. The air filled so full of smoke

Charlie could no longer see the movie-in-the-making. But between the cracks, and pips, and zings and spits of explosive she assumed it was still playing to a camera somewhere.

She'd even lost Rita Latham, who had to be within reach. But it was odd what Charlie *could* see. A lot of stage smoke swirling up from the ground. Mitch Hilsten's head and shoulders in a less dense patch of it appeared to be floating away by themselves around a corner of the fence. She looked for other familiar faces, beginning to feel isolated and anxious.

"Jesus, this whole place is charged." Scrag's unmistakable voice in her ear, no attempt to be quiet on the set. An arm encircled her waist. "You okay, darlin'?"

Charlie coughed in the acrid smoke. Above it the long lean form of Sidney Levit raised a fist toward the sky as his crane chariot descended from the heights, his white head glowing godlike.

Charlie, this is show biz, let's not get carried away here.

One of the pips or pops became a boom. And the milling crowd was growing restless and noisy.

But the fireballs finally began to fizzle. Charlie squirmed out of Scrag's hold and lost him in the smoke. The spark showers dried up. The light show faded. Charlie's hair relaxed and her clothes settled more comfortably. Over the coughing and increasingly perturbed voices around her, calling out names like lost souls, she heard the sirens of emergency vehicles. Headlights rushing up from the street looked like floodlights bouncing through the stage smoke.

An odd smell on that smoke, like burning rubber maybe or garbage? Charlie knew something had gone wrong but wasn't that worried until Mitch grabbed her and pulled her back against the fender of the camera truck to make room for the flashing lights swimming on the smoke. Her eyes were tearing so, she couldn't tell if she'd washed out a lens or not.

She wanted to make some snide remark about heroism to Mitch but was coughing too hard to speak.

He fought their way through a ganglion of milling bodies until the air freshened enough to breathe. But her lungs and throat and eyes felt seared.

As they joined a group at the crest of the hill, lights popped up in batches all over the town below, stoplights blinked red on the main thoroughfare. Rita was there, hovering over John B. He sat with head in hands and bent over his knees. Dean Goodacre and Earl Seabaugh stood against a yellow triangular YIELD sign, crying smoke tears. Mitch deposited Charlie next to John B. and plowed back into the vapor and fumes. Heroically.

It wasn't all stage smoke either.

No stuntwoman had been suited up for that shoot.

The unusual odor over the stage smoke was just plain Tawny.

Chapter 21

Mitch, John B., and Earl decided not to cancel their river trip the next morning. Even Sid and his helicopter pilot, Dean, were going along.

"They might as well," Rita Latham said. "The paparazzi will be back in full force. *Death stalks tragedy-prone movie!* Or some such. Nobody's going to get much done in this town. Including, I'm afraid, you and me. Think I'll head back to Salt Lake for a day or two."

"Rita, Mitch is still speaking to you, right? Think you could get me invited along on that little jaunt?"

The attorney tilted her head back on a long neck and turned it to squint at Charlie. "Wouldn't you rather spend the day with your mother?"

"She's not talking to me either. I need to go down the river."

"Charlie, I'll have to admit I'm confused here. I'm usually a pretty good judge of people. But Mitch will make up his own mind about any commitment to a relationship with you whether you're there or not. You seem so altogether, certainly not the type to chase a man this way." The woman's disappointment with Charlie was palpable.

It's degrading as hell, but I'll seem like whatever I have to, to get in that boat. Time is running out for Edwina and that boat's going to be full of possible ax murderers planning to leave Utah the day after tomorrow.

And what if Tawny's horrible accident hadn't been an accident?

For once both of Charlie's inner voices agreed.

As it turned out, Scrag Dickens invited himself along on the river trip too.

"Damn it, now we can't tell guy jokes and piss over the side of the boat," Earl complained when he saw Charlie, but made a place for her on the seat beside him. Those green eyes weren't laughing this morning.

It was a somber group that climbed aboard two shallow-drafted jet boats, the grim picture of a tortured Tawny still writhing flames in their memory vision, the ghastly smell of her death still a ghost in the air they breathed.

Mitch, John B., Sid Levit, and the guide, Homer Blankenship, rode in the lead boat. Charlie, Dean Goodacre, Earl, and Scrag in the second—Earl and Dean pouting because the guide chose Scrag to drive their boat. To add to the insult, the desert rat explained the workings of the craft to the other males.

If the boats were shallow-drafted so were the engines. They looked like outboards but instead of propellers had pumps that sucked in river water and forced it out in a "jet" of water to propel the boat forward. And unlike the propellers, the pumps were enclosed and didn't snag as easily on sandbanks, logs, and rocks.

These were black rubber boats with white foam coolers holding their passengers' lunch, water, and canned drinks. Homer insisted they all wear bright orange life vests. A colorful, if short, caravan formed on the dark water.

The river looked black down here instead of the chocolate-mud color it took on from above. Maybe because it reflected the vertical rock walls, looming maroon-black with shadow, that channeled it at this point.

Over a hundred feet wide and shallow enough in places to expose rotting tree limbs stuck on sandbars, the Colorado River slithered instead of flowed. Heavy with residue of the canyon it was busy carving, it moved strangely silent for water.

Ducks bobbed along the edges, upending to feed on the bottom, their small pointy tail feathers and paddle feet sticking up from the surface like overturned bathtub toys.

Mitch was avoiding Charlie, which was fine with her. She had to keep her perspective. Of the seven men, six were possible candidates for murderer. And she must study them all on this, the last day she had to prove her mother's innocence by finding someone else's guilt. Not that Charlie felt she should be doing this. Simply that she didn't know anybody else who would.

Perhaps it was learning of Tawny's death, but suddenly Edwina had remembered how she'd propped the ax up against the trailer hitch before they'd sat down to dinner that fateful evening. Charlie had been facing away from it and Edwina was probably too upset to notice any movement around it.

While she and Charlie were arguing, a hand could easily have slipped out of a night shadow and grabbed it, even before Gordon Cabot came back from his tour-bus shoot in the Humvee. The murderer could have lain in wait for him to start off for the concrete johns. Which meant anybody could have done it—including Mitch Hilsten.

Homer Blankenship, a plump man with a benign smile and graying temples, stood knee-deep in the river, his pants rolled to mid-thigh, and showed Scrag how to start his engine. Then he leaped into the other boat. A surprisingly strong current, for what appeared so sluggish a river, had shoved them sideways out into the stream of things before the quiet was shattered as first one outboard roared to life and then the other.

The plan was that Scrag would follow Homer exactly because Homer knew where the channels and snags were. Charlie'd hoped for a quieter trip, where the men would talk to each other and to her and she could watch and listen. But it was hard to talk over the jet engines and she couldn't see much in the way of expressions in the boat ahead of them.

Still, she could hear some of the conversation from the lead boat because the people in it had to yell over their own engine and because sound travels over water and because Charlie's hearing was unusually acute. Not that she expected anyone to conversationally admit to killing Cabot.

And if Tawny had been murdered, it couldn't have been Sid because he was way up on the crane. And if her death was not the accident it seemed (her hair and clothes had apparently caught fire in a wayward spark shower), the chances of it being a different murderer were slim.

Two murderers on one set was pretty far-fetched even for Hollywood. Which meant that all the people here except Homer were at the scenes of both crimes.

Charlie knew she just wanted poor Tawny to have been murdered because Edwina couldn't have done it from her jail cell, which meant she didn't kill Cabot either if one person did them both in.

The giant uranium dump below the mill slid by, abandoned and misshapen. Was it safe to have radioactive material so close to the river's edge? If Charlie remembered correctly, the Colorado nurtured a fair portion of the country. And a fair portion of that in California, where even now Libby might be drinking some.

The morning had been pleasantly warm until the boat started moving. Now Charlie hugged her life vest, wishing it had sleeves to break the cold wind of their passage, which dried out her contacts even behind sunglasses.

She turned around to look at their driver. Scrag smiled intimately. He'd made a ridiculously overblown point of showing off Edwina's ax practically the minute Charlie stepped out of the car her first night at Dead Horse Point. And he'd been even more obvious about what a threat Charlie's mother supposedly was. He could have been setting Edwina up to take the blame for Cabot's murder even then.

Scrag had hung around the fringes of the industry long enough to have developed some grudge against the director. Or he could just be nuts enough to have taken more than an ordinary dislike to Edwina and decided to set her up for disaster.

Charlie was on the canyon's third level this time, at the very bottom. Vertical walls gave way to turrets and spires and ledges. Massive shapes in front of even more massive shapes. Hollywood could make you feel small, but she'd always resented nature for doing it so much better.

Sidney Levit, now, might have seen murdering Cabot as a chance to save the *Animal Aliens* budget and realize a dream of being a director at the same time. Edwina would be a convenient scapegoat to his ambition and business acumen. Or maybe just working closely with Cabot could actually drive one to murder.

Blue and purple shadow hues changed to russets and dull oranges when the sun hit the rock cliffs and formations rearing to either side of Charlie. It was as vast and alien as the other levels but in a different way. It would be so easy to disappear here. The only softness in the whole landscape was the water and it would want to drown you.

In the boat ahead of her, Mitch Hilsten reached an arm around the hunched shoulders of his friend, the director of *Return of an Ecosystem.*

According to the dead Tawny, John B. Drake was going through a life change. In men, that often meant the need to sleep with ever-younger women—as if that proved prowess and youth, rather than privilege and exploitation. Tawny hadn't been able to "deal with it."

So what does life change mean in women, Charlie?

It means hot flashes and mood changes and panic attacks. It does not mean murder.

The hard cliff walls amplified the harsh sounds of the engines. The jarring of the boat against the water brought back all the soreness of Charlie's cliff-hanging experience. One foot had started throbbing again. The tastes of coffee and bacon mixed unpleasantly with sloshing stomach acids and returned, burning, to her tongue.

But why would a life change make John B. Drake want to kill Cabot? Could his hormonal insecurities leave him so easily angered at Edwina's obstreperousness that he'd want to see her accused of murder? Why, when he could just fire her? And if Tawny's death had been planned, why would John B. plan it? They were breaking up anyway. Unless the split was totally her idea and he was that angered by it.

His shirttail flapping in the wind, revealing a hunting or fishing knife worn in a sheath at his waist, Homer pointed out a great ugly bird circling above and shouted, "Turkey vulture."

It glided over them trailing a shadow Charlie could feel when it blocked the sun's warmth. Its wingspan was at least six feet, its feet yellow, and its featherless head an obscene red.

"Looks like an ordinary buzzard, only bigger."

"Yeah, that's another name for them," Earl said, the bill of his cap turned around to shade his face this time, "but there's more of them here for the same reason they're bigger. They're needed as nature's undertakers." He raised his eyebrows and gave her a wide-eyed stare.

She leaned close to his ear. "I'm so sorry about Tawny. You two seemed pretty close."

He simply stared out over the water, as if so fed up with klutzes he saw no reason to bother answering one.

She couldn't blame him. Here she'd narrowed down the list of suspects to six men, largely because they were all in one place. Meanwhile, the real murderer was probably winging his way high overhead about now on his way to California. And feeling pretty smug too.

Canyon walls broadened into layered shelves on one side of them and the APC plant sprawled on a curve up ahead, dump trucks and pickups in the parking lot.

Tamarisk trees laced broad areas of shoreline, their wands fringed with feathers of lavender-pink flowers bowing in the wind and alive with bees. Charlie thought them beautiful. Edwina thought them an abomination. Like most imported plants they were taking over and robbing the natural cottonwoods of a home and of the critters who lived in them.

The boats slowed as Homer pulled over and then stopped at a man-made pile of concrete rubble and aggregate.

"Somebody thought they'd build a hotel in here," he told Charlie as the rest fanned out over the site. "Got as far as the foundations and a wall or two and the river took it out. This is where it landed."

Sid and John B. and Mitch wandered and looked and thought. Earl had his tiny camcorder out again.

"Got a clue for you, darlin'," Scrag whispered in her ear. "What's it worth?" And he wandered off too.

"First, I got to tell you how disappointed I am," he said when Charlie caught up with him, "you fallin' for that old Hilsten line just like any female. I thought you were different. Savvy, special, smart."

"Clue to what?"

"I don't know that I even want to think about it, maybe that's why I'm shoving it off on you." Scrag Dickens looked up at the turkey vulture, which seemed intent upon following them. Pausing for maximum dramatic effect, he then claimed with a totally straight face that he'd passed behind Tawny and Dean Goodacre shortly before the fatal accident. "Darlin', I had the weirdest impression she was using lighter fluid for perfume."

22

Charlie watched the turkey-vulture-buzzard. That was one big bird. She practiced just the right arrangement of words to impress Mrs. Beesom, a neighbor in Long Beach and a bird nut, to avoid thinking of the beautiful dead woman. Funny, Cabot's demise hadn't really penetrated—

The "guys" were climbing back into the boats. Two of them squaring off at each other.

". . . lawsuit," Sidney Levit said, still in a white dress shirt but at least wearing canvas shoes. He stared up at the buzzard too.

Earl Seabaugh, camcorder dangling from one hand, baseball cap from the other, stood toe to toe with the older man, face fused with emotion. "Lawsuit? Ben's dead. Who's to sue? She didn't fucking *have* anybody."

But it was the killer look the *Ecosystem*'s director of photography leveled at his own producer/director, John B. Drake, that brought Charlie up short. She watched everybody watch everybody and tried to catalog looks. Sullen, bleak, suspicious, thoughtful, and afraid.

Once they were moving down the river again, Charlie found her mood had lightened. Even though the buzzard stayed with them. There were six guys here with a lot on their minds and a lot of hostility and just maybe more clues like Scrag's. Some of them might even be true. Just maybe, the noose around her mom's neck was loosening a tad.

She sat next to Dean Goodacre on this leg of their jaunt and asked him about what he'd been doing up in the helicopter the night he'd come to the rescue.

"Started out to scout the power station site, see if there was any need to have an airborne camera. Sid and I decided against it later."

"You weren't over the substation when I saw you first and you were a long way from it when you got to us in so short a time."

"Yeah"—he was chewing on a toothpick now and he parked it to one side to whisper loud enough for the buzzard to hear—"decided to look for that UFO that might have left the night watchman from the uranium mill on that mesa top. The one that ended up backing you off a cliff."

"And did you?"

"Yeah, there was something big there for a bit I couldn't see through. I've seen 'em before. Most pilots have, one time or another."

Sometimes Charlie felt as if she were the only sane person left in this world. Even though she knew certifiable nuts regularly thought so too. "What do you pilots do about it?"

"Ignore it mostly." His honest, steady gaze was a little too much and his long curly hair fanned out in the wind so like a woman's would that the giant arms on either side of the beefy chest looked like prostheses. "Once you fly, see, you don't want to do anything else. And flying jobs are hard to come by. And seeing UFOs is not reassuring to your average employer."

He worked for a company based in San Diego that chartered choppers and pilots to film studios, rescue and medical units, news media, and private corporations trying to impress customers, stockholders, and suppliers.

The U.S. Navy had taught Dean to fly helicopters. "I'd kill to keep this job." He spit the toothpick over the side and pulled a stick of gum out of a shirt pocket under his life jacket. "But I didn't."

He chewed in self-important silence for a while, enjoying the ride and the scenery, and then turned to Charlie with a hard look. "Now it's your turn. What'd you see up there, before you backed off the mesa?"

"Whorls," Charlie told him. "Round swirls in the dirt."

They left the tamarisk shores to explore deepening canyons, the colors changing with the light. The river had sliced through layers of the planet's crust, like a knife through a stack of sandwiches, exposing the hardened fillings in varicolored swaths and crumbling ledges that extended up to the top level two thousand feet above her.

Charlie tried to scratch an itch on her neck with nails filed to nubbins. She'd take canyons walled by buildings any day.

They beached on a porous hardened mud bottom dotted with rotting weeds, a dead rat, driftwood. Homer guided them past a tiny horizontal forest of petrified logs felled aeons ago and back into a cave with a sliver of sunlight coming from a crack in the cliff rock a thousand feet above. The stick figure of a four-legged animal was etched in the wall.

"I tell the tourists this is a deer drawn by the Anasazi." Homer had a gap between his front teeth and whenever he paused in his speaking his tongue would play with it. "Can't help but wonder if some weren't carved by bored cowboys working from the line camps that used to litter the area."

"Or by river guides who want to have something to show the tourists?" Charlie voiced the thought by mistake.

The cave was small and somebody kicked a hole in an old pack rat midden that showed only as a dark patch along one wall. A familiar odor saturated the air and they all stepped out.

"Edwina says the pack rats make their nests by mixing dried pellets of their shit with urine. Kind of like rodent adobe," John B. said and stripped off his shirt. The day was heating up. "Talk about your recycling."

"Be like living in your own toilet." Sid just rolled up his sleeves. They'd all glanced quickly at Charlie at the mention of Edwina.

John B. carried his muscle on his shoulders and back, leaving a chest full of ribs and tufts of black hair in front. He used his cowboy hat to fan himself.

Mitch took off his shirt too and followed the director up a rock outcropping where they could pose while surveying the possible scene from three angles instead of one.

"I'm curious," Scrag said quietly behind Charlie in that country-western-singer voice. "Aren't you the least bit worried being out here in all this vastness, alone with seven guys all wearing their identities in their shorts?"

Mostly Charlie envied them their right to go topless when not doing so made life miserable. She turned to find Scrag wearing his shirt wrapped around his head to keep off the heavy sun and sporting a more impressive chest than either the director or the superstar.

His grin made her giggle. "Aren't *you* a little nervous by the fact that one of these people could be a murderer?"

His know-it-all look wavered and his shirt nodded with his head. "If that *was* lighter fluid I smelled on or around Tawny, they could have the wrong person in that jail cell in Moab for murdering Gordon Cabot."

"Exactly. And Tawny, for your information, was the only one of your little clique who agreed with me that Edwina couldn't have done it." Could Tawny have been murdered for that reason alone?

"You're out here today to pick up psychic ammunition for your mamma's defense, darlin', I suggest you be right careful."

It wasn't difficult to be intimidated by a bunch of guys showing off their musculature. But Charlie didn't have to be psychic to feel the undercurrents, know they had little to do with her. Tawny's "accident" may have gotten them all rethinking Cabot's murder.

"You'll have to admit your mom's one weird duck though," Earl said in tune with her thoughts, as they sat on petrified logs to eat bananas and Oreo cookies, Homer's idea of a morning coffee break.

"That personality change you noticed and her behavior,"

Sidney Levit joined in, "you have to consider the possibility of your mother's mental instability. It can happen to anybody. At different periods in our lives, our bodies are driven by chemical and hormonal reactions nobody can predict or explain."

Finally it had come out in the open. Everyone had been dancing around it since Charlie arrived, including Charlie. "Are you suggesting, Sid, that my mother went crazy and murdered Cabot because she's menopausal? Most violent crime, including murder, is committed by people suffering from testosterone overload not estrogen deprivation."

"Every man has male hormones, damn few commit murder. It affects them in different ways. You women lump all men in some common pot. It might not be politically correct to say so but the fact is, we are individuals."

"Charlie lumps Mitch in a different pot than the rest of us," Scrag said.

Mitch glanced briefly at Charlie, who along with everybody else ignored that remark.

"Sid, that fist you waved at the heavens last night just before the shoot went wrong?" Charlie took a swig from her canteen. "I saw it and *that* looked like odd behavior to me."

Sid glanced shyly away from Charlie, rubbed his hands together. "I really thought we had that one. From up where I sat, Charlie, that was one hell of a take. I felt bigger than God for a minute there. In fact, I think we might still be able to save it. I'll have to see the dailies."

"Sid, did you see Tawny from up there?"

"No, I only saw Koop, our stuntman, set his protective suit on fire. He had his own set of problems and didn't even see her until it was too late. What I can't figure is why the hell she was in there."

"The camera might have seen her. It might show what happened to her. The insurance company would want that footage."

"And I'll be sure they get it, if there's anything to see. Charlie, I'll never forgive myself for that poor woman's death. Accidents like Tawny's are terrible, but they do happen." He was into his kindly, shy, fatherly routine. Charlie could not forget that he'd been closer to Gordon Cabot than anyone here. "Gordon's death," Sid reminded her, "was no accident."

The men wandered around for a while longer, some probably to pee in private, and when they'd all boarded the jet boats for the next leg of their journey, one of the engines refused to start.

It was the lead boat and Homer had a few descriptive phrases for the occasion. Dean wanted to know if the other craft could tow it, but Homer didn't think the remaining engine had the power.

"And we're going downriver now but we'll have to fight the current coming back." He and Dean fiddled with the engine to no avail. Homer asked for volunteers to stay behind and be picked up on the way back to no avail either.

He could well be the only person on this excursion who did not suspect that one of the group was a murderer. Nobody wanted to be abandoned on a strange beach with one of those.

Homer grumbled that he could lose his guide license for putting them all in the same boat. But he did.

This time Charlie sat between a cooler of food and a red can of extra fuel from the abandoned boat, trying to put as much space between her and the testosterone as one could get in the crush. The smell from the red can made her half sick. It reminded her of a flaming makeup artist.

Mitch was watching her again. Just let the bastard watch.

But later, when they pulled over for their last stop and started off across country to view an old cowboy line camp, he dropped back to walk beside her.

"Careful how you handle the menopause angle, Charlie," he warned. "Rita may need it to defend your mother." He was down to two small bandages on one hand and one wraparound on the other.

"You think my mother's crazy enough to commit murder?" And you pretended to like her. Me too, for that matter.

"That's not what I said. But Rita may need all the ammunition she can get. Don't say anything here that can be used against Edwina at the trial. Any of these people could be called back to testify."

He walked off to join the guys all trying to outdo each other in the I-can-hike-faster-than-you-can tournament, leaving Charlie to limp along behind. Feeling sorry for herself. One foot throbbing again.

Edwina probably had ten years on anybody there except Sid and Homer. But they had *all* passed their life's testosterone peak.

Mostof the men—except for Sid—were wearing their shirts like turbans. Earl wore his under his baseball hat more like a Bedouin.

Charlie slapped at something she couldn't see biting her arm and hoped the Arabs up ahead were getting eaten alive. She was still trying to digest the word *trial*.

Somewhere in Charlie's fantasy world, Edwina's innocence would be proven before this whole nightmare reached the trial stage. And old Sheriff Ralph would be eating crow. Or turkey vulture.

Denial fed a good portion of Charlie's fantasy. She simply *had* to get home—to work she much preferred to this detecting. To a daughter who— The pain in her stomach made her foot feel like a coward. Charlie once again switched thought scenes and fast.

Chapter

23

The path was well worn and Charlie had no trouble finding the line camp even though the men had vanished from sight before she reached it. It was past lunchtime and the afternoon weather built as she watched.

A dust devil careened across the path ahead and wind stirred up the scratchy scents of sage and dead wood. Lightning lit the face of the cliff in front of her, etching the desert varnish splashed across it like stage paint.

That peculiar prestorm light, where the sun shines low under a darkening sky, lengthens shadows to stark angles, glows only on one side of things. Charlie notched up her pace despite her complaining feet.

The path ended at a wooden pole fence, unpainted, weather-grayed, forming the outer boundary of a corral. It made a large semicircle closing in on a sandstone cliff face at each end. A wooden chute for loading animals sagged inside it.

Desert weeds of mixed parentage crowded up to the chute as if demanding transportation out of here.

She stepped into a black half-moon hole yawning in the cliff and the weight of the sun lifted off her head and shoulders so suddenly she took a surprised intake of cool damp air. It was like entering a darkened movie theater, the light from outside blinding the eye to any solid forms, causing them to gradually emerge like the rows of seats and the people in them.

Like the seven men in various positions who'd gone still as stones and as silent the minute she'd entered. Not a gallant among them, they'd gone off and left her and now seemed hostile at her approach.

They'd been talking about her.

And they weren't sure what she'd overheard. And she'd been so busy getting herself spooked by mother nature she hadn't overheard anything. Damn it.

During that instant tableau when their shapes firmed up gray out of nebulous blackness, Homer Blankenship knelt in the dirt with a plastic-wrapped sandwich in the hand he was pulling from the mouth of a bag.

John B. Drake hunkered next to him, hand and arm angled over to receive the sandwich. Hunkered in that odd Third World posture that's a substitute for chairs—legs folded double, thighs tight against chest and stomach, buttocks just off the dirt. Pretty limber for forty-five. Three minutes in that position and it would take a crane to get Charlie unfolded.

Mitch Hilsten looked to have been pacing. He lowered a gesturing arm. Earl Seabaugh had been studying the ceiling but glanced down now at Charlie with a flash of anger so sharp and sudden it felt like a blow. He tried to blink it away. Dean Goodacre and Sidney Levit perched on a boulder as if an audience for Mitch's presentation, twisting to look over their shoulders at her. Scrag Dickens relaxed on the dirt floor leaning against the rock wall at the back of the cavern, legs crossed at the ankles, head cocked to study her.

God, why hadn't she stopped outside to listen before barging in on this good-old-boy party?

Or was it just Charlie's paranoia interpreting this scene?

"What? I'm interrupting something?"

There was still a pause after she spoke that her paranoia construed as quick assessments of just how much she'd heard. They didn't know she hadn't listened outside. Lightning flashed white in the sky behind her and the forms in the tableau took on shadow and expression. The men may have been silent, but for a brief moment those expressions talked. Again there was fear and suspicion but it had suddenly been redirected toward Charlie.

And then the world righted and the people in it moved and spoke. Mitch Hilsten took on an oily expression like in *Trophies* when he was about to put the sting on Marlena whatwashername. Sid and Dean got up to offer her their rock. Homer rose to offer her the sandwich intended for John B., who pulled a little boy face and unbuckled his belt to get to his plastic canteen. Earl went back to studying the ceiling and Scrag patted the dirt next to him in invitation.

Charlie sat in the dirt like Scrag but not next to him, the cool dark dankness, the balogna sandwich with mustard and pickle, the sweet warm water, and the relief of being off her sore feet bringing her mood back to conciliatory, if not normality.

She should right now be sitting in her cool clean office on Wilshire anxiously awaiting word as to the fate of Tina Horton's *Southwestern Exposure* pilot for CBS. Barry Zahn at ZIA had called just before she left to say Carl Shapiro had promised to decide by today whether it would be on the fall schedule or put off once again. It had been one of those projects pitched, sold, and developed in record time and then it had languished.

But instead of biting her nails in her air-conditioned office Charlie sat sweaty, dirty, sunburned, with no fingernails to bite. On the dirt. Eating with unwashed hands. Dying to find her own privacy to pee.

Homer munched on his sandwich, trying to clear the residue of the pasty white bread out of the gap between his front teeth and talk at the same time. He explained that the hollowed-out bowls grooved into the surface of a low flat boulder were made by Anasazi women grinding seeds and grains with handheld stones.

The blackened roof was from cooking fires and the layered

chiseled-flat rocks piled to the ceiling in one corner with mud plaster for mortar had once protected food from rats.

Homer was the only one who bothered to stoop and peer into an ancient hole of a doorway. "Last time I looked, it was rats living in there."

Edwina would have loved this.

The Anasazi had made pictures on the walls here too. The larger ones resembled floating Indian rugs hanging from crowned skulls, painted in faded red and blue. The animal drawings weren't stick figures, like the deer in the cave along the river, but crude creatures with bloated bodies and short legs like those children draw before they've mastered the intricacies of proportion.

Rows of orange handprints filled an unblackened edge of the ceiling Earl had been studying when Charlie arrived. Humans had dipped their palms in dye and pressed them flat against the rock. Small humans. Adults and children left their marks, but even the largest was smaller than Charlie's.

The base of this low cliff, eroded away by some long-forgotten river or stream, formed deep overhangs that would come to be human shelters. First for the Anasazi and later the cowboys who shepherded cattle like sheep, living with them, moving them when the meager graze was used up.

Homer offered everybody another sandwich and Charlie was the only one to refuse. Finally, he led his refreshed and cooled, but still uneasy and watchful, crew to the next overhang shelter.

It had a little sign identifying it as Spring Cave. A crevice ran all around the cavern where two different-colored layers of rock met. Water seeped from that crevice so sparingly it dried up before reaching the sand floor. But every now and then a green plant had found a root hold. Some were ferns hanging upside down. One looked like watercress.

At the back, in the deepest recess, the water seeped heavily enough to form a dark puddle on the floor that lengthened to a stream but disappeared into the sand before it reached the point where the overhang met the desert. Homer told them the spring provided water all year.

No ancient Anasazi fires had blackened the ceiling here or cowboy fires either. Both groups may have slipped in for water, but they didn't stay to live. Charlie didn't stay long either. The spring that provided water all year bred the largest, most vicious mosquitoes she'd ever met.

Homer was pontificating outside. "The corral, of course, was built relatively recently by ranch hands and meant to keep the cattle out of the remuda and the cowboys' hair—except at branding and roundup when they were herded inside a few at a time. Trucks hauled them off for slaughter."

Charlie hurried along the corral fence after the others, encouraged by sharp lightning cracks, one hand picking up slivers on the weathered wood. Two untrimmed fence posts with a long pole nailed between—a hitching post. More fencing almost hidden in bushes and tall weeds and a gate wide enough to straddle a one-lane road, a high cross pole above it, but no road.

The wires that had held the gate shut were broken and it hung slack in the sand, propped up by strong wiry weeds.

The overhang here sheltered a large wooden box with a lid. Homer made much over the fact that the air was so dry the metal hinges still worked without squeaking and that the lid had kept the pack rats out of the fine layer of dusty oats once used to feed the horses.

"Charlie?" Earl Seabaugh appeared at her side to help her study the oats. "The night of Cabot's murder? I went up to the *Aliens* campsite to talk to Dean. Cabot roared in, in his fucking Humvee, rushed to his big rig and couldn't get the door unlocked. Big joke, Dean tells me, is the size of Cabot's bladder."

Both John B. and Mitch Hilsten had paused in their euphoria over the boring landscape to watch them, eyes hooded halfway like the clouds trying to squash the sunlight with lightning. "Why are you telling me this now?"

"Mitch says you aren't going to give up. Not smart, but understandable. Maybe you like your mother more than anybody thought." He too noticed the men noticing them and started to wander off.

"Wait." Charlie grabbed a camera strap around his neck so that he had to stop or choke. "He can't get in his motor home and he has to use the john. So?"

"The last anybody but the murderer saw of him was him starting off to the public potty."

"Why didn't he just unzip his fly the minute he got behind a bush?" Like the rest of you've been doing all day.

"Maybe he did. Looked like he was heading for the concrete crappers. I don't know if the autopsy mentioned the condition of his fly, do you?"

"Did you tell the sheriff this?"

"I was too close to the scene of the crime at the time of the crime to tell the sheriff anything. But when I passed your mother's campsite, you two were sitting at the table eating. Her ax was leaning up against the trailer tongue. Next time I see you, you're rushing into John B.'s motor home all torqued at Edwina and wanting to tell us about it at dinner. And your mother and her ax are still running loose out there."

"You didn't see her on the way back to John B.'s for dinner?"

"Didn't walk that way. Sid and I walked the other side of the loop. John B.'d asked me to see if I could get Sid down to discuss the mess Cabot was making of the landscape."

Charlie found it all very curious but couldn't see that it proved or disproved anything. Her own need to find a bush was passing the urgent level.

But she damn near lost it all with the cameraman's parting shot. His earring and green eyes glittered hard in a lightning flash and he patted his little Handycam. "I don't know if Sid's crew got any footage of Tawny's death last night, but I think I did."

Charlie was leaning nonchalantly against the gate while she frantically eyed sagebrush and saltbush, when Dean Goodacre found her.

She clamped her teeth in a false smile and crossed her legs. Either she or the gate creaked in the wind. Her nose was swollen so red with sunburn she could barely see around it.

The helicopter jockey had seen her see him last night talking to Tawny shortly before her death. The bulge of his bared stomach was turning pink with white blotches. "Promise you won't say a word to anybody about this, but I thought it might help."

Charlie realized the man was so uncomfortable he wasn't even chewing on anything. "Not if you don't tell me what it is."

"She wanted me to fly her out of Utah last night. Didn't say why, but she offered me five grand plus expenses to do it. And I said yes."

"Where did she want to go?"

"Vegas. I think she was scared, Charlie."

Charlie raced off to find a big enough bush thinking that the dead woman hadn't seemed afraid during the ride into town from Dead Horse Point yesterday afternoon. And she had looked cheerful enough when she'd waved at Charlie across the substation compound before the shoot.

After half a day of stonewalling, everybody suddenly wanted to 'fess up. What was going on?

* * *

"**Y**ou probably think I'm heartless to be gallivanting around out here after what happened to Tawny, huh?" John B. whispered to Charlie in the next overhang shelter, the largest so far. "Mitch thought I needed to get away, think about something else."

Charlie absently kicked a poof of sand-dirt through the frame of an old-fashioned bedspring of wire coils that had never known padding. The whole place looked like somebody'd dug up a venerable garbage dump on a poverty-stricken ranch and set out the worst of it as a display for tourists. Or filmmakers.

"Hey, my mom's in jail charged with murder and I'm out here gallivanting right along with you. I can't very well say anything, can I? Everybody needs a break now and then."

"I suppose they told you all about Ben. Tawny and Earl, I mean."

Raw two-by-fours formed a trencher table and crude benches, even a chair with a high back but no legs. Just enough to keep your buns up out of the dirt without having to hunker. The table legs were coated with MJB coffee cans.

"The theory," Homer had told them, "is that desert wood rats won't climb metal."

As Charlie remembered, those in Edwina's basement climbed anything. Maybe because they were caged. The men here acted caged, trying to fake their way out of a maze they thought she had the key to.

"Ben . . . Tawny's husband? She told me he was a lot older. Earl said he'd committed suicide. Mitch that he'd failed in a business venture with you and Earl. That's all I know."

He was much taller than Charlie, but he raised his head to look down at her, long lashes almost meeting as his eyes turned to slits and the rubber mouth formed a false happy-face grin.

"Tawny also told me you two were breaking up," she persisted.

He wore his versatile bandanna rolled into a sweatband

around his forehead. His eyes were a deep chocolate brown. In a sort of nerdy way, John B. Drake was good-looking.

Is that possible?

The grin opened to a knowing smile as he recognized her unexpected rush of attraction.

Charlie, your mother's in jail, his latest squeeze burned to a crisp, and you just slept with his best friend. You are here to figure out at least one murder—how would you explain all this to Libby?

That's when Charlie decided John B. was the murderer.

A long stovepipe lay on the floor next to a narrow metal box that once was a primitive oven. A clutter of coffeepots, frying pans, plates, cups, stirring spoons, and platters spread over the tabletop as an open display for tourists. All of them metal, all blistered and blackened, all with holes worn through. Yet none with a speck of rust.

Another table held stiffened dried horse tack—bridles, reins, leather straps.

Sid was the next to sidle over with helpful details, his high forehead beginning to blister like the cookware, his beautiful white hair sweat-plastered to his head like his shirt to his chest.

Sid wanted to know why Scrag's fingerprints weren't on Edwina's ax, since he'd made an oft-repeated display of carrying it about. "That's something you should look into, Charlie."

Charlie looked into Sid Levit's eyes instead and found there the sincere conviction that he could manipulate her in any direction he chose. What, all females are looking for a father figure? That's when Charlie knew for sure that the producer and now director of *Animal Aliens* had murdered his predecessor.

Mitch gave her a secret look. Like, she was supposed to know what it meant. He put an arm around Earl's shoulders, the other gesturing in earnest about the possibilities of this place.

"Sort of a three-generation thing, see? Get some footage here we can discuss later. The Anasazi, the cowboy, and the modern tourist."

Earl concentrated his Handycam on different shots of the intricate prints left by opposing sportswear at different light angles.

You really *can* tell the difference in the prints left by Adidas and Reeboks. Charlie wished she'd thought to look for shoe prints around Gordon Cabot's body while she was losing her cookies three bushes to the left.

She'd no sooner entertained that thought than the river guide slipped her a couple of Oreos. "I saved some back for you."

Jesus, maybe *he's* psychic.

Then he whispered, "Keep your expression neutral. I don't understand it, but *they* all think you've figured out Cabot's murder and came along to force or surprise a confession. And *I* think you're in serious danger here."

They both looked at Charlie's awkward footwear. She was going to flee this danger in a couple of rubber tire slats with canvas straps, right?

"They think you're psychic and 'sense' more about them than you let on. Mitch Hilsten even hinted you would know if the woman who burned to death on the set last night . . . if her death maybe wasn't accidental."

That's what they were talking about when I came into the first cave after everybody else. That's why all the helpful hints.

"I'm not psychic, Homer, and God help me, I want to believe poor Tawny was murdered because my mom couldn't have done that one from a jail cell. And two murderers on the same location doesn't seem likely."

"What I want to know is, have we come too far downriver in an overcrowded boat with half the water and provisions we should have and a murderer on board?"

"If we have, it doesn't mean he has any reason to kill again."

"Unless he feels threatened. Say, by you. Don't do anything to excite him till we get back up the river to Moab? I've got this senseless, unwarranted, crawly feeling somebody dumped sand in the gas tank of the lead boat back there. It sounded weird, started, then choked on something."

In fact, he was anxious to return to the one boat left and be the first there, in order to thwart any more tampering.

"Homer, even a murderer wouldn't want to get stuck in a place like this without enough water and food." Or fax, E-mail, cellular. "If production companies can get cellular phones out here, why don't you carry one with you?" John B. had returned his in a fit of austerity when they'd packed up and left the campground.

"They're of limited use this far out and down," he said as if insulted. "People come this far out and down to get away from that kind of thing. And they're too expensive for plain old river guides." But then he relented, "I could sure use one right now though."

Charlie once again limped along behind the "guys" back to the river, trying to determine if she'd learned anything for all this effort and discomfort.

She was really more worried about the next storm rolling in than the possible sabotage of the boat. Not that the last one had shed more than three drops that made it to the earth. But the lightning was difficult to ignore.

Mitch seemed to be keeping her in sight from up ahead, the last of the gang on a trail marked for tourists with painted rocks lining it on each side.

By the time Charlie and her rubber clogs caught up with the group, they'd formed a dejected semicircle around the remaining jet boat. The slit at one side of the floor (hard to imagine the pliable black rubberlike stuff as a "deck") gaped in an even zag. One section of the pontoonlike rim was underwater and appeared as deflated as the men standing above it.

"No rock did this." John B. was the first to voice the obvious.

"There aren't any rocks on this beach," she pointed out, soaking up the moods around her with stomach-dropping intensity. If they'd been in a room the fear, anger, and suspicion would be bouncing off its walls.

The director knelt to ream the slit edges with a finger, his gaze lingering, accusing each of the group in turn. Even Charlie. "Smooth, like a knife cut."

Homer Blankenship checked his belt to find his hunting knife still in its sheath and gestured above his wounded craft, palms up, as if he were offering it a baby goat with a slit throat. "I'm not going to sabotage my own boats." He raised and lowered the invisible offering and then repeated the action. "Christ, the wife's barely eking out grocery money cooking and slaving in a bed and breakfast, our house. I'm not going to risk my river license and have to move my family back to the city . . . who could have done this?"

Charlie's half-baked idea that the killer was along on this trip instead of back in California, soaking up civilization, was on the money. It made her feel less triumphant than trapped. One thing to ask for something, another to get it.

A totally insensitive idiot could have sensed Charlie was not alone with this inspiration. The difficulty with being accused of psychic sensitivity is you can never tell what's normal intuition because anything you say is held up to you as proof of your superiority to rational thought processes. It was a royal pain.

Mitch Hilsten wasn't the only one giving Charlie slit-eyed, sideways glances. What, they wanted her to make an announcement?

Hard to believe the slam-heavy sun on her head and the parched air smelling of rain. At the same time lightning blazed from a black cloud much too near them and moving closer on a powder-dry wind that rippled the water and shuddered the sunken end of the boat.

Sidney Levit straightened his shoulders, stretched his chin toward the unpredictable sky, and blew a couple of audible breaths through his nose. "This is unforgivable, unwarranted, unnecessary, and banal."

Mitch Hilsten stood slumped and ashen, the California tan overpowered. Then again, he was an actor. "No, Sid, this is one good-sized problem."

Dean Goodacre spit out the weed stem he'd been chewing and wiped sweat off his forehead with a beefy forearm. "This problem could be deadly."

Scrag Dickens rolled his eyes, shook his ponytail. "Let us not get carried away. One night in the wilderness does not a catastrophe make. All kinds of people knew we were coming up here. They'll be searching for us by morning if not before."

That's when Charlie decided the self-styled desert rat must be the murderer. Anybody without an agenda could see one night in the wilderness in such a situation could easily a dead body make.

Earl Seabaugh, however, looked the most suspicious of them all, causing Charlie to shift yet again. He *had* to be the murderer. After all, she could feel the hatred emanating from the cameraman, instead of just the fear and suspicion being given off by the others.

Damn it, Charlie, you don't *feel* anything of the sort and you could miss noticing something important that would help Edwina if you don't concentrate on what you *know*.

Oh, help Edwina. Sure.

Charlie's mother might be up a creek without a paddle but Charlie was down the river with a killer.

Chapter

25

The intelligent thing to have done would have been to stick together by the injured boat until discovered by a search party.

But the earth jarred with the force of a lightning strike. Smoke rose from something on the other side of a mound of slickrock across the river. The palpable static charges in the air on this side were reminiscent of the fatal shoot at the power substation last night. Everybody dove for cover.

And thus separated. *Not* the intelligent thing to do.

An onrush of wind blew sand into Charlie's face and it wasn't until she opened her eyes that she realized she'd lost a contact. She closed the good eye with the lens still intact, leaving her operating with the nearsighted one.

She flattened herself in a dry arroyo next to somebody else. Maybe the murderer.

"Be over in a minute," Homer Blankenship said close to her ear. Thank God. He was the only person here Charlie did not suspect. "Weather moves through pretty fast in this country."

"Don't you have a patch for the boat?"

"Nothing strong enough to withstand that load."

You don't think of rain as your biggest worry on a desert, but Noah would have been hunting building supplies about then. Not so much where Charlie winced next to the river guide as upslope from their shallow depression.

"Well, wouldn't it hold enough for one or two to go upriver for help?"

"Might. Have to wait out the storm to know though." He added in apology, "Never rains hard in this country until it decides to."

There was moisture seeping under Charlie, trying to get to the river but soaking up in her clothes instead.

"Think we might have to move." Homer pointed out the obvious. "Just kinda roll up on the edge next to you, but stay flat."

Charlie did and ended up buffeted by alternate waves of blowing grit and gigantic drops of cold wind-driven rain. She'd gone from sweaty hot to shivering chill so fast her body couldn't adjust to the change if she continued to breathe normally. Sort of like Edwina used to before beginning estrogen-replacement therapy.

Well, I sure as hell better stay in better control than she did. This is no time to lose it.

Uh-oh, there we go, admitting to ourselves that our mother's change of life could make her dangerously unstable. Playing right into the hands of Sheriff Ralph Sumpter and those who won't vote for women in government.

Oh my God. Now what? There was Scrag-the-desert-rat and Earl-the-cameraman duking it out by the boat. Charlie changed eyes quickly, realizing she couldn't have identified the fighting figures if she'd been protecting the one with the lens. And immediately the battle degenerated to a blur.

A blur that both Homer Blankenship and Sidney Levit were crawling toward on hands and knees. Them she could see, even nearsighted, because they passed her on their way. Being either wiser or more cowardly, Charlie followed on stomach, knees, and elbows. Her focus was not on the macho histrionics but on what appeared to be a plastic bag she imagined to contain patching material and maybe glue to repair their boat. It looked in danger of being kicked into the mighty Colorado River. Even when she checked out the scene with her one good eye.

She was wrong again. It was a Ziploc which, when she un-zipped a corner, smelled like more bologna sandwiches with mus-tard and pickle. So much for psychic intuition.

But she held on to the bag and inched an awkward reverse crawl out of the scuffle, nearly choked by the kicked and blowing sand. Somehow keeping both the correct eyelid and her mouth closed at the same time was too much under the stress of the moment.

Hey, I survived backing off a goddamned cliff a zillion feet high. I can handle this. We're talking one murderer and five people in the same boat I am, right?

Poor choice of words.

It was clear that Scrag was merely defending himself, and quite well, when Homer-the-guide and Sid-the-producer brought a struggling Earl to the ground with a knee tackle, ending the fight.

Scrag wiped blood from his nose with the back of his hand. "You are really overreacting, Earl-my-man. All I said was it would be logical if anybody torched poor Tawny on purpose, then it must be somebody from our crew, and if it was an accident, it was some-body from Sid's. I didn't say you'd killed her."

"Yeah you did." Earl struggled out from under Sid and pushed Homer off him with an ease that made Charlie uneasy. But the cameraman didn't advance on the desert rat, who obviously took time from his hitchhiking to work out and had biceps to go with his chest. "You accused me of scuttling the boats. Same thing."

"Not if you were just trying to trap her murderer. That's what I meant."

Earl scuttled the boats?

Where were Mitch and John B.?

Scrag winked at Charlie. The consummate ham. Ever aware of an audience.

Charlie pushed herself up to a sitting position. Hell, most of the men were standing. Lightning didn't strike them. Earl followed Scrag's look at Charlie as if contemplating a conspiracy. Dean braced behind him.

And the drama dissolved, not because of the threatening weather, but because of John B. Drake's laughter. It dripped scorn. "Earl, you scuttled the boats?"

"No, you did. The first one at least. Where're the sugar packets you keep your pockets stuffed with for that sweet tooth, Drake? Dumped them in the gas tank, didn't you?"

"Why would I use sugar when there's all this sand?"

Charlie sat on the sidelines munching on the bologna sandwich, watching the interplay, the personalities revealed under stress. Everyone would be afraid of the murderer and he afraid of exposure.

Where was Mitch Hilsten?

Dean watched Sidney Levit for orders but every now and then glanced at Charlie Greene for approval.

Sid was talking up a storm trying to smooth over hard feelings and to encourage them all to plan a strategy for survival until rescue came. His was the voice of reason—listing the options, greasing the wheels to smooth out life, particularly this sticky part at hand.

Good film producers are like building contractors. They can keep their cool and convince others to keep theirs when the plumber doesn't get there before the dry wallers and both are scheduled elsewhere into the next century and starting tomorrow. Or when the director's fired halfway through the filming and the new one hasn't read the script.

Pleasant, relaxed, practical—Sidney Levit used his cool on them until it was obvious it wasn't going to work. And then he lost it. He was about as wrinkled and wet as his white shirt. His white face had lost its sunburn, his white hair its part and the air of aplomb it helped him give off. His deep voice cracked. And he was just an angry, helpless, old man.

His ace pilot looked to be chewing on his cheek as he glanced around the group hoping for another leader. Dean Goodacre, Charlie decided, couldn't be a murderer because he was such a follower.

Not that the ace detective sitting bedraggled and stringy-haired and smelling of bologna and mustard was that great an inspiration at the moment.

Homer rose stiffly to his feet to deliver an incoherent diatribe. But Charlie couldn't hear it and nobody else seemed to be listening anyway. He finally backed up to sit deflated, a fellow noncontender, next to her.

"Homer, where's the patching stuff?" Charlie asked when there was nothing more to eat and her discomfort refused to be ignored.

He squinted at her in disbelief. "Those jerks aren't going to let me near that boat."

"They might not notice. But then again some people just sit back and watch." Feeling guilty for baiting him, she crawled on hands and knees between Dean Goodacre and the bullying match. When she reached the boat she found the deflated section hadn't widened so the pontoon rim was, as would seem logical, segmented. The tear in the floor was still pretty ugly though.

Homer, suddenly beside her, reached into a compartment next to the thing that held the jet engine onto the boat and extracted a thick plastic bag and cut it open with his knife. Its handle was wrapped in leather strips.

The bag held smooth-edged patches in graduated sizes, a tube of what Charlie hoped was glue, and a disposable plastic air pump.

The patch, if it held at all, might help the boat hold the two of them, he explained as he worked. And the rip in the bottom, too large to patch, wouldn't sink them because the pontoon would keep them afloat. But not dry. So Charlie spent the time piling anything movable onto the beach.

She was soaked anyway, sick of detecting, and just wanted out of here. But where was Mitch?

She'd been staring at rocks and into bushes awhile before she realized both the weather and the combatants had grown quiet on her. The guys were hovering all of a sudden.

"Just what is it you are doing here?" John B.'s exaggerated confusion sounded more threatening than it should and seemed to rally the other warriors to his allegiance.

"Well, Homer and I are going up the river to bring help back and the patch won't hold up with any more weight than ours and . . . and we're leaving all the supplies for the rest of you and—"

"And leaving the rest of us alone with the murderer."

Seemed like a good idea at the time. "We don't know the murderer is along on this trip." Just because someone wrecked the boats doesn't mean anything—much. "And just because he murdered once or even twice doesn't mean he has any reason to again." There wouldn't be anybody left on earth if they never quit. "Anybody know where Mitch is?"

Blank stares all around.

"I thought he was right behind me." John B. looked over his shoulder and then called, "Hey, Hilsten?"

No answer.

What to do? Leave the boat unprotected to search for Mitch and risk the murderer returning to sabotage it for good this time? Or leave one person behind to guard it and risk the one person chosen being the murderer? Or leave two people behind and risk one of them being the murderer and killing the other as well as destroying the boat? Charlie wasn't sure that's what all but one of the disheveled little group was thinking but it should have been.

There could be more than one murderer.

Oh great.

And it could be somebody else wrecking the boats. Someone wanting to force the killer's hand for instance. Someone single-minded enough not to care that he's endangering us all in the process.

Charlie, so miserable her stomach forgot to hurt, wished mightily that there *were* such things as Unidentified Flying Objects. Real life was too unpredictable.

Chapter
26

The storm had been a late afternoon affair and it never did warm up afterward. Charlie began an awkward freeze-dry process—sitting with her back against a cooling slickrock shelter that wasn't really high enough for shelter. It brought to mind a lump of scrambled dinosaur eggs or a heap of nature's gallstones.

She sat on the river side of it, facing the ruined boat and load of supplies. The men decided she was the only one they'd trust to guard these items while they strode off to search for Mitch Hilsten, superstar.

Charlie sat there, aware that suspicion itself had become the enemy that might destroy them all. That she'd be a sitting duck if the murderer returned to do her in with the boat as Homer Blankenship had warned/worried when forced/persuaded to march off and lead the search, leaving Charlie behind.

When Charlie suggested she and Homer go up the river for help while the others looked for Mitch, Sid insisted that if the movie star were hurt, he should be the one to go out on the boat with the guide. Charlie could think of all kinds of arguments against this logic now that she had nothing else to do, but then she'd been too tired and too worried about Mitch to demand her say. Homer was delegated to pair up the searchers and choose the appropriate directions for the teams since he was the one least suspected of murderous intentions.

Even shivering and scared, Charlie began again to think through the list of suspects. It was motive that threw her. If there were two murders, were there two motives?

But Earl Seabaugh interrupted her deliberation by wandering alone onto the beach without his hat and camera.

"Run, Charlie, anywhere, Charlie, hurry." There was something mechanical in his hoarse whisper and something strange about his eyes. Earl wasn't wandering, he was staggering. Charlie thought briefly of the rat staggering onto the road when she was changing the Corsica's tire but the cameraman fell on his face before he reached her, Homer's hunting knife buried in his back.

Charlie's adrenaline rush was so strong it made her dizzy and she had to crawl over to him. She was never more mindful of the scarcity of odors out here than now with the unexpected potency of the metallic scent of his blood.

He raised his head a few inches. "No, sand, Charlie, run. No sand . . ." he said and dropped his head back down on some.

The sea-green eyes stuck open halfway through a blink. Faint blond fuzz coated patches of a scalp he probably hadn't shaved today. And wouldn't need to tomorrow.

Reminded of the squashed tour bus, Charlie felt for a pulse in his neck as if she knew where to feel. But the sigh of a slow fart as Earl's body did the ultimate relax job convinced her he wasn't faking the blood seeping from his mouth into the sand either. She grabbed her jacket from a nearby rock where she'd spread it to dry and made it out of sight of the beach before stopping to think.

Three murders, if Tawny's death wasn't an accident, were moving this situation from the realm of necessity, expediency, or whatever to serious insanity. Of the remaining five suspects, Charlie figured only four were candidates. Dean was real. Okay, he was a blowhard, but he was tethered to nonmurderous reality.

That left Scrag Dickens, John B. Drake, Sidney Levit, and, yes, Mitch Hilsten. If only because he was here. But Sid alone seemed to have a motive to kill Cabot. And that wasn't much of one. But none to kill Earl or Tawny.

You've only known these people a few days. They could have motives and shared histories you know nothing about.

Charlie worried about Homer Blankenship. He was an innocent bystander pulled into the fray here. It might have been his knife but she couldn't believe his hand had . . .

She crawled under a bush to hide. Her jacket hadn't dried to the lining and only made her colder and stiffer in her cramped position. She was crying silent tears and trying not to wash out the remaining lens, remembering poor Earl's stuck blink. He'd worn contacts too, but his were heavily tinted. One of them had been dislodged enough to—

GodCharliedon'tthinkoryou'llstartscreamingandthe killer'llfindyou!

"Charlie, I don't want to startle you, okay?" a voice she recognized whispered behind her. "Try to back out from under that bush without making noise and then come over here. Hurry."

It was Mitch. Charlie stayed where she was. She'd almost got him killed and now he was getting even. And he was on the shortening list of candidates for murderer.

"Charlie, I know you're terrified, but your legs are sticking out in plain sight." He sounded ever so patient. Yeah, *wrong*.

But Charlie opened her good eye to stare down along her body. He was right.

"Please, Charlie, I know it's hard to trust anybody at this point, but there isn't much time."

She would never remember making the decision, but Charlie was suddenly snuggled up to his warmth in a vertical rock crevice with scratchy weeds for cover.

"Earl . . ." she breathed in his ear.

"I know," he whispered back. "I saw it."

"You what? You saw—"

"I didn't see who stabbed him. But I saw him fall on the beach. I was watching the beach and you."

"Everybody's looking for you. We thought you were lost or murdered—you were watching the beach?" She had the urge to

slug him and stomp off, but even a jackhammer couldn't have dislodged her from this embrace she had no business believing was
safe.

"Remember when you did something stupid? Backed off a
cliff and nearly got us both killed? Charlie, I think I've done the
same thing."

And Mitch Hilsten explained in whispers in her ear that
he'd decided to use her as a lure. That he'd hidden out to watch the
beach, expecting the killer to come back for Charlie. "I was going to
rush in and save you and unmask the killer."

"Like the hero."

"Like the hero. I'm sorry, Charlie."

Could anybody that convincingly contrite be a murderer?
You bet.

"I couldn't believe it when poor Earl dropped dead at your
feet. Did he say anything?" Did Mitch's body stiffen a little with
that question?

Yeah, he did but it didn't mean anything. "No, he didn't.
Well, he wanted me to run away."

Had Mitch's body relaxed a little against hers with that answer? "Shit," Mitch said, "he was the hero and he died for it."

Mitch had schemed with John B. to lure everyone else away
so that the murderer could come back after Charlie.

"Why would he want to kill me?"

"Because I convinced them all you knew who he was and
were trying to trap him to clear your mother. At least I tried to."

"By telling them I was psychic and that's how I knew.
Thanks a heap."

"Who *do* you think is the murderer, Charlie?"

"Everybody. It's motive I can't figure. Earl and Tawny might
have angered John B. or Scrag somehow." Or you. "But I can't fit
Gordon Cabot into that scenario. Sid might have had reason to
want Cabot dead but not the other two. Unless they figured out he
killed Cabot and needed to be silenced." Actually, you were furious
with Cabot and closer to Earl and Tawny than Sid ever was. "Scrag

and Earl squared off a little bit ago, but Scrag was with me when Tawny . . ."

"At least you've stopped trembling." And he kissed her, wiped a tear from her cheek, and buried his face in her hair. "I'm sorry I put you in danger like that, Charlie. I just wanted to get it over with."

"Who do you think murdered Earl?"

"I know all those people well, Charlie. I can't believe any of them would do such a thing."

Charlie wouldn't have believed she could let down her guard, feel warm and safe enough to fall asleep there. After all, she'd just seen a man die with a knife in his back and only the night before a young vibrant woman writhing in flames. But maybe murder gets easier to live with or the system overdoses and you go numb. Or maybe the stress sent her into shock and made her sleep. She'd never know. But she woke to darkness and cold. She was alone.

Next to falling off cliffs, crashing in airplanes, drowning, becoming one of the youngest grandmothers in history, or having to take Libby and go live with Edwina, Charlie's worst nightmare had always been being lost and alone in the wilderness. She'd prefer a dark alley sprawling with drunks and junkies any day, but it was beginning to look like she was on a roll this trip.

She peered through the weed cover to see several shapes, definitely male, standing off at a distance and gesturing as if in deep discussion. One wore a cowboy hat à la John B. One wore his jeans like Scrag Dickens. One had Sidney Levit's white hair, glowing now in moonlight, and the other was Mitch.

Charlie's legs were tingly asleep, but she decided she had to get out of here regardless. One of those dudes was a murderer. Anybody who'd killed three times would have little to lose by making her a fourth.

And thanks to Mitch Hilsten, whoever it was thought he knew that she knew who he was and probably why he done it. If it wasn't Mitch, that is.

How to unwedge herself from this rock without attracting

their attention. Then find Homer and Dean. And then what? Charlie was in a real mess here. But she couldn't die and leave Libby with a demented grandmother. She couldn't leave this planet without telling off Richard Morse and throwing this job in his chauvinist teeth.

Charlie realized suddenly she'd paused for a fantasy about lining up a power job with William Morris first and throwing that at Richard as well. She had to get control of herself and think of a plan before Mitch brought the others over to her hidey hole. Maybe they were all together against her. She probably had only seconds to—

The guys looked up as if one and ran straight at her, shouting obscenities. Charlie froze, too shocked to react, not that she'd have had time to get out of the crevice and escape them. She closed her eyes. When she opened them, the men were gone and she was alone. Was she hallucinating or what here?

Then Charlie became aware of what she'd been hearing too, over the thunder of her pulse. What had sent them all running. The unmistakable tear in the quiet of a desert night. The roar of the jet boat engine.

Chapter 27

Charlie filled the plastic canteen, mostly by feel, in the puddle at the back of Spring Cave. She drank half of it and filled it again. The water tasted metallic but good. The upside-down ferns looked like shrunken heads hanging by their severed necks in the shadowy recesses. It must have been too cold for the mosquitoes but Charlie didn't linger anyway. This would be the obvious place for the men to look for her.

Aren't we being a little melodramatic?

Listen, I don't know about you, but I want to be alive to see that smirky runt of a sheriff's face when Edwina walks out of that jail a free woman. Charlie covered her mouth when she realized she'd carried on this conversation aloud.

Now that she had water she had to find a place to hide until morning. Glancing longingly at the wooden box with the dusty oats and hinges that didn't squeak, she passed it by. That would be too obvious.

The best way to survive this situation was to keep from panicking and feeling sorry for herself. The latter being almost more difficult because Charlie so loathed discomfort. Edwina used to rattle on about all sorts of things one should know to survive in the wilderness when she'd hauled Charlie off on research trips, not a word of which her daughter could remember. She'd been too busy loathing the discomfort and being away from her friends.

The moon was cold and bright and had highlighted the white-painted rocks lining the path that brought her here and would take her back to the beach at the first inkling help was arriving. Charlie had only to survive until then. That moon was also casting some heavy shadows for her to hide in.

She'd reached the slickrock jumble near the river and peered over it in time to see the jet boat round the bend heading upstream, the shapes of two men on board. Had to be Dean and Homer because everybody else was dancing around on the beach waving fists.

Earl's body had been covered. It looked as if someone had thrown the plastic tarp over him that once covered the supplies still piled where Charlie left them. By the way the covering bulged at one point, it was obvious no one had removed the knife.

Charlie'd turned and ran before they saw her, found the rock-lined path and raced, well, hobbled as fast as she could, along it to the spring. Her tire-tread sandals were neither warm nor swift, but she was not going to feel sorry for herself.

She didn't think they'd be able to see her tracks at night and by morning help would be here. What she needed to do was to stay off the path but follow it back toward the beach from the sidelines. Where, unseen, she could flit between shadow puddles if need be, but stay close enough to meet her rescuers. Sounded like a good plan.

One problem. A chorus of coyotes sent up a harmony only they could appreciate and Charlie made a wrong turn, chills rising everywhere. She'd heard coyotes often when traveling with her mother and even in town on a quiet night, her home but a few blocks from Boulder's mountain backdrop. Charlie had even heard the critters in the canyons of Southern California when visiting reclusive clients.

They'd always sounded so much farther away than they did now. But she wasn't going to panic or feel sorry for herself. Nor would she wig out over the fact that, although she was sure she'd retraced her steps exactly, the white rocks of the path were still nowhere in sight in any direction.

The coyotes keened and yipped lonely sounds she sincerely wished they'd stifle. Charlie visualized them ringing a campfire, pointing their noses at the moon, wearing bandannas around their necks.

The thing to do was to stop going in circles, find a safe shadow, and sit quietly to think what the thing was to do. Again it was a sound that set her off—a footstep or a hoofstep or a pebble dislodged from a path or . . . Charlie found her shadow and sat down fast.

"If you're out there, darlin', you stay put, hear?" Scrag's voice came low and somber. "This shit's going to work itself out."

She could hear him repeat the message twice as his footsteps faded away. He was probably walking the trail and if she moved in that direction maybe she could find it. If Scrag was warning her not to show herself it meant either that he was on her side or it was a trick.

What she would do was sit quiet as the proverbial mouse until he came back and then she'd know it was safe to leave her shadow. Wouldn't she? Sounded like a good plan, but she didn't have the patience to sit there and wait in gross discomfort and seriously substantial fear.

She experimented by moving a shadow puddle closer to the area from which she'd heard Scrag Dickens and the sky didn't fall in, no night creatures out feeding made a grab for her. So she moved on, a shadow at a time, keeping low, from bush to bush to . . . no white-painted rocks, no trail, no overhang shelters or cowboy line camps, no river. God, where was she?

By the next morning the swelling in her feet had completely disappeared and tighten the straps as she might it was a major effort to keep her tire clogs on. And, yes, she was lost but she figured she couldn't be that far from the river and if it was big enough to carve the Grand Canyon it was big enough for her to find. And if she found it, the rescue squads sent out by Dean and Homer would find her. Logically, if she found a wash or arroyo or whatever and followed it downhill she'd come to the river.

And the sun was rising in the east, which should give her some direction as well as warm her. Charlie was so cold she'd lost the battle to keep from feeling sorry for herself hours ago. But every time her stomach rumbled she forced herself to see the body on the beach and the burning woman at the electrical substation and her hunger went away. She'd taken not one sip of water and her canteen was still full.

She worked up the nerve to climb a pile of slickrock and stand above the scrub forest and weeds to look out on a veritable garden. A garden of buttes and buttresses and pinnacles and sculpted ribs of rock, monoliths that rose blood-red out of swirling purple shadow, ground mist, and night, their tops flaming with sunrise.

Definitely big-screen stuff that would have had a lot more appeal from a cozy theater seat. But from their position she figured the river could be in any of three directions. Or all, when you thought about it, because it curved and wound so. No matter, the sun would warm her soon and there would be airplanes in the sky and maybe Dean's helicopter and she would jump up and down and wave and be rescued.

On that happy note Charlie took a breakfast swig of water, rolled it around on her tongue and teeth before swallowing to get the full benefit.

As the sun continued to move down the buttes and cliffs, birds took up singing and flitted from bush to bush as she had bush shadows half the night. Bright, strong twitters and tweets and trills—no chorus of them—they were individual and far flung. But they sounded ridiculously happy and at home in this ghastly place.

Charlie searched the sky for rescue planes, but saw only a contrail too high in the friendly skies and too busy to notice her speck of a life in this universe.

As she lowered her eyes another bird circled ahead. Turkey

buzzard. Vulture. They like dead meat. Circling over Earl Seabaugh of the once-laughing sea-green eyes? Very likely. And if so, that was the direction she should head.

Here's to the buzzard, the body, the beach, and the boats to the rescue. Charlie took another swig, giggled, and started off. She was kind of proud of herself for not running around banging her head against rocks and screaming by now.

The buzzard kept circling, then descended out of sight. Charlie planned to hide behind the same pile of rock she had last night when Homer and Dean took off in the wounded jet boat and case the scene carefully. She hadn't spent the previous horrible night saving her skin to have it exposed by walking into a trap.

She noticed her course was weaving, but that was because of the ill-fitting footwear. Wasn't it? She slipped into a fantasy in which she was describing her heroic escape and calm calculating demeanor, at a time of terrible danger, to her daughter and Maggie Stutzman. Libby and Charlie's best friend were awestruck.

Get real, they'd be yukking it up. Probably have to hang on to each other to stay upright.

Where have *you* been?

Right here. You just haven't been listening. I'm a little worried about our present direction. Should we maybe slow down and scout the scene . . .

Charlie's inner voice was too late and she was reminded of why they have serious medication for people who hear voices.

The vulture rose at her approach just as three others appeared from nowhere but pulled out of their dives toward the body on the ground to soar off with their brethren. They voiced no sound but their giant wings whumped the air as they ascended. For a moment the big sky filled with feathers and an obscene stench.

It wasn't the river, the beach, or Earl that had attracted them either. It was Mitch Hilsten. He lay sprawled on his stomach, a bloody wound on the back of his head.

Chapter
28

Charlie didn't know whether to use her precious water to try washing out Mitch's wound (maybe the blood already had) or try to force some down his throat. She'd turned him over so that he was bleeding on the collar of his sheepskin jacket. But he was breathing. She could almost see his beard growing.

She pulled the lapels of his jacket together to keep him warm, found one side decidedly heavy, and reached into a pocket stuffed with two cans of soda.

Charlie sat back and studied the unconscious man while downing a warm Dr Pepper, not wanting to admit how relieved she was not to be alone.

The guy's out, Charlie. How much more alone can you get?

Yeah, but he's still warm.

The other pocket was stuffed with Oreos. Charlie ate only two before guilt overcame her and she dribbled water between the beautiful teeth. The first dribbles ran out the corners of his mouth but then he swallowed, eyelids fluttered.

"Mitch?"

"No."

"Mitch, open your eyes, it's Charlie."

He did. And his eyes were crossed. Did that mean concussion?

She rolled him on his side and off the wound. The movement

pulled up his jacket and revealed something red sticking out of his pants' pocket. One of those thick pocketknives that have more attachments than a vacuum cleaner. She slipped it into her own pocket thoughtfully.

Charlie had forgotten that a lot of men carry pocketknives. Homer's cutlery had clearly killed Earl, but any of the rest of them could have wounded the second jet boat with one of these.

She wished she had something to wrap Mitch's head with, but neither of them possessed a clean inch of skin let alone clothing. Edwina would have plucked a strip of skin off a cactus or plastered leaves from the bushes together with spiderwebs and spit or something equally gross.

He closed his eyes again and she offered him water, Dr Pepper, an Oreo, and a kiss. His response to all was the same.

"No."

"Well, I can steal the rest of your cookies and soda and go off and leave you to the buzzards, you know."

"Vultures." One eye opened to a slit. "Turkey vultures."

"Mitch, do you know who I am?"

"**W**hy would Scrag hit you over the head with a rock?" Charlie's gnat bites oozed. Some had crusted over and they seeped again when she rubbed off the scabby crusts trying to scratch without nails. The most maddening were those inside the outer curling of her ears.

"I don't know. Always liked the guy. Even lent him money once. Maybe it's because he can't find work. He can't think of anything else."

She'd tried to convince him they should stay put and await rescue. But he knew that he knew the way to the river. Charlie knew he was not acting right. She'd even tried to hold him back but he shrugged her off and kept wandering. No telling where they were by now.

"Yeah, but why would he attack *you* because *he* didn't have work?" Charlie knew that by "work" he meant work in the "biz."

"Terrifying, not having work. It does things to you. I should know," Mitch told her. "When you're trained to do one thing and no one can afford you. No reason to leave the house. But the house is empty. I have three houses, a condo in Aspen, and one in Switzerland. I don't want to live in any of them. It's hard to make friends when people look at you and see an image instead of a man. Even my kids get lost in the image. My own flesh and blood. My wife couldn't live with the image and didn't want the man."

"Please, Mitch, if we ever get out of here you'll hate me for having heard all this." Part of Charlie ached to respond to the staggering loneliness in the dazed eyes, part of her wanted to believe in the image, the rest of her couldn't believe they were having this conversation at a time like this.

He told her he'd met and married his wife in New York and their relationship had been good while he'd studied his craft and found small roles on the stage and in television commercials to help her support them and their growing family. She held down steadier jobs—waiting tables, clerking. Then he landed several bit parts in movies and started traveling too much.

He was discovered in one of those small parts and offered a leading role. He moved his family to California. "Janet hated it out there." His career zoomed, his marriage died. "Now I have nothing but an image and three houses and two condos."

"Hey, more good scripts will come your way. They'll have to. You're Mitch Hilsten, for God's sake."

"I'm either too old or too young. Or the role doesn't fit the image." His speech was getting less slurred, his gait steadier. But Charlie waved his sheepskin at two flies buzzing around the clotted blood at the back of his head. She'd ended up carrying both their jackets because he'd just wandered off and left his.

"Mitch Hilsten can be convincing as a fool or a villain or a weakling, Charlie. I've seen you consider me all those. I've seen it in your eyes. But the public won't like to see that happen to the image they've invested part of themselves in. I'm the invincible hero. And that's all I can be. Shit, I can't even grow old."

Charlie knew this happened to actors. She just didn't want to believe it had happened to this one. Like giving up finally on Santa Claus when you're a kid. "When I moved Libby to L.A. from New York, it was just the opposite. I had trouble adjusting and she took to it so fast I haven't really known her since. It's a paradise for snotty blondes out there."

They should be sitting still and keeping still in whatever shade they could find and conserving energy. But she just kept following his wavering course like a goddamned squaw. She did *not* want to be alone out here.

Charlie heard herself go on to explain how Richard Morse came to offer her a job on the West Coast. She'd talked to him by phone from New York while working for Wesson Bradly Literary Agency, negotiating options for film rights on books his clients might be interested in—sometimes studios, usually actors looking for stories with possible starring roles from which they'd like to see scripts written for them.

An option tied up the property while a producer looked into financing and scripting possibilities. It paid the writer and his agent some pocket money to keep it off the market. Rarely did an option result in a film going into development and even more rarely showing up on the big screen or even television, but it all somehow added to the gambling allure and helped keep people like Charlie employed.

"Richard said one time on the phone that I had a voice like a gravel pit and it didn't sound very literary and he just had to see what I looked like. Next time he came to New York, he took me out to dinner and explained that Congdon and Morse had come far enough up in the world to have its own literary agent. He didn't feel qualified to judge screenwriters or to screen the literary properties coming his way. He needed someone with East Coast contacts in publishing in his office.

"He offered me the job and boy have I just found out what all it entails. He offered me the job and enough money to support us so we wouldn't have to make up what I couldn't live on by being a drag on Edwina. Libby and I joined the middle class. We were blessed with California sunshine, freeways, and debt. You won't believe what Richard's latest demand is though. Mitch?"

"Charlie, look," he pointed to a really deep shade puddle and then headed for it. "I think we should stop and rest, don't you?"

And the squaw carrying the jackets and Oreos and Swiss army knife and what water they had between them followed obediently. "I just don't want to be alone right now, okay?"

"What? Oh, Charlie, I'm sorry. I'm still a little groggy. Feels like Scrag used an ax instead of a rock. Here, let me carry some of that. Christ, have you got a sunburn."

They crawled into an abscess in a rock formation, not deep enough to be called an overhang, but offering blissful relief from the heat. Charlie's feet had swollen again, which was probably not a good sign, but did help to keep her tire clogs on. Charlie's hands were swollen, too, and sticky with sweat, a fine layer of grit coated her face, and more itchy bumps were forming. Those on her neck were along the big veins that ran close to the skin. Wonderful, some living thing too small to see was feasting on her blood.

"Do you think Scrag hit Gordon Cabot over the head with Edwina's ax like he did you with a rock? Maybe Cabot wouldn't give him a job."

"Maybe it's just me. Maybe even my friends are turning on me." Mitch's eyes were no longer crossing but he'd never looked less like a superstar. Dark patches puffed under bloodshot eyes, a scraggly beard was growing out dirty and uneven.

Still, Charlie could look at him and see Lawrence of Arabia deciding to do something heroic, romantic. She could swear she was looking at box office. Stereotypes do die hard. So do images.

They sat silent as the sun began to move down the buttes and rock ribs. One bird went, "Twee, twee, twee." Another, "Toy-toy-toy,

toy, toe-o-oy," as if winding down. They sounded so small and delicate in this vast and brutal land.

Lawrence of Arabia began to cry.

"Oh, Mitch, oh please, not now, not here. I know you're depressed. Who wouldn't be? I mean, you're bashed on the head and dirty and yucky and lost and hungry and thirsty and miserable." Which is as good as it's going to get if we don't find the river or rescue planes don't find us pretty fast. "But you can't give up. I need you. The world needs you. Think of how many people would go into mourning in a minute if something happened to you. Mitch, you're an institution."

And boy, Charlie, do you sound like an agent.

"They'd mourn for the image. They don't give a shit about me. They don't know me." Dirty tears cleaned streaks down his cheeks and disappeared in the stubble of his beard.

Before it was quite dark, he fell asleep beside her and she wrapped his sheepskin around him and snuggled up against him. She had no idea when he was demented by injury and fatigue, when he was acting, or when he was sincere. He could still be the murderer. But right now it didn't matter. If she died out here, she didn't want to be alone.

When the cold and dreaded discomfort prodded Charlie awake it was still deep night and moonlight and her one remaining contact lens had gone dry and brittle. And, like the night before, she was immediately aware of sneaky noises—large paws padding, the whoosh of wings and cries of small animals captured and carried aloft, the rustle of bushes, the slither of snakes . . . the electric lights on the horizon.

"**I** can't."

"Yes, you can. Don't look down."

"If I don't look down I won't know where to put my foot and I'll fall," Charlie said. "If I do, I'll panic and fall anyway."

"I'm right below you. I'll place your feet as we go. Trust me, Charlie."

"Why should I trust you? I never know when you're acting. I don't know that you haven't murdered three people already. I don't know that you're not nuts after that blow to the head."

She'd watched the lights blinking in the far-off night long enough to determine they didn't move and then woke him up to point them out. He'd groaned and gone back to sleep. Charlie had slept little. Dawn erased the lights but Charlie knew where they were.

Mitch seemed back in control of himself this morning. They'd finished off their meager rations, and with half a canteen of water between them, set out to find that beckoning civilization.

And they'd arrived at this steep unending rock-strewn incline.

"You want me to go off and leave you here alone? That what you want, Charlie?"

"I want this whole scene to dissolve," she whined, "and life to cut back to normal."

But he gripped her ankle, pulling her foot down to the next foothold. Which also pulled her off balance, forcing her to release her handhold on the flaking rim of a tiny projection in the cliff and follow her foot. She found a tenacious weed to hang her hands on. "I'm going to be sick."

"Very soon now there's a nice wide ledge where we can stand and rest."

Charlie made it to the ledge before the dry heaves racked her body. She was even too dry to sweat. She could feel her pores trying, in sympathy with her stomach.

"Charlie, look across the canyon or up at the sky. If you keep your eyes closed, you'll get dizzy."

Don't patronize me, fella, you didn't sound so brave yourself last night when you were crying in your beard.

But she opened her eyes. One focused on a blurry world. The other on something shiny wa-a-ay over on the other side of wherever they were.

"Oh, God." Where they were was on an incredibly minute ledge.

"Don't look down." Mitch lifted her chin and thus her eyes.

The shiny thing glinted from across two canyons but there was something familiar about the protrusion upon which it sat. She'd seen it from below while riding in Mitch's Bronco to meet Lew's plane. But then there'd been jet fighters darting across it. She'd be willing to bet she'd seen its lights last night too. "Mitch, that's Dead Horse Point over there."

"All those mesas look alike."

"The one shaped like the bow of a ship with the metal roof or RV or whatever glinting back the sunlight."

Mitch shielded his eyes and squinted across the canyon. "Looks more like a whole fleet of bows, all lined up in a row."

But one of the rusty-red sandstone ships sailed ahead of the others. And it was the one with the metal glint.

"You know, you could be right," he admitted after a second

look. "Because there's the APC holding ponds over there. Lines up about right."

The ponds stood out crisply blue in the dun-colored landscape.

"There'd be water and help either place."

All they had to do was get themselves down the rest of this cliff and across several miles of open sage, rock, scrub, full sun, and rattlesnakes to the edge of the canyon within a canyon. Then find a way down a thousand-foot cliff, cross a hundred-foot-wide river, climb another thousand-foot wall out of the river canyon. Then cross more open benchland and walk miles and miles to the APC plant or just a few to the thousand-foot wall of the outer canyon where there would at least be that Jeep road. Once on top of the mesa, if they didn't get lost in the bush forest, they could cross it to the ranger station next to the campground.

And all without water, food, sun protection, a map, decent shoes, ropes, or a boat. Piece of cake.

Mitch scratched his scalp and gazed out at the prospect. "That river can get real shallow in places. But it'd be a long way."

"Beats wandering aimlessly." Charlie turned around to face her wall again.

There is something to be said for having a goal, even an impossible one. She didn't look at the bottom of the canyon, only as far as to where Mitch was managing to find footing and handholds. They used the long string, meant to gather in the bottom of her discarded jacket, to bind her tire clogs to her ankles and the makeshift shoes actually fit in any toehold his boots did.

When they made it to the shelf, Charlie wished it were night again as she and Mitch started off across the open wasteland. There had been the shadow of the cliff overhang to protect their descent from the sun. Out here there was nothing.

Still, she was pretty proud of herself for making it down that cliff. They wouldn't have to do the whole gig. A helicopter would swoop down and rescue them or a ranger would come along with a van filled with water by the gallon and ointment and sunglasses and stuff.

"Okay, so I don't think you're the murderer," Charlie conceded at one point, and gave him back his pocketknife. He'd had ample opportunity to do her in accidentally. And it was getting heavy to lug around.

"Christ, after that night we had together, you still really thought—" He snorted disgust and proceeded off into the sage. "Women."

"What, murderers don't do sex?"

He stopped and turned on her again. "Is making love no more to you than 'doing' sex or lunch?"

"How the hell would I know? I'm in estrus." When did love get into this? Probably his head wound talking.

"Sun's getting to you," the grimy superstar pronounced after peering into her eyes and feeling her forehead. He pulled off Charlie's sweatshirt and tied it around her head.

From above it had looked like maybe a mile across the benchland. Down here it felt more like twenty.

Their trudge had turned to a stagger by the time they reached the rim of the inner canyon. They hadn't bothered to speak for what seemed hours.

Mitch stood swaying, looking for a place to descend. Finally, he lay on his stomach to look over the edge. "No way here," he said. "You walk one direction, I'll walk the other. Look for a crevice or deer trail, anything."

This, of course, was hopeless, but it was doing something. Charlie knew they'd both run out of steam long ago and would soon have to give up. In some ways she already had. Like, she could no longer get worked up over Libby having to live with Edwina, over missing out on Edwina's triumph over the sheriff, or not being able to get even with Richard Morse. She even managed to peek over the edge a couple of times as Mitch had ordered. What the hell.

His shout startled her so that she had to sit down fast to keep from toppling over into the abyss. In the glare of the sunlight it took her a moment to find him, on his stomach again leaning over the rim. "I think I've found a way down."

Charlie figured he was hallucinating but started toward him on her hands and knees. The red bow of the ship that was the Point seemed no closer than it had when she'd spotted it from their meager shelf on the cliff above. It had been a worthy goal. Her goal now had shrunk to reaching Mitch. You do what you can.

Charlie lounged in the smooth hollow of a rock shaped like a hand, in a freshwater pool on the island of Kauai. The water washing over her naked body rocked it gently. On one side of her, a narrow waterfall rose out of sight behind the lush foliage of tropical trees and giant ferns. On the other, white foam and white gulls flecked the blue sea crashing against black lava rock, sending shimmery spray into humid air. She reached a languid hand toward the sweating glass of lemonade on the grass verge next to her. Her fingers were wrinkled from soaking so long.

"Charlie?"

"Go away."

"There's going to be water down there and shade." Mitch sounded drunk. He fell to his knees a few yards away and motioned to her. She put her gritty sweatshirt back on to cover tender skin and crawled over to a crack in the earth, two feet wide where it opened on to the rim. A wonderfully cool breeze wafted up from it, carrying the scent of water.

"Hard telling if it's passable all the way down. I'll go first. If I get stuck, I'll yell up to you not to start out."

"Then what do I do?"

He was already out of sight down in the darkness, but his answer echoed up to her on an ominous, hollow note. "Then you can die up there alone, Charlie Greene."

Chapter
30

Charlie decided she suffered from claustrophobia as well as acrophobia, even though she'd been able to see daylight out the canyon side of the fissure for most of the way. She'd squeezed through some places and slid down others but she hadn't stuck in a narrows or fallen through a wide space. Yet.

She hadn't waited for Mitch's permission to enter this creepy shaft either. Charlie was not about to die up there alone.

But she felt awfully alone where she wedged now and it was a relief to hear Mitch's swearing echo up between her legs. "Damn it, Charlie, you were supposed to wait. You're kicking stuff down on me."

She slid further into the narrow space, the pause offering her unwelcome opportunity to feel the stinging and prickling of all the abrasions on her sun-abused skin. She lay in a diagonal position with her knees propped against the opposite wall and her head turned toward the opening. There were pearly cloud puffs in the sky, but the sun still tortured the barren moonscape below. The cool draft through the shaft was absolute heaven in contrast.

A shout echoed up to her and she decided it was permission to continue. Charlie had no idea how long it took her to descend the rest of the way. She did know there was no way anyone could get back up this damn thing. Her jeans were torn and sweatshirt in shreds by the time she came sliding out of control on a curved rock slide as smooth and hard as polished marble. It deposited her on a rough floor of deep sand mixed with jagged pebbles.

Mitch Hilsten sprawled against a fluted wall. He raised the canteen to her in a toast. "Glad you could make it."

And "make it, make it, make it" entered curves and swirls of pink, red, and lavender rock and returned to them as it might in a cathedral. Aeons ago, water had shaped a lovely grotto here, quiet and sheltered. Soft, diffused sunlight reached them indirectly through several curved openings in the cliff high above the river as well as the opening off this chamber.

"Beautiful, isn't it?" the sorry-looking superstar croaked.

"There're certainly worse places to die."

He crawled over to offer her the canteen. "We're not dead yet. Here, drink it all."

There were only a couple of swallows left but she took them gratefully. Real people who lived in houses with faucets would never believe how wonderful just plain unflavored, uncarbonated water could be. "We can't very well drink river water. This is downstream of uranium tailings at the mill."

"It's running half-mud this time of year. Wonder if we could make the Point by nightfall."

"You go ahead, I'm staying here." But she followed him to the narrow lip of the cavern that overlooked the river.

It was a good ways down to the water still, but getting there would be no problem. The bank sloped gently for such a perpendicular place, with a swath of mud and weeds covering it most of the way. Getting across the river would be another story.

They lay on their stomachs again, side by side, the lower halves of their bodies still inside the grotto. The river smelled of mud but just the dampness rising from it was pleasant after the aridness above.

"Not a bad place to die at all," she said, feeling drowsy already.

"And Edwina kept telling everybody how tough you were. Charlie, we're almost halfway there, you can't give up now."

"Edwina said I was tough?"

"'Strong-willed and independent, she gets things done, my Charlie does.'" The actor beside her imitated Charlie's mother without really trying to be exact, which would have failed, but by hinting and exaggerating at the same time. And so well, a vision of Edwina sitting gray and stooped and defeated in a jail cell flashed right up in front of her inner vision. "She said it with a great deal of pride, I thought."

"She never said that. When did she tell you that?"

"The morning I cooked you two breakfast. But she was using you as a threat against John B. So she could have exaggerated."

"Was this before or after you took a swing at Gordon Cabot?"

His eyes had been restlessly searching upriver above her head but came now to rest on hers. "I never took a swing at him, Charlie. But I almost did. John B. and Sid stopped me. How did you know?"

"Because I'm psychic, remember?"

"Have any intimations about whether or not we're going to get out of this alive?"

"Not without my crystal ball."

"You've revived enough to be sarcastic. We might get you out of here yet. Hell, we're almost halfway to Dead Horse Point."

"We've done the downhill stint, the easy part. It's all uphill from here. Where are we going to get the energy? With no food, no water? Much more sun and we won't have any more skin. And how are we supposed to get across the damned river? There's probably quicksand and suckholes and God knows."

"Well, it is spring, and we generally get an afternoon shower or two that tend to leave water in the potholes in the slickrock. Once we get across the river, and before we leave it, we rub mud all over our skin to protect it from the sun, and if you'll glance upriver a ways, you'll see a sandbar you have seen before. Which means we don't have to cross the whole width of the river at once. You've seen that sandbar before because it happens to be just past the concrete pile that was once a washed-away hotel or something."

"Where Homer stopped the boats the first time?"

"Exactly. I may not be psychic, but I know where I am."

"Bullshit." Since she was about to die she might as well quit trying to quit swearing. If she'd had the chance she'd have given up struggling not to clean up her plate even. All the little perks life offered must seem very dear to the dead. "How could you know?"

"Because I saw the rubble from above before we started down here and the sandbar too. And you know what else? I saw the outline of the road they built to get the concrete rubble there to begin with. It has switchbacks, Charlie, it's not that steep or exhausting. That takes care of everything but the food and who killed Gordon Cabot and Earl. You really can't have it all, you know."

"Why do they call it Dead Horse Point?" Charlie asked when they sat sodden and exhausted on the narrow tail of the downriver side of the sandbar. They were now supposedly, officially halfway to the Point.

The Colorado River might have been shallow in places but it was damn deep in others and the strength of the current belied the silent stealth of its flow. They'd started as far upstream of the sandbar as there was navigable beach to traverse and still almost missed it in the crossing.

"There's a neck that narrows where your 'bow' juts out from the headland between the campground and the overlook. And the story goes that some cowboys once put a gate across it to keep the horses corralled out there and then never got back to let them out and they all died."

"The horses."

"Yeah. Haven't you been down to the basement at the Visitors' Center? They've got talking displays on everything."

"I didn't even know it had a basement. I no more than got

here, remember, when murder started happening. Which brings us back to who killed Gordon Cabot."

"I'd be interested to know why you've decided it wasn't me all of a sudden. After suspecting me for so long," he said as they threaded their way through half-drowned tamarisk and fanciful bushes coated with tiny yellow flowers and fair-sized bees.

Was he being patronizing again or was she especially edgy with the wind drying the river water on her skin and clothes already, leaving a gritty coating to chafe literally every wrinkle, dimple, or crevice her body possessed when she moved it or her clothes moved against it?

Charlie wondered what kind of deadly germs were getting into the clotted wound on the back of his head. "Because you believe in psychic powers and that I possess them. You'd have left me to die out here long before now so I couldn't psych out some clue to prove you did it. My decision is based on logic and has nothing to do with one enchanted evening in the honeymoon suite at the Pit Stop Motel."

When they reached what looked to be the narrowest part of the other half of the Colorado River he took her hand. "Maybe I just didn't want to die alone out here either."

They waded in wearily and were toppled by the current about the time the water reached their knees. Probably getting slowly nuked by all the uranium tailings seeping in from upstream anyway. They soon lost hold of each other and he yelled as he was swept by, "Or maybe I'm just acting."

And the accusation he managed to convey in the accompanying but swift glance made her what-should-have-been-torpid-by-now blood boil.

"Oh right," she sputtered and coughed up half a lung full of nuclear waste when he pulled her on shore by her poor hair, "just punch my guilt buttons like Edwina. See where it gets you. 'Maybe I'm just acting.'" She flounced up on another natural-sucking-yucky beach. He was right about the mud in the water. It left grit on her teeth.

He pulled off her tattered sweatshirt and plastered her with more mud, cool and soothing but smelling like buzzard breath. Then did the same to himself. Then gave her the famous smile. If his smile gleamed when his face was clean, the world should have seen it encased in a muddy beard.

"How much does a mouth like that cost?" she asked in wonder when he turned away so she could muck up his bare back.

"Let's just say it's insured by Lloyd's of London." His answer came in that oily voice he used to convince an audience he was the villain instead of the hero when the audience knew better by the way the billing was organized.

"Scrag must be the murderer because he hit you on the head. I think it's bleeding again by the way." They walked mud-coated, heads covered with shredded shirts woven into makeshift hats. "Doesn't it hurt?"

"A tall bottle of aspirin would look pretty good about now."

Charlie realized the softening of colors and blurring of edges in the landscape around her didn't mean just that she was having a near-death experience. "Mitch, I've lost the other contact lens."

"You wear contacts? I didn't know that."

"That's the whole point." But I'm very nearsighted without them. You want to walk off and leave me now, it sure won't take you long to get out of sight.

His stomach was growling, but hers wasn't even hungry. Maybe she was working off thigh fat cells.

"I'm not actually sure it was Scrag. I didn't see him," Mitch admitted. "But I knew it couldn't be John B. or Sid, and Scrag was the only one left out here with us by then. I heard kind of a low chuckle and a crunch when my head caved in. And I think I remember a sort of sweaty smell."

"Which used to be Scrag Dickens, but now it's any of us. Why did you three separate?"

"We split up the provisions and fanned out to look for you."

"Why couldn't it be John B. or Sid?"

"Because I know them well enough to know they aren't capable of murder, just like you knew your mother wasn't."

"Anybody's capable of murder, Mitch, given the right circumstances. The circumstances were not right for Edwina. And she wouldn't have used an ax."

"What would she have used?"

"I don't know. But we all know she didn't, especially after Earl was killed while she was in jail and maybe Tawny. Which is the problem. I can see the connection between Tawny and Earl, but Cabot doesn't fit anywhere. There's no sense to this. Maybe John B. killed Tawny and Earl, and Sid killed Cabot." All of which doesn't matter anyway, since you and I are going to be dead soon too.

In their deteriorating condition the thousand-foot climb up out of the inner canyon turned out to take a lot longer than they'd thought it would even with the switchbacks. And Mother Nature decided not to bother raining that afternoon. They made it about halfway up and found a rock to shelter against to spend a silent, mostly sleepless, and very cold night.

When a blurry dawn finally made the vestige of road even vaguely visible they started off again to get warm and make as much time as they could before the sun got too hot.

Charlie thought her misery complete, until Mitch Hilsten stopped her dead in her weary tracks.

"If we get out of this alive, Charlie . . . I heard the scuttlebutt when the press blew into town . . . is it true Eric Ashton has backed out of the engineer's role in *Phantom of the Alpine Tunnel*? I also heard that your agency handles Cyndi Seagal and you handle the screenwriter, who wrote it from a jail cell. Charlie, do you think it's possible I could be considered for the part? I'm not that much older than Ashton. Could you at least mention my interest to your boss and the producers?"

Chapter
31

It already seemed as if they'd been walking for days under an unmoving, unrelenting sun by the time they'd crossed the arid benchland to the wall of the outer canyon and the next thousand-foot climb. This was the illicit road to Moab from the Point and a lot steeper than the one they'd used to get to this level from the river.

"It'll be a pull, shape we're in," Mitch said as they stood, swaying, at the bottom of the road looking up. "But there'll be some shade on the curves. It's once we get to the top that's got me worried. It'll still be a long way to the ranger station and Visitors' Center, and damned easy to get lost."

They stopped to rest in the shade of each curve so it took longer than forever. At the first curve-rest-stop, Mitch asked, "Why are you so pissed all of a sudden?"

"I'm not pissed, I'm livid. And it's not all of a sudden, you were just too dense to notice." And she told him the reason for Richard Morse's phone call to Room Eight at the Pit Stop Motel.

He chewed on that in silence for the next two curve stops and then exploded. "Shit, we'd already screwed half the night. I didn't think you'd ever get enough. What's the big deal?"

"If you have to ask that question, you wouldn't understand the answer."

"Oh, pardon me," he said with a punch-drunk bow. "Sorry

if I'm being politically incorrect here. But I'm the one worn to a nubbin."

"Well, just put in a claim to Lloyd's of London, why don't you?"

At the next curve they took a look at each other and grinned. They would have laughed had they the energy.

"Nubbin," said she.

"Is it the mud, or do all nearsighted women have such huge eyes?" asked he.

"Do you really believe in UFOs or was that just a come-on to get sympathy for a romantic evening?"

"I really do. And, hey, you're the one who backed off a cliff trying to get away from one. And you saw what happened to the bats and rats around here."

"Why are you so sure the two are related?"

"For the same reason I believe three murders are related. But like you, I haven't figured out the motive."

By the next curve they began to doze in each patch of shade. Charlie decided that, if the impossible happened and she survived this ordeal, she'd never take a walk again. Not even around the block.

"You know," she said as they started off once more, "it's funny, everything hurts but my stomach. Used to be the other way around. Maybe nature stress is different than city stress." Maybe this ordeal had shocked her stomach into submission. Maybe it had given up hope for survival, so considered burning a hole through her middle not worth the effort.

By the next stop it didn't matter, and the dozing was less helpful. It was difficult to gather strength from a rest period while working so hard to avoid the thought of water. When she dozed off, she dreamed about water. When she woke, it was the first thing on her mind.

The only consolation was that her myopia made the heights less threatening and the vast distances less noticeable.

But, after an incredible grind, they made it to the mesa top. The patches of shade and their mud coatings had saved them. And at the top they found the tire tracks from the production company's illicit supply missions to guide them across the scrub forest.

Charlie was watching those tracks when she walked headfirst into a dead-tree skeleton. She fell over backward and lay looking up at the fuzzed rings in the sky that harbored the deadly sun. She tried to call Mitch, but her throat wouldn't work.

She closed her eyes against the sun rings and felt the coolness of a shadow flow over her. She thought Mitch had come back but instead it was the shadow shape of a bird. A bird the size of a sailplane. It moved like one too, tipping instead of flapping. A wingspan that filled the sky. An obscene breath. It sailed low enough to become more than a shape, lowered its landing gear and hissed.

A blink later it was gone and Mitch bent over her. "We're going to make it, Charlie. We're almost there. Don't give up on me now."

"Rings and wings—"

"I chased the vulture off with a rock. Where's your shirt? You were supposed to keep it on your head."

"My shirt—"

"Take off your pants."

"My pants—"

"Put them over your head. You've got to protect your brain, Charlie."

"Put my pants on my brain."

When the Visitors' Center appeared out of the blur, Charlie cried dry tears and gravelly sobs.

Mitch pulled her along by one wrist, his mud mask faded and evened out until he looked like a blue-eyed Indian. "Where the hell are your pants? You lost them too?"

Charlie whimpered an apology that didn't quite make it to words—just weepy "I'm sorry" sounds.

He hauled her into the shade of the covered breezeway that connected the building's two sections. There was a soda machine, an ice chest, bundles of wood for the cooking grates in the campground, and a water fountain.

Charlie drank. Mitch drank. Charlie drank. They splashed water at each other and on themselves beneath a sign warning them not to waste a drop because it all had to be trucked in. Charlie noticed her feet calling to her. They were stained with dull red sandstone dust and bright red blood.

His chin still dripping, Mitch lurched up the redwood steps to the door that led to the information desk, the phone you could never use, and the rangers' offices.

Charlie opened the door on the ice chest and lifted out one of the plastic bags of crushed ice that had to be hauled in by truck too. She stood there in her dirty bikini panties, her bra, her mud-streaked, sun-blistered skin and cellulite, hugging the bag to her as she would a lover. "Libby, baby, I'm coming home to you after all."

The plump, healthy, and cheerful young ranger, Tim Pedigrew, offered Charlie more scrambled eggs and fried potatoes, which she hated to refuse. But she was so sated with water, orange juice, and coffee she thought she'd float.

All the other rangers were out searching for the superstar (oh, and his latest squeeze—what's-her-name) except Tim, who was holding the fort here.

Charlie and Mitch had showered and lathered and shampooed recklessly. They'd slathered themselves and each other with Vaseline Intensive Care Lotion with Aloe and Lanolin, and ointmented abrasions with antiseptic salves. They sat dressed in borrowed uniforms, looking more like convicts in their bruises and

Band-Aids than like park rangers. Tim had even found a pair of soft bedroom slippers for Charlie.

Mitch accepted the offer of more food. Guys could go through ordeals and come out robust, looking rugged and cute. Women looked like shit.

"You know," Mitch said, holding a potato slice aloft on the tines of his fork, "why we made it, don't you?" He popped the potato in his mouth and chewed while staring at her expectantly.

"We could be the luckiest people on earth." And your ideas about keeping our brains and skin covered probably didn't hurt.

"I don't know about you, but at times I felt guided either by your psychic responses or by an alien presence. We did not do this astonishing thing alone. We had help."

Which is not what our hero told the press and TV crews, for whom Charlie refused to appear. But she could hear most of it from a back bedroom where she hid with an EMT who checked her injuries, sunburn, and feet. He decided she wouldn't die right away and then got irate when she refused medical evacuation. Instead she crawled into some ranger's bunk, pulled his blanket over her head, and refused to play.

It wasn't simply that Mitch was acting the hero that society expected him to be out there with the press. Or that he could never be her hero if he was dumb enough to believe in "psychic responses" or "alien presences." And Charlie *was* grateful for his intuitive man thing (the logic of the mud and head covering bit).

What she could not stomach was his insistence that now they'd conquered the challenge of imminent death, could she not see her way to reconsidering his modest request that she mention his name to the producers of the upcoming epic *Phantom of the Alpine Tunnel* for the role of the train engineer?

Okay, part of it could have been that her stomach was acting up again. Because she was back in civilization or because she'd cleaned up two plates of scrambled eggs, fried potatoes with onions, garlic, and chopped peppers, and watched him start in on a third just as he questioned her reasoning about "one goddamned simple role in a movie to a man out of work."

"You're Mitch Hilsten, you don't need some little literary agent in a two-bit agency you'd never even heard of a few days ago mentioning you anywhere. Talk to your agent." Here they were saved from the jaws of death and . . .

The poor rangers still hadn't returned from their search—to discover Charlie wearing their clothes—before John B. Drake, Scrag Dickens, and Sidney Levit arrived. And shortly thereafter, Rita Latham and Sheriff Ralph Sumpter. (Their former river mates had all been rescued at the beach within hours of losing Charlie and Mitch.)

Somehow they all ended up in the bedroom which Charlie had refused to leave.

"You look great, darlin'," Scrag whispered, and pulled back the blanket. "You don't have to hide."

"Well, she looks alive, at least," John B. said. She was on the lower bunk and he had to hunker next to it to be sure.

"God, Charlie, I was so worried about you." Sid just sat his fanny on the floor and took her hand.

"I hope you guys can talk some sense into her," the EMT man said. "This woman should be in a hospital. She won't move, even bit me."

"Do you feel that bad, Charlie? Or is this guy trying to hustle you?" Rita Latham asked.

"I've got a lot of questions to ask you, Miz Greene, and I don't want you talking to anybody until you're debriefed," the sheriff of Grand County told her. "You understand me?"

"I've got a few questions about all this," Mitch said as they huddled in the ranger bathroom to avoid their friends.

"If you mention *Alpine Tunnel*, I'll knee your nubbin."

He sat on the edge of the bathtub and she on the lowered

lid of the stool, unable to believe how exhilarating in the face of overexertion, bodily harm, and sleeplessness, simply being alive was beginning to feel. The emergency medical type had treated his wound and left a dramatic swath of bandage around Mitch's head before being forced off without a paying patient to justify his trip. Charlie had little doubt they'd be charged regardless.

Mitch, too, was doomed to death in a few days or hours if he didn't let himself be sirened off to the expensive magic of a hospital.

Rita Latham had insisted upon sitting in on the sheriff's debriefing when Charlie and Mitch went over where they were and what they saw at the time of both Earl's and Tawny's deaths. And Edwina was still in jail.

"Could just be, we have two murderers here," Ralph maintained, trying to stifle the overflow of Charlie's sputtering anger. "I'm not letting one go until I'm sure." What's more, no one on that river trip would be allowed to leave the county until the little sheriff had himself some answers. "And all Mr. Seabaugh said before he died was, 'There wasn't any sand'?"

"And for me to run away."

Scrag had denied hitting Mitch over the head with a rock. He'd apparently been teamed up with John B. on the search for Mitch. And they hadn't parted before Earl's death.

Sid had teamed up with Earl and they'd gotten separated and Sid became lost himself.

"Somebody's lying," Charlie whispered now.

"I know. I just don't know who." Mitch was dejected and disgusted with himself again because after everything else, and posing heroically for the paparazzi, he'd been kneed in the ego when the rangers began to return from the hunt.

The first one achieving access to the room where they'd all gathered was absolutely furious. "When you made it to the river after being lost for a day and a night, why didn't you stay put? There's boat traffic up and down it all day. If you'd waited somebody would have come by, tour boats, or search boats—somebody. That suicidal walk out of there was just plain dumb."

Mitch had been speechless, everybody else exceedingly uncomfortable. Charlie was hastily trying to arrange some form of damage control to ad-lib their way out of the embarrassment when Ralph the sheriff-prick came to the rescue of his matinee idol.

"Well now, let's not be so hasty to judge here, fella. Mr. Hilsten is not a native of these parts and what seems obvious to you might not to him. Plus which the man had been hit on the head with a rock and could not be accountable for the state of his reasoning, plus which he was shackled with this female . . . that's an awful lot to load any man with who's suffering from heat, exhaustion, thirst, and hunger."

Chapter
32

Mitch Hilsten was finally coaxed out, but Charlie refused to leave the rangers' bathroom.

"What are you going to do, sleep in the bathtub?" Rita said outside the door. "I've got a nice motel room for you two lovebirds in Moab. It'll be a lot more comfortable than in there and the people who live here need the bathroom."

"What lovebirds?" Charlie opened the door long enough to yank Rita into the room and then lock it again.

"You and Mitch. Charlie, what's wrong with you?" Rita looked absolutely stunning in a lavender suit, with bright cranberry-colored blouse, earrings, lipstick, and shoes. The only wrong note was the perspiration beading under the makeup on her forehead. "Do you realize how narrowly you escaped death? The press has been playing up your liaison to the hilt, makes for good heartstring coverage. Charlie, you're from Hollywood, you know the ropes."

"Well, now for sure I'm not leaving this room. Look at me. Would you want to be splashed all over the tabloids looking like this?" And if you had a history like mine and a rebellious daughter as well as an unreasonable, judgmental mother would you want to add fuel to the press-driven fire? "Rita, has the sheriff decided for sure that Tawny's death was murder?"

The lawyer nodded. "There wasn't much left of the poor thing, but after Earl was murdered, the state lab did further tests and found a residue of acetone in fragments of her boots. It's used in nail polish remover, solvents, that sort of thing. It's highly flammable and there was a bottle of it missing from the production crew's supplies."

"Scrag thought he'd smelled lighter fluid on her." Charlie hugged her stomach and turned away.

"If you come back to Moab with me you can call your daughter and reassure her you're all right and you can visit Edwina. Please, Charlie."

"The murderer's still out there."

"I can't imagine why you'd feel safer here."

What you don't understand, lawyer my dear, is that I can't face Libby or Edwina at this moment. Not after all the publicity that's gone out about me and Mitch. "I'm too stressed by my ordeal to make any decisions right now, okay?"

Rita put up her hands, palms outward. "Okay, but I do think you're a little old for this kind of behavior."

Charlie did too. She just wasn't in wonderful shape and didn't completely trust her own judgment either. She used up the rest of some ranger's Intensive Care Lotion to soothe the tormented skin of her entire body. She gave herself a good talking to and then tried some deep-breathing exercises. She would have loved to crawl back in that ranger's bunk and cover her head.

The rangers' quarters were built barrackslike, with old linoleum tile and no wallboard over the studs in places, and the windows were not spacious. But Charlie managed to crawl out of one. Almost.

Rita Latham had been dressed to meet the press. Charlie would find another way out of here. It was fairly dark night by now and she had vague plans to commandeer a vehicle or something.

You're going to have to face your kid and mom sometime.

Well, maybe I'd like the privilege of doing it in private.

One of your most treasured dislikes in print, on the screen, or especially in reality has always been some dippy victim trying to save her self-esteem by walking into danger on her own. Even if that's all the guys are buying now in Hollywood, you resent it and you know it.

I'm not walking into danger, I'm climbing out a window and this place is crawling with reporters, rangers, sheriff's deputies, and tourists. Nobody's going to pull anything funny now with so many witnesses around. And I need some space.

Charlie lived in the modern world, thrived in Hollywood, and had just survived her second near-death experience in a week. What more could happen?

"Hey, darlin', let me help you there."

"Oh shit." I can't do anything right.

The window was farther off the ground than it had looked from inside and she was in the awkward position of having part of one leg still in the room and the other unable to reach the earth, trying to support her weight with already sore hands gripping the sharp edges of the cheap metal window frame. Scrag helped her pull the second leg over the sill, while holding her around the waist from behind.

"Listen, Dickens, you don't let go of me, I'm going to scream loud enough to blow your eardrums down your throat." He had a viselike grip on her waist that kept her from squirming around to face him. She tried to kick him in the shins with her heels but the slippers she was wearing were too soft to be much of a threat.

"It's Mitch. Charlie, you've got to help him."

"And you've seen too many movies. He's a big boy, he can take care of himself."

"He's hurt."

"Tough titties, I'm no doctor." Charlie's scream ended in a croak when he clamped his other arm around her chest and deflated it of all her screaming air.

She wanted to tell him to give her up, that with all the people around here now, there was no way he could drag her off unnoticed.

But she didn't have much talking air either and the minor squawks she did manage wouldn't alert anyone not within touching distance. So she tried to make scuffling noises with the soft slippers, which was also futile. All the while, Scrag was dragging and pushing and otherwise moving her along.

On the way around the side of the ranger barracks, they passed a lighted window. The shapes of two men in the room gestured in hot debate. The shapes most certainly brought to mind Scrag Dickens and Mitch Hilsten.

Ooops.

If that weren't bad enough, when Charlie and her captor started across the road toward the Visitors' Center—she, held so her feet were off the ground by now and his hand clamped across her mouth—the lighted parking in front of the barracks was all but empty. Just a few blurred lumps, sort of truck size. Even worse, the parking lot at the Visitors' Center was completely empty.

What, Charlie had told everybody to go away and leave her alone, and they did? She tried to bite the hand clamped across her mouth but that hand had her lips pressed together so she couldn't get her teeth out.

Where was the press now? The sheriff's department, the lawyer, Rita Latham, when she needed them? Aha, they had driven off into the desert, hidden their cars behind the bushes, and were even now sneaking back this way to the rescue. Oh no, better yet, all the cars and people were really there, she just couldn't see them without her contacts.

Charlie, get a life. This is serious.

I know.

Her last desperate struggle earned her a constellation of stars behind her eyes and a nasty pain in her head.

Voices and lights, many of them and from different directions, all alien and talking gibberish. Oh God, Mitch Hilsten was right. There are such things as UFOs and Charlie was on one.

That's why there were two Scrags, one holding on to her and another busy elsewhere. That second one knew everything she and Mitch and Edwina and the Army and even the President didn't know. Even Universal Studios didn't know!

Oh boy.

Chapter

33

A coyote squinted through dried grasses that matched the
color of its coat, its sharp ears and pointed nose trained
on Charlie. It was not wearing a bandanna.

"Venom in the scorpion's stinger is used to subdue struggling
prey . . ."

"Charlie, I'm over here . . ."

A mule deer with a doe's sweet face regarded her with glinty-
glass eyes. A bobcat slunk toward her with a frozen snarl.

Charlie lay on a rock floor surrounded by critters behind
glass, each in a lighted habitat not much larger than its body.

"After shedding their first skin, these . . ."

"An ability to veer suddenly makes the bat's flight conspicu-
ously erratic . . ."

"Don't know where you are, do you, Charlie?"

Wrong. Charlie knew exactly where she was and rolled out of
the light on her section of floor. She came up against a turkey vulture
hunkering, its enormous wings folded against its body, its featherless
blood-colored head turned so it could inspect Charlie squarely with
one black bead eye.

She crawled between it and the next display and tried to pull
herself up by bracing between them, the pain in her head and the
scrambled eggs and green peppers in her belly vying to see which
would achieve critical mass first.

Bats, their pinned wings outspread, their eyeteeth agleam . . .

snakes, lizards . . . big rats standing on their hind feet, little staring mice . . .

"One of America's largest birds of prey, the vulture also forages for carrion. Usually silent, this massive bird makes a hissing sound when . . ."

Each display had its own canned message available with the push of a button and someone had pushed all the buttons. There was only one recorded voice but all the messages came out of sync, sounding like a one-man crowd.

The dead wildlife, fuzzy in Charlie's impaired vision but quite recognizable up close with such dramatic stage lighting, ignored the educational intonations and watched with suspicion as Charlie crept past.

The room was dark, the only light coming from the displays as she rounded a dark corner trying to stay out of their illumination.

"This erosion process has taken approximately 150 million years. Much of it is caused by the river's slicing down into the earth's crust as land is forced upward." The recorded voice had moved with her from wildlife to geology.

"Two thousand feet below, the Colorado River winds its way from the Continental Divide in Colorado to the Gulf of California, a distance of 1,400 miles."

"'No sand,' Earl had said, 'No sand.'" A dark form stood outlined against the lighted display of a molded relief map covering most of a wall. "You know what that means, don't you, Charlie?"

And Charlie did all of a sudden, partly because she had by now identified her attacker. She was in the basement of the Visitors' Center. He would block off the exit up the main stairs. There would have to be a fire exit in a place open to the public. He was only one person. He couldn't block off two exits at once. She looked for a red sign.

"For centuries streams undercut walls and cliffs collapse. Mesas shrink to buttes and then to spires and they collapse, too, and disappear . . ."

"Couldn't resist the old Hilsten charm, could you? Tawny

couldn't keep her hands off him either." Her tormentor's voice came from a different part of the room each time he spoke and his shadow was gone from the map wall.

"Cracks of thunder split the air, clouds roll across the sun, streamers of rain stretch out to the canyons, but only under the darkest clouds do the drops reach the earth before evaporating . . ."

"You and Earl and Tawny, quite a threesome, weren't you?" The whisper was that of a deeply angered man and it came from behind a movable partition at the corner of which was a red glow. An exit sign?

". . . Stronger, more resistant layers of rock remained to form a rim. Today, the inner crater is 1,500 feet deep and surrounded by cliffs of the Wingate Formation . . ."

"They found out about Ben, didn't they? And they told you. And the three of you planned to destroy me."

This time he was right behind her and Charlie swung an elbow fortified by the hand on her other arm pushing with that arm's strength against the fist of this one. She connected with tooth-jarring precision.

He went down with a thud and she took off in the direction of that red glow, only to be dropped as he caught an ankle and pulled it out from under her.

Charlie hit her head on the back of the buzzard display and if she thought things were out of focus before . . . She had the illusion that the bird raised its massive wings and turned its own head to look down at her. She could have sworn she heard it hiss.

". . . outer valley of the Kayenta layer, and finally a second and final lip of cliff formed by the sturdy Navajo sandstone . . ."

"I was always finding the three of you huddled off together in a corner somewhere."

"The uranium-bearing layer is in the Chinle Formation."

"I'm not good enough for you, but Hilsten is."

Charlie had lost the soft slippers somewhere and he had no trouble removing the overlarge ranger pants even while they struggled.

"The benchlands and white rim belong to the boundary line between the Mesozoic and Paleozoic eras and form . . ."

"That was a mud beach. There wasn't any sand to put in the jet boat's gas tank. So it *was* your sugar that wrecked the engine. That's what Earl . . ."

"And Ben's death was not a suicide." John B. sounded euphoric. Surely he could see, whether he raped and killed Charlie or not, his number was up. "Got drunk as a skunk and I drowned him in his own pool. Poor guy'd gone bust. 'Must have committed suicide,' everybody said. I was going for accidental death due to drunkenness but suicide was okay by me. Worked out fine."

He was playing with her like Tuxedo, Libby's goddamned cat, played with injured birds, mice, bugs—played with anything injured that was smaller than itself. She squirmed out from under his hands and to her bare feet, knowing damn well he'd catch her again when he felt like it.

"And you thought Tawny and Earl had just discovered this and decided to tell me?"

"Oh no, they knew long before. But they didn't know I was on to them. That's why I assembled this crew for this shoot, at this place. They knew, Charlie. And then they told you." He grabbed her shoulders and slid her down against the buzzard display and to the floor again.

"You meant to kill Tawny and Earl all along." Like you mean to kill me. "I didn't know about Ben, honest. I don't think they did either."

"The APC mines make economic use of the Cane Anticline core by using a solution process. Water from the Colorado River is pumped down through the dome and then upward into huge evaporation ponds."

"Ben found out I was using the money to put together a film on the side, instead of for a housing development. Why Cabot you want to know, right?"

Actually, Charlie was past caring about anyone but herself,

about anything but survival. Her eyesight diminished without corrective lenses, her strength nearly gone, her head and stomach threatening to explode in unison, no fingernails even to mark the bastard . . . he already had her legs parted so she couldn't do the knee thing mothers always encourage their daughters to resort to . . .

"I'll show you why, Agent Greene." He got to his knees and pulled them both to their feet. "You're not a very good psychic, you know."

John B. Drake turned her around and bent her over the buzzard. She thought he was going to enter her from behind, but he pushed her head down on top of the display. "I made a mistake. People do. You've sure made a bunch lately. See?"

And Charlie did see.

She also could not believe her luck. He turned her around but forgot to spread her legs before he moved his hands from her shoulders to pull her shirt away from her chest.

And for the first time in an incredibly long life Charlie got to use her mother's sagest advice. She gave it everything she had left.

The producer/director of *Return of an Ecosystem* careened off her with a roar of pain and the canned voice continued calmly, unaware of breaking glass, grunts, falling signs, and crashing room dividers. "The river itself has cut deeply into the Paradox Formation. The Paradox . . ."

"And I'll show you something else, Charlie Greene, I'll show you I'm twice the man I ever was . . ." His voice was soft and silky now but his S's hissed like an angered buzzard's.

The struggle must have reached the source of the recorded voice because it had finally gotten the message.

"Paradox," it said clearly, "Paradox, Paradox, Paradox."

Chapter
34

Maybe it was the fact that Charlie was completely naked now. Maybe it was because the producer/director of *Return of an Ecosystem* was concentrating more on his self-delusions than the reality of his chances of getting away with one more murder. Everybody knows about DNA and semen and stuff these days. And if the sheriff and the press had gone home, the rangers were still here, weren't they?

Whatever the reason, Charlie managed a last emergency squirm out of John B. Drake's grasp and nearly made her getaway good.

But she slammed into Mitch Hilsten at the bottom of the stairs and they both went down hard.

Charlie staggered to her feet first, only to be bowled over by Scrag Dickens as he vaulted down the stairs. This time she just lay still.

And the manic electric voice kept repeating, "Paradox" over the sounds of rage and scuffle and swearing.

Actually, it did seem paradoxical that someone so concerned over ecology as to make award-winning film about it thought nothing of murdering four people. It didn't fit anywhere in Charlie's stereotype file. Then again, she drew most of her perceptions from the writers she worked with and they were almost all liberal to the core. Any environmentalist would be the hero in their works because that was the natural order of things.

"Charlie?" The voice belonged to Mitch.

"Go away."

"What's happening?"

"Scrag and John B. are slugging each other somewhere between the Kayenta and the Mesozoic. Where the hell's that twit of a sheriff?" Charlie intended to live at least long enough to make Ralph Sumpter's day.

But Mitch was off to join the fray before she'd finished speaking.

It took her a while to figure that out. And to become aware that the "Paradox" voice had stilled, the lights in the displays had gone out. In her present and injured frame of reference, time was not a stable commodity.

There was still plenty of commotion from the men though, but it sounded far enough away for her to try again.

Charlie, still buck naked, was on her hands and knees at the top of the stairs when the press arrived. Somewhere between camera flashes Rita Latham, still dressed for the press, tried to block Charlie's present image from exposure while yelling lawyer talk about legal ramifications if they persisted.

Charlie did notice Sheriff Ralph getting in a self-righteous ogle or two first, though.

But it was Sidney Levit who removed his starched white shirt to cover her battered nakedness. Not only that, he lifted her, once wrapped, in his arms like the big rat had the fake ranger in the *Animal Aliens* army scene and carried her off.

She buried her head against his bare chest to ignore the media demands. "Sid? I'm sorry. I had to suspect everybody."

"You don't have to be sorry, Charlie. I even sort of suspected your mom, just because it was easier. But I began to suspect Drake after Earl's death. I just couldn't understand what he had against Cabot."

"That's just it. He didn't have anything against Cabot."

* * *

"Poor Mitch." Charlie rode beside Rita Latham on the long road out of Dead Horse Point State Park, dressed once again in borrowed ranger clothes.

"It would have been 'poor Charlie' if Mitch had gone off with the rest of us," the lawyer said ruefully and rolled down her window to let the chill air in to poor Charlie. "I can't believe I let myself get suckered in that way. Or Scrag Dickens either."

"I can," Charlie said.

"You're just lucky Mitch didn't fall for Scrag's story."

John B. Drake had offered Scrag Dickens the only human role in a proposed nature series to be aired on prime time cable. John B. offered this morsel to the desert rat while the two were teamed up to look for Mitch at the cowboy line camp stop on the fated river trip. The series with Disney was a done deal but still a secret until certain financial matters were settled. Scrag was a perfect "character" for the part of host-narrator. No question, the one-time camp follower would accrue fame and fortune and travel the world.

"He even described how the show would open, with me in front of a campfire, playing my guitar and singing." All Scrag had to do was to lie then, and again tonight.

Scrag had to claim that John B. and he were together the whole time when in fact the director/producer planted Scrag in the shadow of a rock and went off to kill Earl Seabaugh. He smashed Earl's camera and exposed its film—the possible incriminating evidence of Tawny's murder. John B., meanwhile, had stolen Homer's knife before the teams had even parted to search for Mitch, simply slipped it carefully from its sheath before Homer or anyone else noticed. The director was good at shell games, and the river guide wore the weapon more for his image than for actual need so he didn't miss it.

Scrag claimed to have been terribly shaken by the cameraman's murder but the lure of fame, fortune, and world travel is very powerful to someone whose libido demands an image that life consistently thwarts. And so tonight, he had been asked to lie again, this time to prove his prowess as an actor.

"'An audition,' John B. called it," Scrag told them after the sheriff and his powerful deputies had pulled the fighting men apart. This time Scrag had been supposed to convince as many people as possible that a UFO sighting had happened out on the tip of Dead Horse Point.

While Charlie Greene had been greasing herself up again with soothing lotion in the bathroom—the press, the sheriff, a good many campers, most of the rangers, Sidney Levit, and even the lady lawyer had fallen for Scrag's acting and hurried out to the overlook at the end of the Point.

Looking out the car window at the alien scenery now, Charlie could see how all those people could fall for the desert rat's story. Jagged black tree skeletons pointed at dark heavens blinking with misty starlight. Every bush, every cactus, every stunted tree, every mound or weed or sand hill had an angular moon shadow. It was like driving through an unfocused cubist landscape. It could all easily put you in an "alien" frame of mind. Then again Charlie had experienced near-death, near-rape, and been hissed at by a big live buzzard.

"It'd be dead easy to see flying saucers and little green men and stuff in this place. That's why Hollywood comes out here to make it all happen," she told the lawyer. "Did you see anything out at the overlook?"

"No, but we wasted a lot of time looking, or imagining we saw something. Then we noticed Scrag, who'd sent the rest of us packing out there, hadn't bothered to join us. That alerted the sheriff and Sidney Levit."

Scrag had stayed behind to try to convince Mitch, who should have been an easy target for that sort of thing, but Mitch began to smell a rat (a human one) and started looking for Charlie. Scrag eventually let his conscience catch up with him and began worrying about her too.

"I wonder why Mitch didn't fall for it," Charlie said. "He really believes in UFOs."

"Maybe he was more worried about you. Or maybe he's not as naive as you think," Rita said and suddenly stood on the brakes.

"What?" Charlie hit the end of the seat belt and bounced back.

"That stupid rat, it ran right out in front of me."

Charlie let that sit in her weary brain until they reached the highway and headed for Moab and the motel and Edwina before she asked, "Was it—the rat—like, staggering drunk?"

"Yeah. Really weird."

"Did we hit it?"

"Yeah, yuck."

They drove in silence for a few miles, then Charlie asked, "Would you really have used menopause as a defense for Edwina?"

"If it came down to it, I'd have used anything. And you know, from what I've learned of the whole situation tonight, that was a large part of the problem." Rita shivered, and sent the windows back up to close out the night. "Except it was male menopause."

Chapter
35

Charlie sat ensconced in the breakfast nook of her modest but costly nest in Long Beach, scarfing down Mrs. Beesom's hot tuna noodle casserole with peas and potato chips. And Maggie's homemade rolls and salad.

"Tastes like hot lunch in grade school." Libby's elegant features warped with distaste. She pushed the Tuna Supreme to the edge of her plate and buttered another roll. "Why does she always bring this over?"

Charlie thought it tasted wonderful, real comfort food. She was so grateful to be alive. And home. And sitting across from Miss Pucker Puss.

Maggie Stutzman grinned at Charlie and passed the beautiful brat the salad bowl. "Try some veggies. You need more than bread and milk."

Libby speared a tomato wedge and a carrot slice. Everything else was the wrong color.

Besides the casserole, Betty Beesom, who lived behind Charlie's patio, had brought over a clip from one of her birding magazines about turkey vultures. Charlie had thanked her profusely and dumped it in the trash with a shudder the moment her neighbor left.

The house had been returned to reasonably good order, but Charlie would have to replace most of the blinds. What had they done, swung on them? There was not a lot she could say now though.

Libby's indiscretions had at least been passably private, while Charlie's were broadcast worldwide in living color. When Charlie reluctantly broached the subject of her own misdeeds, Libby blushed a deep red with ugly white blotches.

"I just don't want to talk about it, okay?"

Charlie'd been stunned. First of all, because she didn't know the kid could blush. And second, Libby never missed a chance to criticize her mother or gain leverage in the Greene household's battle of wills.

"She's not sick," Maggie had assured Charlie. "But nobody wants to think of their parents in a sexual context. How would you approach Edwina if she were the one on national television accused of an affair with a famous sex object?"

Charlie got the point. She also knew she hadn't, by any means, heard the end of this.

Mrs. Beesom had blushed, too, when she handed over the casserole and buzzard clip. Charlie didn't even want to think about what was going on in that mind. It was a toss-up as to which topped the woman's priorities—her church, or wild birds, or her neighbors' private lives.

Maggie was all cool amusement and patient smirks, knowing she'd get the whole story in due time. And then, of course, there was thegoddamnedcat. Tuxedo took a header into the side of the refrigerator while riding the area rug that had been in front of the sink, did a 180, and gallumphed back into the dining/living room and up the stairs. The gallumphing continued above their heads.

"Probably just took a dump," Libby informed Maggie, throwing several feet of platinum hair over a haughty shoulder. "Always turns him on." The kid pried a tomato bit out of her braces with a fingernail and asked Charlie, without quite meeting her eyes but with the return of the interesting coloring, "So, uh . . . is Grandma going to be all right?"

"Well, she's no longer in any trouble with the law obviously—but something's still the matter and was, even before Gordon Cabot got his brain carved with her ax. She won't talk to me, but I know I haven't heard the last of that one either. I sure hope it's not her job. I will *never* understand that woman, never."

Edwina had presented her daughter a hangdog look and a pat on the arm when they parted, and given a long weary sigh.

"Oh Jesus, there's trouble coming down the freeway on that one," Charlie said grimly now. "But all I can do is wait for the collision."

Her daughter and her best friend rolled their eyes knowingly at each other. They always sided with Edwina when Edwina was safely off in Colorado.

"Was she really in that much danger of being accused of Cabot's murder?" Maggie asked.

"Boy, was she. Those dried blood chips in Howard's Jeep *were* Gordon Cabot's. We all wondered what had happened to the murderer's clothing." John B. had owned several sets of his standard locationwear—jeans, red-and-black-plaid flannel shirts, and hiking boots. He'd stashed those with the blood and brains somewhere outside the campgrounds and hitched a ride back on the generator truck, appearing to Mitch to have been the last of the diners at his RV to arrive that fateful night.

In reality, he'd been among the first and had sent Earl Seabaugh off to invite Sid to dinner to discuss Cabot's misuse of the landscape as a ruse. He'd grabbed Edwina's ax and set off to murder Earl.

"You see, both Earl and Gordon Cabot were bald as buzzards." And in the dark and in his haste, the director had struck down the wrong man. "He thought that Earl and Tawny had discovered his murder of Tawny's husband, Ben, years ago. I don't think they had a clue, but it must have been working on him all these years and living with Tawny had to keep reminding him of Ben. She told me he was going through some kind of change of life and that might have made him unstable.

"John B. planned for Tawny and Earl to meet accidental

ends on a dangerous location. But then when he saw me and Edwina—who was acting like a true nut case—arguing over dinner and the ax so handy, he suddenly had an even better idea."

When Lew flew in the reporters and John B. took Howard's Jeep to intercept him, the director had picked up the incriminating set of clothing on the way, leaving the blood chips. Then he threw the clothes over a cliff into an all but inaccessible canyon before he reached Lew's plane.

Only recently, and after two more murders, a group of rock climbers had brought out the plaid shirt and alerted authorities, thinking there might be the body of a fallen climber somewhere below.

"Well, what about the rats and bats?" Maggie dished herself another helping of Betty Beesom's casserole and then dished half of it back, ruefully.

"There's this hilarious show on the local cable channel I watched my last morning in Moab." Charlie slid out of the nook's high-backed bench seat to make coffee. There were still plenty of sore places on and in her poor body to remind her of the Canyonlands of Utah. "And this guy, sitting behind a bouquet from the sponsoring local mortuary, was wondering if the strange animal behaviors around Moab lately had been caused by the release of uranium into the Colorado River from the tailings pile next to the shut-down mill at the edge of town. And the APC's pumping of that water into the potash holes. Something about wildlife getting nuked from the evaporation process, or getting into its salty leftovers, or something."

Only blank looks from the two at the table.

"Potash, it's used as a slurry in oil drilling and in fertilizers and it's a basic mineral for all kinds of things, even dietary supplements." Charlie had learned this from one of the canned messages in the Visitors' Center's basement that fateful night at Dead Horse Point State Park.

Still no reaction that made sense from her audience.

Charlie tried again. "Hey, the drunken rats and bats I saw were two thousand feet above the river. That's not where they get their drinking water and they don't take vitamins."

Maggie and Libby stared at Charlie expectantly, waiting for the punch line.

"But Edwina thinks their strange behavior is because of all the filming and tourist disruption in the area. Mitch Hilsten and the *National Inquirer* now, they think it's an alien presence that we can't see or hear that disrupts the bats' sonar system and drives the rats drunk because they, too, can hear what we can't."

Charlie stopped laughing when she realized she laughed alone. She ought to be the expert on aliens. She lived with them.

"You know, after the weird time you had in the Canyonlands," Maggie said, "that doesn't sound so far-fetched."

"Potash—potassium carbonate, hydroxide, any of several compounds containing potassium—particularly soluble compounds such as potassium oxide, chloride, and various sulfates," quoth the blond metal mouth, fresh off a chemistry exam cram. Full of half-digested facts she'd soon forget when her brain cells were needed for something more important. Cute guys, for instance.

Libby wrinkled her forehead with effort. "One of those is also used, I think, to help out the way hormones work or something . . . maybe the guy behind the funeral flowers is right."

"Libby!" Charlie burned her finger on the stove burner under the teakettle and grabbed a paring knife to cut an end off the aloe plant she'd picked up in Oregon several years ago.

The goo you can squish out of the cut ends of the cactuslike leaves seems to erase the pain and prevent blistering. It was the only houseplant his royal highness hadn't eaten down to the potting soil and then barfed all over the carpet.

"I wonder if rats have PMS."

"Maggie!"

"What," the most formidable teen in the world said, meeting Charlie's eyes head on now, "you're such a big deal you know everything? You know for a fact everybody else's ideas are wrong just because you can't explain it all? Like, who are you to say there's no such thing as an alien presence?"

Chapter
36

Mitch Hilsten arrived at the party at Richard Morse's home in Beverly Hills with Cyndi Seagal on his arm. They made a truly stunning pair. She, tiny and dark, with her medically enhanced tits blossoming out of the top of her dress. He, darkly tanned against a white dinner jacket.

Of course everybody watched Charlie for her reaction and even some of the cameras were aimed her way. Her escort, however, was even more gorgeous. He managed to guide her away from approaching reporters without touching her.

"Okay, I can almost believe you'd sleep with him," Larry Mann said, "but not for the good of the agency. Independent guy that you are."

"I didn't." Charlie snagged a glass of champagne off a passing tray and a cracker covered with ground black pepper, capers, and a huge naked shrimp from another. Then the shrimp reminded her of herself at the top of the steps at the Visitors' Center when press and posse arrived together and she dropped it in an artificial floral display.

"Didn't sleep with him? Or didn't do it for the agency?" Larry enjoyed the camera and video attention. People at all savvy to Charlie's particular echelon in the industry (lower) knew that he was her assistant (secretary) and both were here on command. But Congdon and Morse was hardly a well-known agency and many of those present were impressed by her "date." And who knew but what some producer would see his picture in the trades and think, "Who is the hunk? Get me that hunk. He's perfect for the Handsome Hunk part. We'll make him a star!"

"Thanks for helping out with the condo damage in Long Beach, Larry. I really appreciate it and I don't know what Maggie would have done without you." They were speaking through false smiles and sounded weird. But right now it was what they looked like that mattered.

Charlie was wearing about thirty-four layers of makeup over peeling skin. (Superstars tan, agents peel.) She was, however, more slender than she had been recently (okay, for years) and thus able to wear a knockout cocktail dress Libby'd worn to one party at the Long Beach Yacht Club and outgrown the next day. It had enough shimmering net to appear revealing while masking the ravages of healing skin.

"How else could you get *the* Mitch Hilsten to sign on for the train engineer's part?"

"Maybe some of us have exceptional people skills, powers of persuasion."

"Maybe somebody got a fabulous raise too."

Actually, it *was* a pretty good raise. "What happened had nothing to do with the agency or *Phantom of the Alpine Tunnel*. It's hard to explain, Larry, but . . . there was a peculiar set of circumstances and it happened to be a . . . peculiar time of the month."

And as soon as the economy picked up, Charlie would get a job at William Morris or TNT or ICM and give Richard Morse the bird. The old buzzard.

"Is there truly nothing a woman can't blame on the exigencies of her monthly cycle?" the hunk asked with a sigh and cocked a dramatic eyebrow in case someone worth noticing, was.

Richard's mansion was a typical Beverly Hills pastiche. English Tudor on the outside, art deco on the in, all uncomfortable harsh angles and corners, glass tops on tables, black and white marble tiles on the floor.

An ancient dance orchestra on the raised dais at the far end of the room was playing even more ancient music for people too busy networking to dance.

Richard Morse appeared suddenly, one foot on a black square the other on a white. He too was smiling through his teeth and talking at the same time. Certainly makes for interesting expressions. "You're a real trooper, babe. Thanks."

And you're a real bastard.

"Kid." The boss recognized Larry Mann, known around the office as Larry the Kid. Richard looked as elegant as someone with pop eyes and a twitch or two could. Wearing a zillion-dollar shiny gray suit made to fit better than his skin. Hair allowed to whiten at the temples only. "He wants to talk to you," he said to Charlie, nodding importantly. "Privately."

"He?" Charlie told herself she put up with this guy only because Libby would need college money in a couple of years. Maybe it was his energy and cunning. Maybe it was the challenge.

"Himself," Larry explained, sardonically, and sauntered off.

"I told him you'd be out behind the lemon tree in two minutes." Richard screwed up one twitching cheek and sighed like Edwina. He was still nodding and the bulging eyes tried to register pity. "And, Charlie, I also warned him you don't like men, unless they're like the Kid, there."

"I *love* men, Richard." Respect takes a little more time.

"I wanted to thank you for the kind word," Mitch Hilsten said out behind the lemon tree. "I really appreciate it, Charlie."

"I didn't say a word, kind or cruel, about you and the train engineer part to anyone. Not a soul." She really hadn't. But she deserved the raise anyway for all the damned notoriety.

"Your boss called my agent for *some* reason." That searching, sensual, hurt look.

"I told you, Richard wanted you for the part the minute Ashton dropped it and he found out I had access to you. Why won't anybody listen to me?"

"Beats me." Mitch Hilsten either assumed his most sincerely vulnerable look or felt sincerely vulnerable. "Charlie . . ."

"I don't think so."

"Are you sure?"

No.

But Charlie stood her ground. It wasn't that time of the month. "My life's a zoo already, Mitch."

The lemon tree was between the requisite swimming pool and a hedge made of solid, pruned, scratchy greenery. Looking every inch the wounded hero, Mitch Hilsten turned away from Charlie to return to the house just as a guy with a minicam rose from behind a planter on the sandstone patio.

Charlie resisted the urge to go after Mitch. Like the superstar had said, "A woman's got to do what a woman's got to do."